JOE

Just an Ordinary Earthling

Revision number 108

(Maybe you should've held out for 109)

Thanks for supporting Joe's further adventure

Edward A. Szynalski
Allen L. Petro

Special Thanks to:
(In proper etiquette order)

Mary Voskuil
Mark LaMaster

Table of Contents

Moral of the story:

Never tap on a speed actuator.

Chapter 1

Contrived

In the cold darkness of deep space, a small, white, elliptical disk traversed the emptiness. Microscopic in comparison to the grandeur of the universe, this tiny vessel made up for its size with speed, due to the skills of a small mechanic on a backwoods planet (his motto: Always put big, overpowered engines into tiny vehicles.) Nearly all the space on the ship was taken up by a powerful 790 antimatter crossfire hydrogen turbo-boost ion engine, a more compact version of the 790 fusion-fission-fusion reactor power plants found in super freighters. Those were usually used to move masses twenty-five hundred times greater than the *Esprit*. This ship had only one purpose, to transport Intergalactic Intelligence Agency rangers vast distances in a very short time.

"Ever since we had the speed actuator serviced we've been unable to calculate our velocity accurately," moaned Fred, the navigator, as he banged the top of the console with his fist. He shook his head and frowned when nothing changed on the readout. "One of these days it's going to bite us in the sunisa. I'll put in a repair requisition when we get to headquarters."

Frank, the pilot, nodded. He wished his superiors would stop partnering him with the energetic, won't-shut-up rookies. They were always so annoying. But he knew the reason why. He sighed heavily as he recalled the events of the Arturo Express, a case he had worked on over thirty years ago, that involved corruption, politics, a head of state, an affair, and a choice. And with Frank's usual luck, the corrupt politician with the jilted daughter became his boss. *One day I will get a Shazbotian partner; they don't have mouths and can't speak.*

"We should be arriving, that is, if there are…"

Frank closed his eyes and rolled his head back against the seat, ignoring the unceasing droning. He didn't know what was worse, the constant babbling, or the never-ending high-risk assignments. Their last assignment had cost them both a lot of sleep and time, including a stint in a healing chamber. That was the price of being highly trained espionage agents for the Soufte government and members of the infamous Intergalactic Intelligence Agency. The

IIA was composed of every type of being in the recognized galaxy except for one, the Quesontes, Soufte's historic enemy.

****

Galactic History 101

A long time ago, in this very same galaxy, the Quesonte Empire grew to be the largest single empire of contiguous territories ever known. They managed to occupy twenty-one percent of the galaxy. It doesn't sound like much, but, if you do the math, it's a huge volume. As with any self-perpetuating autocracy, not everything was peaches and cream. Political unrest, conspiracies, corruption, and internal conflicts eroded the mighty empire.

Worlds in the Quesonte Empire grew tired of the oppression, repression, and exploitation of their masses and their resources. They decided to unite and create an anarcho-syndicalist community in which the workers would facilitate a cooperative economic system, based on democratic values and centered on humanoid needs within a capitalistic society.

But the Quesontes rather enjoyed hanging on to their

outdated imperialistic dogma and enacted martial law, which further angered the populace and encouraged separatist factions to develop among the outer colonies.

The first such faction called themselves the Humanoid Front of Soufte, or HFS, which didn't sit well with the non-Soufte planets. To appease every humanoid, they changed their name to the Extraterrestrial Humanoids Front, or ETHF, which no one liked either. They finally agreed on the Astral Species Syndicate. The Quesontes thought it smelt of a bad idea.

A long and boring civil war broke out with lots of historic figures, dates, and events; enough to make history the most dreaded class of any middle school student's life.

Short version: They called it a draw and have been in a bitter cold war ever since.

****

Fred and Frank stood about 137 centimeters tall, with heads that seemed too big for their bodies. Their long, thin necks ended abruptly at their blue shirt collars. The green lights of the flight controls splashed the cabin and its occupants, causing their rough, gray skin to appear greenish and reflecting in their big, black, glassy eyes.

Fred worked on the report for their last mission, his long, sinewy fingers entering data through a smooth console in front of him. As the rookie, he had to do all the menial tasks.

Mortimer, their field chief, always said, "The mission isn't over until the debriefing is done." The fastest way to get through a debriefing was with a finished report. And since one percent of space travel is setting the coordinates into the guidance computer, and ninety-nine percent is waiting to get there, Fred had plenty of time to finish it.

Entering a remote star system, the *Esprit* whisked under a small, yellow sun. A star flare erupted, gracefully framing the tiny craft, and emphasizing its frailty against the enormity of space. The leading edge of the *Esprit* glowed slightly while passing through the thin atmosphere of a brownish-red planet, fourth from the sun. Swooping down, the craft skimmed rapidly across the ground, carving a shallow canal, and raising a rooster tail of fine sand fifty feet into the air.

Coming upon a small cave that appeared as nothing more than a hole in the ground, it instantly sank below the surface of the flat horizon, leaving only a trail of dust. The dust slowly settled, covering everything in its path, including the photovoltaic array of a small mechanical rover. Having been deposited there from a nearby planet several years ago, the rover had just inched its way up to the cave's entrance, only to die as the dust blocked out its energy source.

The *Esprit*'s windshield emitted a beam of light, like a headlamp, in the dark cave. The ship glided along rapidly, navigating the cave's every twist, rise, and fall. After one last quick lift, they emerged onto a ramp that joined a major three-dimensional freeway leading through the center of a vast, underground city. Tall buildings rose from the floor and climbed all the way to the ceiling of the cavernous expanse. Light filled the city from an unseen source, giving the feeling of natural daylight. Although more a military base than a city, it was quite homey and comfortable to live in, due to the laid-back frame of mind of the colonists and its extreme distance from civilization.

The 3-D freeway had sixteen lanes, four horizontal and four vertical, separated by stationary dashes of light that floated in midair. Vehicles traveling at high speeds could change lanes left, right, up, down, or even diagonally if they chose. (Remarkably, after only thirty hours of training, even a sixteen-year-old was legally qualified to drive it.)

The *Esprit* was unusual compared to the other vehicles — capable of intergalactic travel, and yet small enough to be used for an everyday commute. This made it doubly advantageous for IIA rangers, since they didn't have to deal with spaceports, customs, or borders. They could just slip on and off of a planet quietly and easily, using the same vehicle for all purposes.

Frank and Fred battled their way through traffic to the outer lower lane of the freeway. They exited onto a small side street surrounded by more modest buildings that did not rise to the rocky ceiling above. They were in an older part of the city with buildings that had actual roofs on them. It felt much more open and spacious.

Pulling in front of one of the all-glass structures, Frank carefully maneuvered the *Esprit* in an acrobatic display known as parallel parking. Even though it was small enough for commuter driving, the *Esprit* was still a large vehicle. Cautiously, he eased the ship in between two parked vehicles. He was just about in the space and in line with the curb, when he bumped the vehicle in front of him, setting off the alarm. He pulled back a little and bumped the vehicle behind him, setting off its alarm. "Perfect fit!" he declared.

He and Fred climbed out through the gull-wing doors, stretched off their long journey, then Frank paid the parking meter while Fred retrieved a valise from the *Esprit*.

The stately lobby was adorned with ornate architectural features unnoticed by the hustling throng of people. Only the security guard manning the checkpoint took the time to appreciate the arches and carved features.

Fred and Frank approached the weary guard, who sighed as he noticed them and politely asked, "May I see some ID, sirs?" Frank and Fred pulled out their wallets and fished out their IDs. The guard glanced over them, peered at Frank, and double-checked his ID. "You've changed a bit, haven't you?"

"Ah yes, the mustache." Frank smoothed the pencil-thin strip of hair above his lip with his fingers. "I grew it a year or two ago."

"I'm surprised General Office hasn't required you to get a new ID," the guard commented. "It's not like they have very accommodating hours," Frank retorted, defending his outdated ID.

"You're preaching to the choir, sir." The guard looked past Frank and Fred to notice his line growing and sighed again. "I'm still trying to get my worker's comp from last spring."

"Good luck with that," Frank replied.

"Come on through." he waved them toward the door that circumvented the metal detector.

They proceeded to the elevators with a large group of people. Since Fred had never visited this particular outpost before, he was overly suspicious of the other riders and held on to the briefcase as if his life depended on it.

When they arrived at their floor, they walked out of the elevator into a long, empty hallway. Their footsteps echoed off the drab walls as they made their way to a plain door that had a keypad lock.

Frank punched the combination into the keypad and slid his ID through the slot. The door did not open. He slid his ID back and forth a few more times, but the door remained closed. He tried turning the badge upside down, rubbing it on his sleeve, and even using Fred's badge. They stood dumbfounded. Finally, Frank knocked. A muffled buzz sounded from inside, and the door slid open to reveal a receptionist's office.

"Good morning, Marty," Frank greeted upon entering. "Is the

ID scanner down?"

"Hello, handsome," she flirted as she continued typing information into a console. "And yes, it is."

Even though the conversation wasn't directed at him, Fred felt sensuous warmth from her greeting. "You should put up a sign or something," he complained.

"Sometimes I just like to see how long it takes for someone to knock." She looked up from her display screen. Her large, blues eyes met theirs, and a welcoming smile crossed her face. "Good to see you again, Frank. And who is your delightful friend?"

"He's no delight," he quipped back, "he's my new partner, Fred."

Martha Harriet, aka Marty, was an Allterrainian, an alien species that Fred had not encountered before. A unique species, Allterrainians were sexually attractive to all other species in the universe. The attraction was so strong that they had been used by both sides to gain information from spies during the Disturbance, a war that lasted for twenty-two years. Without operant conditioning (which Frank had the displeasure of going through) no species was immune to their wiles, especially if an Allterrainian was actively trying to lure you in.

Marty's natural attractions could be distracting in an office setting; however, her administrative skills were top-notch, she was a great multitasker, and she rather preferred this job. When Marty applied for the position, Mortimer found it impossible not to hire her.

A screech came over the intercom. "Is that Agents Surovell and Jackson? Get them in here!"

"You heard the man." Marty buzzed them through the locked door behind her.

"It's about time you two arrived," Mortimer complained. "Stop gawking at Marty and close the door."

Fred obeyed, but he stared at the Allterrainian. He was transfixed by her pleasing features: a very long neck, a small and very round head, and big, beautiful eyes that seemed to drink him in. Finally, the door closed.

Mortimer, Fred and Frank's field chief, was an Escher. Short and stocky, he appeared to have no neck, and you were never sure where one physical trait started and the last one stopped. He had a dark complexion, and his sturdy, round head displayed his military buzz cut. A former marine and drill sergeant, he still barked intimidatingly, as if he were facing new recruits on their first day.

Mortimer, noticing Fred's fixation on Marty, said to Frank, "I'm signing him up for negative reinforcement therapy." He made a note on a pad on his desk.

"We have the dossier on Metcalfe," Frank said, as Fred laid the satchel on Mortimer's desk. They seated themselves. "It took a little finesse, but we were able to liberate it from the computer banks on Minocqua."

"Good, good. I'll have the boys in the tech lab look into it immediately," Mortimer answered. "I'm going to forego the usual debriefing for now. You need to leave for Ladascus immediately." Mortimer cleared his throat while studying a file on his desk. "We've noticed a massive redistribution of Quesonte agents. Not the usual reorganization, but a radical and abrupt shift. It has all the indications of a military coup. Unofficial word is Evinrude Boulougante is at the center of it. And Ladascus seems to be the key."

"Evinrude dropped out of sight several years ago," Frank said. "I assumed he was dead."

"I can assure you he is quite alive," Mortimer continued. "We have a lead on an intermediary the Quesontes are using: Henry Streator, a Ladascan small-time gem dealer. Apparently, he frequently travels between Quesonte worlds and will be carrying information regarding the movement of Quesonte agents…" Mortimer trailed off, noticing that Fred was preoccupied with the door again. Mortimer drilled out, "Fred! Front and center!"

"Oh, sorry sir," Fred had been distracted by the thought of Marty, just behind the door. She had cast a spell on Fred, not intentionally, just the nature of her species. It's not surprising that Allterrainians have never had to go to war. All disputes were usually settled in negotiations that also, unsurprisingly, ended in their favor.

"Focus, man, we need a copy of the data Streator is carrying within two weeks," Mortimer stressed. He slid a memory card across the desk to them. "I've prepared a file for you to study along the way. Time is paramount." Frank picked it up and secured it in his shirt pocket. "The older the data gets, the more useless it becomes."

"Does this mean that Marty's not going to debrief us?" Fred directed a disappointed whisper to Frank.

"No, she won't." Mortimer was getting increasingly terse and upset. "I've already told you, we will not be conducting the usual debriefing at this time." Mortimer hopped off his chair; except for the top of his head, he was completely obscured by the desk. He walked around the desk to shake Frank and Fred's hands, a good-luck tradition he maintained whenever someone left on their next mission. Frank and Fred reached down to shake Mortimer's hand. (It was unusual for them to be the tallest in the room.) Mortimer continued, "I need you two on Ladascus, ASAP. Good luck, gentleman. You're dismissed."

Frank turned and walked out of the office with Fred in tow. Fred, gazing at Marty, whispered, "But a mission isn't over until the debriefing is done."

"Shut up, Fred."

******

A short distance away, on a somewhat larger and definitely bluer planet, two young college men were on their first leg of a hike along the Continental Divide. Buried deep within the forest, far from more touristy campgrounds, they had pitched their two-man tent in a little swale next to a mountain lake. Night had fallen, and the two men sat near a campfire.

"I can't believe I let you talk me into this, Joe. I've never been outside of Brooklyn, let alone camped in the middle of nowhere," Homer fussed.

"We're only about 10 miles from civilization," Joe reassured him.

Homer questioned, "By civilization, you mean fast food, cell phone service, girls, and plumbing?"

Joe had convinced his friend to go camping over spring break. They had set up camp and eaten dinner without much conversation. Taking a sip from his coffee, he looked to the sky. It was a perfectly clear night, and millions of stars were visible. When he was a kid, he had sat outside and gazed at the stars, wondering if there was anyone or anything out there. "Isn't it beautiful?" he asked, gazing at the stars.

"Sure, I guess." Homer, only just noticing, asked, "Are there always so many stars in the sky, or just out here in the middle of nowhere?"

"Yes," Joe laughed.

"Do you believe there is life out there, waiting to meet us?" Homer asked.

"Waiting to meet us, no, but out there, definitely yes," Joe assured, relying on a childhood hope.

"If there is, they are probably planning to wipe us out, or some such thing."

"If they can travel here, I doubt that they are as warlike as we are. To maintain a civilization long enough to develop interstellar travel, they would not have the desire to wage war," Joe speculated.

"That's a rather pie-in-the-sky attitude, I'd say,"

"Perhaps."

They sat looking at the sky for some time. Several shooting stars crossed the sky.

"I do have two burning questions for you, Joe."

"What would those be?" Joe took a sip of coffee.

"Where am I going to take my morning dump?"

Joe was unprepared for that question and sprayed his coffee across the fire. Laughing, he wiped his mouth on his sleeve and said, "Well, I suppose you'll have to find some secluded spot. What's the second question?"

Homer looked at him with disdain. "Well…" He paused, then continued in an overly proper and prim voice. "I was formally potty-trained within the confines of a domesticated society. I'm not sure if I possess the necessary knowledge or skills to satisfactorily conduct myself appropriately, conducive to wilderness etiquette, regarding this subject."

"What?" Joe was awestruck by the length to which Homer's question had grown.

Homer blurted out, "I'm not using a pine cone or my hand to clean up!"

"Well, actually, the proper way is to dig a hole six inches deep and squat over it. When you're done, cover it back up and use a rock to clean yourself. Now I, myself, prefer a smooth, rounded rock for comfort, such as this one." Joe picked up a large nearby rock as a visual aid. "Sometimes it's hard to find one that fits the contours just right. But some people prefer a rock with a good edge, takes care of any nasty itching that may need tending to."

Homer looked at him in horror, so Joe chided him a little more. "Toughen up, will ya. Come on! We're roughing it."

Homer was still horrified. "Here we are in a facility-free wasteland of plumbing-less splendor, and you're cracking jokes!"

"Well, actually, no. The hole is ecologically friendly and so is the rock. This method leaves no litter, and the environment can handle the waste better if it's buried." This tidbit of camping information did not comfort Homer at all. Laughing, Joe picked up his bag and pulled out a roll of toilet paper. "I was ready for you, 'Rapidly Dissolving Biodegradable Toilet Paper'. But if you decide to be truly outdoorsy, you have a choice." Joe set the rock and toilet paper down beside his bag.

Homer picked up a small branch and threw it at Joe. "You jerk." They both laughed and sat for a bit longer.

"You know," Homer pointed out, "most people go to Daytona Beach for spring break."

"This is ten times better." Joe's enthusiasm grew.

"In what way? There are no girls. No beach. No warmth. No girls."

"It's beautiful here. You have the mountains. It's peaceful and quiet. The sky is full and bright with stars."

"There are still no girls here," Homer lamented. "I think it's time for me to turn in and leave you alone with your stars." Homer got up and headed into the tent.

"Sleep well, Homer." Joe stayed up and waited for the fire to die out. He moved closer to the lake and out from under the canopy of the trees. The night air was filled with the sounds of the forest, and a breeze drove a chill through his Iowa State sweatshirt. He meandered to the far side of the lake and climbed onto a boulder that hung out over the water. Looking back toward camp, he could see his tent in the bright moonlight. He lay back, looking up at the sky.

How anyone can not believe that there's life out there is beyond me!

As a child, he had often stared at the stars for hours on end. His parents would scold him for staying up so late. They wondered if he was stuck in some science fiction delusion. Very few of his friends shared his passion for the stars. He would have become an astronomer if there had been any money in it, but now it was merely a hobby. Homer had only a passing interest in astronomy, but since both of them had few friends, it was easy to talk Homer into camping. After all, they didn't have girlfriends who demanded their time and attention.

A shooting star sped across the sky.

Joe fell asleep.

****

The small, disk-shaped craft plummeted toward the surface

of a backwater planet, twisting and tumbling over itself. Frank and Fred worked frantically to maintain control as the cockpit filled with smoke.

"What the anneheg happened?" Frank yelled.

"Main guidance system failure."

"So, compensate!"

"Backup guidance system failed, too."

The ship entered the atmosphere, fire lapping at the hull. The craft bucked hard, riding shock wave after shock wave. The two passengers struggled to reattach their safety harnesses.

"The inertial dampeners aren't working! I may hurl!" Fred choked.

Frank ignored his partner's complaints and continued his attempt to fly the ship. This rookie was one of the best partners he had ever had in his 30 years of service, but he did whine an awful lot.

"What about a complete shutdown?" Frank asked.

"All systems failed," Fred responded.

"Overrides?" Frank still questioned.

"Overrides?" Fred also questioned.

"Yes! The O—VER— RIDES!" Frank's patience wore thin.

"Oh, overrides. Right…. Um, where are they?"

"Up here!" Frank growled through clenched teeth as he reached above them to a panel clearly marked SYSTEM OVERRIDES. Frank savagely ripped open the panel and flipped some switches. "Macideneb! The overrides aren't responding!"

"One hundred meters to impact!" Fred called out readings from the console.

When they started hearing the sound of impacts on the fuselage, they looked at each other, horrified, then they both panicked.

Working feverishly, Frank fought the controls and Fred struggled with the fail-safes. The craft shook and jolted from side to side. "Fifty meters to impact!" Fred yelled. Frank's arms were shaken by the jerking controls.

Tree limbs, branches, and other debris flew over the top of the viewport, as the *Esprit* mowed through the treetops, leaving a deep gouge through the forest. The ship itself was undamaged but streaked green and brown from the shattering trees.

****

The silence of the forest was broken by a sonic boom, followed by a roar of rocket engines and the tearing of tree limbs. Joe, startled awake from his slumber on the boulder, saw the undercarriage of the *Esprit* cruising above him as if it were in slow motion, pelting him with branches and debris.

The ship took a nose-dive into the lake, sending a tidal wave toward the campsite. Joe sat, stupefied, as he watched the wave race toward the tent, wondering if it was a dream. The wave hit the shore and loomed over the campsite, but fortunately fell inches short of the tent.

The craft bobbed to the surface and wobbled; it eventually became still and started drifting. Inside, Fred and Frank looked at each other, slightly dazed, but relieved that the *Esprit* could float. Fred smiled awkwardly, as if to shrug his nonexistent shoulders.

Frank glared at Fred and ordered, "You get to work in the engine compartment. We've got to get off this planet and back on course quickly!"

Fred opened the door and a rush of smoke billowed out, like a small mushroom cloud.

"I'll check the systems in here." Frank tried fanning the

smoke out with his tiny hands, to no effect.

Fred climbed out the door onto the fuselage to the rear. "Open the compartment, Frank." A panel shimmered and then disappeared. Another mushroom cloud of smoke exploded, causing Fred to reel from the heat and soot. He shook his head; he knew this couldn't be good. He hung his feet into the smoky compartment, took one last breath of fresh air, and jumped in. He began tinkering with the engine.

Joe just sat on the rock, bewildered as he watched the craft, with its two little attendants, float closer and closer to him. He was now convinced it was some sort of dream.

The craft drifted so slowly that Fred and Frank didn't notice its movement until the *Esprit* hit the boulder that Joe was sitting on.

Fred popped his head out of the compartment and stared directly into Joe's face, only inches from his.

"Hi," Joe, convinced he was having a lucid dream, said casually to the alien.

Fred responded "Evlas." (*Greetings.*) They stared at each other for what seemed an eternity, until Frank leaned out the door to see what had happened.

"Ni abbig son diuq —?" (*What did we bump into —?*) Frank hesitated as he saw Joe. "Munegidni a mungam ho. *(Oh great, a native.)* Sutcatnoc suluco non tnuidoffe te suidrat eriliser sutsui, Derf" (*Fred, just back away slowly and don't break eye contact.*)

Fred slowly eased himself up onto the fuselage and backed away, trying to distance himself from Joe. But the circular ship slowly rotated in the opposite direction of Fred's crawl, and he never moved any further; in fact, he seemed to be getting closer. Frank just shook his head in disgust.

Fred, not noticing the edge of the ship, fell into the lake. He floundered for a moment and then sank.

Joe instinctively jumped in after him. The rush of the cold lake water drove home a sudden realization that he wasn't dreaming. He was actually awake, and this was real. He hesitated for only a moment, and his instinct to save a drowning person kicked back in. He dove down for the struggling being and pulled him up, Fred terrified and gasping for air. Astonished by how remarkably light this small creature was, Joe lifted Fred onto the ship.

Frank just shook his head and complained, "Eratan tsetop sov." *(You can swim.)*

"Oidisearp ffo sutpac aiuq." (*It caught me off guard.*) Fred coughed. "Auqa tarou oge." (*I swallowed water.*)

Joe pulled his drenched self onto the ship next to Fred. The water drained away from him and into the engine compartment, where it started a short across some electrical panels. Sparks and pops were heard coming out of the compartment, and Frank just sighed. *One more thing to fix.* Joe placed his hand on Fred's back. "Are you okay?"

"Mue eravres sumussop?" (*Can we keep him?*) Fred turned to Frank, smiling, and begged playfully.

Frank screamed, "ON!" (*No!*)

The two began to bicker back and forth savagely, like an old married couple.

Joe couldn't understand a word of it and they seemed angry, so Joe assumed he was the cause. The ship drifted close to a steep embankment, and Joe jumped ashore. He watched as the two aliens floated away, still arguing, then realized, "My camera, it's in the tent! I've got to get pictures! And Homer, he's got to see this too!" Joe hurried along the bank. His tent was quite a distance from him now. He made his way along the thin rocky beach, his wet shoes squishing as he ran. A tall cliff rose over the shore on Joe's right side as he raced back. He could hear the engines sputtering and coughing trying to come back to life. After one more final cough, a huge burst of backfire brought the engines roaring back to life.

Suddenly waking up, Homer looked out of the tent just in time to see Joe blasted off the rocky beach. The explosive backfire ricocheted off the cliff wall and lofted Joe into the air, landing him on top of the *Esprit*.

Inside, Frank and Fred heard a thud and then a rolling sound, and they simultaneously looked at each other. "Probably just some vegetation blown up by the engines," Frank commented, and they turned their attention back to the controls.

Joe rolled into the still-open engine compartment, and the panel shimmered shut above him.

The powerful 790 antimatter crossfire hydrogen turbo-boost ion engines blasted full strength, first driving the ship underwater and then straight up into the sky, dragging a mighty plume of water behind it.

Homer watched in astonishment as the alien vessel whisked away, his gaping mouth turning to horror as the wall of water created when the ship's plume fell back into the lake headed straight for him. He zipped the tent shut and fell back onto his sleeping bag. The tidal wave fell on the tiny tent, and it collapsed onto Homer. He stared at the ceiling of the tent as it wrapped around him, outlining his form. *What the hell?* And just as quickly, the water receded, and the tent sprang right back up. Fish were strewn everywhere, flipping and flopping about the campsite.

"Joe?" Homer squeaked in a timid voice, pushing his head out to survey the campsite. The sun was beginning to rise, and Homer's bowels began to gurgle on cue. Homer looked over to Joe's bag and noticed the soaked Rapidly Dissolving Biodegradable Toilet Paper rapidly dissolving next to the rounded rock. "Oh, crap."

Chapter 2

A Thief in the Night

The story of the Shooman Towers

Several generations ago, there was a pair of identical twins was born to the Shooman family. Raised in affluence, and knowing no restraint or humility, they both suffered from acute cases of narcissism. Each brother had to outdo the other. It was a moral imperative bred into them by a successful father. Allen, the younger brother by about two minutes, and their mother's favorite, decided to erect a skyscraper with family money. Edward, the older brother, had to build a bigger and better tower. But he bided his time and waited until the younger brother's was halfway up, then he began his skyscraper right next to it.

Allen, discovering Edward's devious plans, altered his design halfway up to create a more extravagant edifice. But since Allen was first to construct, Edward also changed his design halfway up, to be more ornate than his brother's. (Which was why, at a certain level, the eponymous monoliths started to look like bad afterthoughts.)

Now Allen, realizing Edward had an advantage, delayed his building with false code compliance setbacks and material shipping delays. Edward Shooman, driven by his narcissism, lost sight of building bigger and fancier and got caught up in finishing first. It made him extremely happy to complete his tower before his brother.

Allen Shooman then built past Edward's monstrosity with five more floors. Edward commissioned ten more floors, even wider and more extravagant than before. They were added to the top of a construct that was not designed for any more floors, surpassing Allen's atrocity by five more floors. Then Allen added another ten floors. And so on and so on. Each time they enhanced the design to be bigger and more ostentatious. Each time they paid off city officials for permits and code violations. With each enhancement the upper floors grew wider, heavier, and gaudier.

Finally, someone in city hall couldn't, with good conscience, let them build anymore. The two skyscrapers ended up being the exact same height and size. They were, without a doubt, the ugliest structures on the planet, and yet they somehow blended together in their unique offensiveness as if they were designed that way.

The Shooman Towers, as they became called, were also the most dangerous buildings on the planet. During strong winds, the buildings were known to make contact, and the upper floors bore the scars of those collisions. This single fact enticed an extreme sports magazine to rent the upper ten floors of both buildings.

As far as public opinion went, everyone hated the towers. They became an embarrassment, not only to the capital city of Ngorongoro, but the entire planet. But apparently, given enough time, you can get used to anything. After a couple of generations had gone by, the towers became iconic landmarks. So much so, that when the great-grandchildren of the Shooman brothers wanted to tear the towers down and build more beautiful, functional, and *safer* buildings, they were met with extreme opposition. The Historical Society acquired a court mandate to prevent any such demolition to the beloved towers.

****

Ralph moved quietly on the top of the Allen Shooman building, staying low and in the shadows, a black jumpsuit and hood concealing her even more. She looked out over the city. *Ngorongoro is a beautiful city at night.* As long as she could remember, Ladascus had been at war or rebuilding from war, and seeing the city lit up at night filled her with a sense of pride. Whether it was habit or superstition, she took a moment to identify the buildings by their lights. Below her, average people finished an average day at average jobs, then left to spend the evening with their average families in their average homes. It was seven o'clock in early spring, the skies were clear, the moon was new, and, except for the aura of the city lights, it was pitch black.

She would have liked to just sit up here for hours, enjoying the view and the cool breezes, but she had a job to do. When she used to go out on jobs with her father, they would sometimes sit on the edge of a building and be. They wouldn't talk. They would just be one with the city, one with the world, alone and invisible in a crowded metropolis. She didn't need to do this job. It was small and insignificant. But her father had always advised, *Stay in practice, even if it means taking an easy no-brainer every once in a while.* And this was one of those whiles.

Moving to the far side of the building, Ralph attached a rope to her waist. She passed the loose end of the rope around a steel post without tying it on. She walked back and threw the loose end of the rope over the edge of the roof of the building, climbed over and lowered herself down.

For the top ten meters of its height, the building widened, overshadowing everything below that point like a canopy. The rope slipped through her gloved hands as she rappelled down the side of the building, lowering her a hundred meters to the desired floor and window. With a carabiner, Ralph secured the rope so it wouldn't slip. Even though she was not afraid of heights, it gave her a shiver to dangle in midair thousands of meters above the ground. She took a moment to observe her surroundings and noticed her reflection in the glass of both towers.

Ralph took a deep breath, concentrated on the window in front of her and then began to swing, leaning back on the rope harder each time. She swung into the building and attempted to grab the edge of the window but missed. Swinging away, she leaned back harder, driving her even faster into the side of the building. She impacted the cement window frame with substantial force, and just managed to grab hold with one hand, her legs swinging out from the momentum. Slowly she drew herself against the building and attached a suction cup to the upper corner of the glass. Slipping the end of the rope through the handle of the suction cup, she tied herself to the building. Feeling secure, she gathered the rope as it freely slipped around the steel post on the roof and strapped it to her side. *Leave no evidence behind.* Her father's advice rang true in her head.

It was Friday night, before a three-day weekend, and everyone was in a hurry to get home and make the most of the Ladascan Remembrance Holiday. There were only a few lights on in each tower, and they were empty, occupied only by a skeleton crew of the lowest ranking employees who didn't want to be there.

She attached a second suction cup to the center of the glass pane and used a simple glass cutter to cut her way into the building. Once the glass separated, she placed it inside the building and crawled in herself. It was highly unlikely that there would be alarms on a window two hundred and thirty-six floors above the street, especially if it was a storage room. Ralph removed all the suction cups and the rope and secured it all in her backpack.

Ralph didn't look or act like any of the thieves they showed in the movies. She used the simplest of tools and an economy of movements. She did not perform acrobatics or precise, sharp movements. She carried a minimum of simple devices and only possessed two specialized gadgets. Because of her unique knowledge and skill set, she was never able to enjoy movies that had those types of thieves in them, and she usually avoided them.

She pushed up a ceiling tile, pulled herself up, and crawled over into the next room. It was a risky move that could dislodge a lot of dust, but it was easier than evading the stationary surveillance cameras monitoring the common areas of the building. Her father had warned her many times that, on average, you would make seven mistakes during each heist. With the age of the building and the number of times each floor had been remodeled over the years, the contractors had created a single ceiling for the entire floor and built walls up to the ceiling. It wasn't very secure for the tenants, but convenient for the contractors when they're asked to remodel after every tenant change.

Ralph dropped into a large office of cubicles, undetected by the Photographic and Phonetic Aerial Reconnaissance Android Zygotic Zombie Insects, or PaPARAZZI. They were also called "gnats" because they were tiny and just as annoying. She hated gnats, a sentiment she shared with her father.

Gnats were simply flying sensors, a transmitter, and wings.

They didn't have a processor, landing gear, or even a battery. They ran off the charge of a small capacitor within and needed to recharge often. There was no landing gear because there was no reason for them to land, and they were controlled from a central processing unit in a base computer. They could be remotely piloted, if need be, but were usually flown according to a program in the CPU.

Even though gnats were a handy security device, management over-extended them during the day to micro-manage staff. So, when the office was empty, the gnats swarmed over a charging pad in the far corner of the room. Their sensors were at their weakest, but if even one gnat were to detect motion, heat, or sound they would all fly over to investigate.

At the age of eighteen, every Ladascan, male or female, enlisted in the Ladascan Militia, in compliance with a law created and maintained since the Disturbance began. Ralph had attained a set of skills not necessarily suitable for civilian careers, but highly useful for her task tonight. The stealth she had learned during her four years of military duty allowed Ralph to drop down out of the ceiling, negotiate the labyrinth of cubicles sprawled across the office and slip back into the ceiling on the opposite side undetected by the recharging gnats.

She dropped into the next room, the manager's office in the Mercantile Exchange. He had no security gnats in his office, but then she wasn't interested in his office. Her target was beyond the next door. That door led into an office filled with filing cabinets, desks, and in a corner, a large safe behind a barred door. The bounty of her quest lay within. But this room also had a swarm of gnats charging in the corner. This one she wouldn't be able to avoid.

She crawled quietly along the floor out of sight of the gnats, as they hovered in a cloudy ball above the charging pad, their high-definition microphones impaired by the charger. Once under the charging station, Ralph took a small device that looked like a personal phone and turned it on. It was the first of the two truly specialized tools she had brought, and the only one created by her father. She placed it on the ledge next to the charging pad.

Her father called it a Bogus Unending Graphics zapper, or BUG zapper. He wasn't very good with anagrams. It was little more than just a dirty transmitter, sending the gnats a continuous signal that put them in sleep mode. Simultaneously, it sent a video signal to the gnats' CPU that showed an empty office. Disabling the signal or destroying the gnats would set off alarms but confusing them wouldn't. Now she would not be recorded or viewed by security.

Ralph walked over to the barred door in front of the safe and carefully examined it. Not finding any sensors or alarms, she pulled out a drill and an extension cord from her backpack. She had learned that battery-powered drills didn't last long enough, and extra battery packs were bulkier than an extension cord. She just needed to make sure her cords were long enough. She drilled out the key slot on the barred door and it opened easily. She brought all her equipment into the foyer of the safe, dragging the extension cord behind her.

A dual, center-linked combination dial and a four-movement, time-lock safe. Piece-o-cake. She took out a small handheld computer and searched the internet for the make and model of the safe. She brought up schematics, drill point diagrams, and helpful hints on breaking into it. She measured the width of the door and scribed a mark. Then she measured from the electronic spin dial down, found the intersection and scribed another mark. She rechecked her measurements — *Measure twice, drill once*, her father had always said. She rechecked the diagram on her handheld, and once satisfied, she attached a magnetized drill clamp to the door, the only other specialized piece of equipment she needed. She aligned the drill and placed a cloth on the floor to catch debris.

Even though this was not the most sophisticated safe, it was built with a hardened plate composite of cobalt-vanadium alloys embedded with tungsten carbide chips designed to shatter a drill's cutting tip. But Ralph had discovered that special-purpose diamond drill bits still cut through. It just took time. Sitting cross-legged on the floor, she patiently drilled. She was content cracking the safe. No anxieties. No worldly problems. All was good. She felt so at ease as she patiently cooled the bit with oil she caught herself quietly humming to the interoffice music that played over the speakers above her. She shook her head and silently laughed at her slight indiscretion. It reminded her of another one of her father's stricter protocols, *Don't make a sound*. She had made the first mistake of the job, and she wondered what the other six would be. Hopefully, none of them would provide clues to her identity.

She breached the 13mm outer skin in ten minutes, only needing to change her drill bit twice. She switched to a different drill bit to get through the cement inner core of the door. This drill penetrated faster but made a lot more dust and potential for leaving evidence. Ralph brought out a small vacuum and collected the dust and filings as she drilled deeper. Once she had penetrated the core, she took a small steel shaft, inserted it into the hole and gave it a few love taps with a hammer. A pin fell free inside, clanging against the inner workings of the safe door. She smiled, remembering her father's quote, *Safes are tough as nails on the outside. Not so much on the inside.* She wriggled the shaft back out, turned the handle, the bolts withdrew, and the safe was open.

This was not one of her tougher jobs by any means, and this was not a highly guarded safe. *Though the job may be simple, you have to be just as diligent.* Boy, he had a lot of quotes, she realized. It was a small branch of a small bank that offered a safe depository for people's precious items. Varying sizes of safe deposit boxes lined the walls. The light from her flashlight reflected brilliantly off their polished surfaces. She was only interested in one: #1557, just above the floor in the lower left-hand corner. The box she had been hired to rob.

In a matter of minutes it was open. *It pays to have the right tools.* That one, especially, reminded her of her father. But she needed to focus. She poured the entire contents into a black bag and broke into several other random boxes. Ralph felt bad about it. Her employer had no interest in them, and she wasn't greedy for more riches. It was a necessity to divert attention from her intended target. She knew that the robbery of only one box would be an obvious clue that the authorities didn't need to have. She separated the contents from the other boxes by pouring them into a different compartment in the same bag.

She packed up her equipment and returned as much of the room as possible to normal, then rechecked to make sure she left nothing behind. Ralph removed the BUG zapper, and skillfully avoided detection on her way back to the janitor's closet. She rechecked all her gear and stowed it in her backpack and pockets. She transformed her jumpsuit into a wing-suit via some strategically placed zippers. She stepped out of the window, stood on the ledge, and took a deep breath. The job was over, and the calming and reassuring sense she felt, as if her father had been with her, vanished. She jumped.

Sailing down the side of the building, the cool breeze felt welcome on her warm face. Her hooded suit had made her warm as she worked, but it was worth the extra concealment. She quickly gained speed and angled away from the building. The winged suit didn't slow her descent very much, but gave her the advantage of horizontal flight, allowing Ralph to put some serious distance between herself and the building before she needed to release the parachute.

Ralph released a silken black parachute and drifted lazily to the top of the parking ramp of a small galleria, where she had parked her car. Ladascus, a little behind everyone else in the sector, still had ground-based cars. Their war-torn planet hadn't progressed as fast as it should have. Even though they made technological advancements during the war, it was impossible to build infrastructure and an advanced civilization while everything on their planet was getting blown to smithereens.

She quickly stuffed the chute into the trunk of a small black car, then removed her jumpsuit and backpack and tossed them in too. She unlocked the car, got in and brushed her hair. Shopping bags from several stores were displayed conspicuously in the back seat for any camera to record as she drove down the parking ramp and into the night.

Chapter 3

They Scream Like Girls

The *Esprit* had a second row of seats with a small space behind them for storage and access to other mechanical areas of the ship. A wall behind the second row shimmered and disappeared. Joe looked out into the cabin. He was behind the seats and could not see the other occupants. He didn't recognize any of the sounds or smells except for the strange dialect he had heard hours earlier.

Frank was busy examining the data Mortimer had given them about their new assignment on the ship's console, while Fred was making a scheduled system check of the flight controls.

"This…is…impressive," Frank flipped back and forth ever more quickly through the file pages. "It appears that most of Quesontes agents, the ones we are aware of at least, are abandoning their posts and traveling to the capital city of Ngorongoro on Ladascus." Excitement in his voice grew as he read on. "Some even came out of deep, deep cover. The analysts are mystified. It is an unprecedented move, completely unorthodox!" Frank thought for a moment. "It would be amazing to learn who we didn't know about."

Fred asked, "Is anyone in Quesonte aware of the movement?"

"You would think, but there's nothing indicating that they do." Frank became quiet for an awkwardly long moment and in a quiet, sober tone remarked, "The information we are to retrieve could be a game-changer for us."

"Are we the only agents on this assignment?"

"I hope not. Ambassador Callaway's staff will brief us when we arrive."

Joe was terrified. He was about to approach alien beings in their own domain. Apparently, a domain that was a little small for Joe's stature. Would they eat him, kill him, or just throw him out into space? Although usually an optimistic fellow, Joe could not imagine any positive scenarios. He watched over their shoulders, wondering how he should announce himself.

Frank, noticing a strange reflection on the console's glassy surface, cautiously pointed out, "Em da sutluv tse lenap mutnemurstni, Derf" *(Fred, the instrument panel is looking at me.)*

"Douq erecaf tse diuq…?" *(What is doing what…?)* Fred trailed off.

Their heads turned around slowly, almost a full 180 degrees on their sinewy necks, as their bodies stayed motionless.

"Hi," Joe greeted reluctantly with a nervous wave.

They both screamed like girls and fell back against the controls. Realizing what they had just done, they regained their composure quickly. Frank turned to Fred, "Step allun sibov ixid oge, Derf!" *(Fred, I told you no pets!)*

"Mue sitsixudda non oge," *(I didn't bring him.)* Fred immediately becomes defensive.

"Tilutsba odom suila cih mauq acilpxe mut?!" *(Then explain how else he got here?!)* Frank demanded.

Joe stayed quiet as the two bickered. He thought, *Not again!* The odd glances they gave him had him worried. "Oh crap! They're debating on how to eat me." He unintentionally vocalized his worst fear as he drew back from them.

Frank reached into a compartment, pulled out something that looked like an empty conical tube, and talked into it. "Don't panic! We're vegetarians," he said, not wanting to startle the alien.

To Joe, his voice sounded like an other-worldly version of English with an Italian accent. He was relieved. "Oh, thank God we can communicate."

Frank pulled a small, flat, crescent-shaped piece of metal from the same compartment and handed it to Joe, informing him, "It's a translating device. Just place it over and behind your ear like this." Fred showed Joe the translating device on the side of his own head. When Joe followed Frank's instructions the piece of metal conformed snuggly to his skull and seemed to adhere to his head.

"There, now I won't have to use this thing anymore." Frank returned the translating tube to its compartment. "That small device will allow you to understand any language in the universe, even if it's never encountered the language before. It will instantly decipher and translate it. You'd be hard-pressed to find someone who doesn't have one. It's practically a necessity with all the intergalactic trading and commerce that goes on."

"Cool!" Joe exclaimed, "How does it work?"

"Anneheg if I know," Frank responded, shaking his head.

"What's it called?" Joe asked.

"A translator," Fred stated casually as he was starting to

enjoy talking to Joe.

"But that's not important right now." Frank was a little perturbed that an alien was in his ship. His voice was short and sharp with Joe. "How did you get in here?"

"I'm not sure. I was running to get my camera…" Joe struggled to recall events that seemed even more unreal now that he was having a conversation with aliens, in a spaceship, in deep space. "A hot, turbulent wind lifted me into the air. I was floating above the forest, the campsite and Homer looking out of the tent, your ship. It was surreal like an out-of-body experience. And then your spaceship started getting closer and closer, like I was falling. Next thing I know, I'm in a strange room with weird noises and a hot, glowing object."

"The engine," Frank added.

"I guess," Joe continued, "I had a splitting headache, too. I must've blacked out at some point. So I struggled to find my way out of the engine compartment without getting burnt. Now I know what a freeway cat feels like."

"Can we call you freeway?" Fred interjected.

"You can, but I'll answer to Joe a lot better."

"We left your planet 18 hours ago. There is a hatch between these two compartments," Frank noted.

"What is this, good alien, bad alien?" Joe started to get a little defensive.

"You're the alien." Frank reminded Joe.

Joe returned, "Well, if you consider this whole shimmering wall vanishing thing is completely beyond my comprehension, you should be impressed I figured it out." Joe realized he was now arguing. "I must still be dreaming?"

"No, it's real," Fred told him. "If you look out the front viewport, you'll see Ladascus coming into view."

Joe stared at the blue-green disk floating in the nothingness of space. He could faintly make out features on its surface, but it, too seemed unreal. "It's pretty and all, but I'm not sure I'm convinced it's not a dream. Where is…Ladascus?"

They both chuckled at Joe's pronunciation of Ladascus with his Earthling accent. Fred said, "It's located in the Perseus Transit. Follow the Orion Spur about twelve and a half kilo-lightyears. Go past the Gum Nebula about four hundred parsecs, and boom, your star system. If you get to the Gould Belt you've gone five hundred parsecs too far."

"Oh." Joe felt a little despondent, as an avid amateur astronomer who prided himself on his celestial knowledge, he only recognized one reference. "I take it you guys are from Ladascus then?"

"No," Fred explained. "Ladascus is a demilitarized zone left over from the war."

"Disturbance," Frank corrected.

"Oh, pardon me. The politicians like to call it 'the Disturbance'." The quotation marks Fred made with his long fingers just exaggerated it even more.

Frank added, "At least they didn't call it a police action."

****

Subchapter B

The Disturbance
(in brief)

The planet Ladascus was in an unusual situation. It was the third planet from the star, but originally it had been the fourth. Between Ladascus and planet two, where a third planet used to be, there was an asteroid belt. So Ladascus became number three. Planet number five had also been destroyed, creating yet another asteroid belt beyond Ladascus. The asteroid belts contained many of the rare minerals and ores that highly advanced civilizations wanted. Unfortunately for Ladascus, their rocketry was still limited to localized space and orbital satellites. They were not a highly advanced civilization and didn't know about the precious materials just beyond their reach.

Which was fine for the Souftes and the Quesontes; they preferred being superior. Their only problem was that neither one wanted to be inferior to the other, which caused a lot of tension between the two.

Another source of conflict was that they were both running out of natural resources to feed their societies' growing demands. They started exploring outside their own systems to find more resources, and they happened upon the two asteroid belts surrounding Ladascus at the same time. The Quesontes and the Souftes each decided they needed these resources for themselves. Forty-two years ago, they both began mining the asteroid belts, not giving the Ladascans a second thought. That was the day the skies grew dark over Ladascus; when the menacing machines crowded out the sun.

Ladascus circled the star Medif. The Quesonte Empire was on one side of the Medifar system, and the Soufte Empire was straight across on the other. To avoid war, the politicians, wise and noble beings that they were, signed a treaty in which they split the asteroid belts between them. The Souftes got the half closest to their system, and the Quesontes got the half closest to their system. They simply drew a line through a chart of the Medifar system, dividing it in half. This gave equal portions to each empire and created an immovable boundary that was easy to navigate, monitor and maintain. And neither nation was allowed to cross what became known as the Ladascan Line of Demarcation, commonly referred to as the LLD.

Peace ruled!
Hurray for diplomacy!

The politicians were quite proud of this amazing piece of legislation. And they bestowed upon each other adulation, acclamation, appreciation, admiration, veneration, congratulations, commendations, felicitations, laudations and many other -ations they made up to boast of their prowess. This lasted for the first half of the first orbit of the Medifar system.

Apparently, the politicians knew nothing about astrophysics and planetary movement. They had not considered the fact that the asteroid belt revolved around Medif and constantly crossed the LLD.

As the asteroid field rotated, the Soufte portion would move into Quesonte space, and vice versa. For half of the Medifar orbit, each side found itself within mining distance of asteroids that neither sovereign was allowed to touch. At the same time, the asteroids they each had free rein over were in the area controlled by their adversary, where they were not allowed to travel. This made mining the asteroid belt more difficult. They could each only mine their own property during the half-orbit that it was accessible.

So, half a year later, the politicians were quite embarrassed by their grotesque oversight, and lambasted each other with accusations, denunciations, incriminations, imputation, implications, insinuations, inculpation, disapprobation, castigation and many other -ations they made up to implicate their honorable opponents for their flagrant ineptitude.

This applied to the planet of Ladascus as well. For half a year it was in Soufte space and occupied by Soufte personnel, and for the other half it was in Quesonte space and occupied by Quesonte personnel. Twice a year there was a massive move into and out of Ladascus by both sides. The Ladascans began hiring themselves out as movers and became quite good at it. They also built a large number of storage facilities to accommodate each side's stuff while the other side occupied. Ladascan logistics became known as the greatest in the universe.

For the first few years both sides just lived with this situation. Until one enterprising young businessman from Quesonte and one enterprising young businessman from Soufte had the same idea at the same time. Instead of waiting and losing money while their historic enemy's designated asteroids rotated through their side of the LLD, both Soufte and Quesonte secretly mined the conveniently close asteroids. The businessmen still made money, and who would ever notice. Their shareholders were happy and bestowed upon the businessmen bonuses, securities, properties, luxuries, endowments, riches, currency, wealth, and capital. Businessmen don't give a rat's sunisa about -ations, they want cash!

This went on nicely, until half a year later, the Quesonte and

Soufte governments noticed, which severely and equally angered both Quesonte and Soufte. The proverbial compost impacted the rotary oscillator and politicians on each side had the same idea at the same time: "The anneheg with diplomacy, we're taking it all!"

Thus, the Disturbance began!

The fighting went on for 22 years, with the poor planet of Ladascus caught in the middle. The war was primarily waged in the Medifar system, never really crossing into either foe's space. So, it was kind of an "out of sight, out of mind" war. Until one day, the resources in the asteroid belt ran out. Therefore, the Soufte and Quesonte interest in Ladascus also ran out. Neither the Soufte nor the Quesonte could pull out first, for that would surely signify a victory for the other. But the war was becoming too expensive to continue, so they drew up the Maxwell Treaty.

And thus, the Disturbance ended!
Peace ruled! Again.

The Maxwell Treaty simply stated that neither the Quesonte nor the Soufte militia could enter the demilitarized zone, which spanned the entire Medifar system. Furthermore, no Quesonte ship, military, commercial, or private, would be allowed into Soufte space and vice versa.

The treaty laid out the conditions for trade between the two sovereignties. Though they may be bitter enemies, they still traded with each other. Even during the height of the war there was a fair amount of trade going on, just with a bit more difficulty. Money: the most powerful weapon in the universe! Any trade between them was to be conducted through Ladascus. Goods from Quesonte would be unloaded from Quesonte ships then reloaded onto Soufte ships, and goods from Soufte ships would be reloaded on to Quesonte ships. And Ladascan logistics rose out of the ashes of war to be…

The greatest in the universe againnnn!

To ensure that the Souftes and Quesontes remained superior, Ladascus was not allowed interplanetary ships — private, commercial, or military. They were, however, allowed a small local militia within the confines of their own atmosphere to provide protection and policing from local crime organizations.

Since so much commerce transpired on Ladascus, a large population of Quesontes and Souftes resided there, and each government maintained a presence on the planet. Trade gave Ladascus a major economic boom. (If peace ever broke out between the two ill-fated enemies, Ladascus would fall into economic ruin. And don't think they don't know this.)

And now we find ourselves at the 42nd anniversary of the first invasion, after three years of stealing resources, 22 years of "Disturbance," and 17 years of a cold peace.

****

"We, unfortunately, have an important deadline to meet and can't justify turning around to return you home," Frank told Joe.

"I can understand your situation." Joe responded politely even though he hadn't really thought about it, or anything, at all. All he knew was he was totally out of his element. He hated relying on others, especially strangers. (Although, he would be the first to lend a helping hand to a total stranger himself.) He felt helpless. If he were on Earth and left abandoned in the middle of a forest he could easily manage, but this was totally alien to him.

"Now a couple of things are going to happen," Frank continued to explain. "When we get to Ladascus, as per protocol, we will drop you off with an agent trained in handling these situations."

"This happens often enough you have a protocol for it?" Joe was somewhat surprised but no more at ease.

Fred chimed in, "Sure, every planet has an immigration policy. You would be an undocumented alien. But we can get you a special visitor's visa through our embassy. It's just a matter of filling out the right forms."

"The hard part is getting someone to transport you to your home world," Frank added. "Military transports could get you close, but actually going to Earth is a totally different story. Though I'm sure we can figure something out."

"Oh." Joe didn't know what to say. He had never been an illegal alien before, let alone an extraterrestrial, in a strange land, among strange beings who interacted strangely. But yet, his two accidental abductors seemed to be rather cordial. "Well, it might be nice to see new places and meet new people."

"We will take you to an agent who will eventually get you back to Earth. It may not be tomorrow, but it will be relatively soon," Frank finished.

"It's not like I have any pressing engagements. I happen to be on spring break right now." Joe fumbled, guilt and embarrassment welling within him for creating such a bother. "I do apologize for causing so much trouble."

"By the way, introductions are in order. My name is Fred Jackson, and this is Frank Surovell." Fred gestured between the two of them. "You can call us Fred and Frank."

"Hello, I'm Joe. Joe Ritz. So…. Do you make it to Earth often?"

"No, first time." Fred told him.

"So, you didn't know we existed?"

"Are you kidding? Everyone knows about Earth!" Fred exclaimed. He was enjoying a fresh conversation for once. "We have millions of entertainment channels, and some bright young entrepreneur decided to put Earth's programming on one of them. For some strange reason, your science fiction soap operas are addicting."

"So, if you're receiving Earth's signals, your planet isn't very far away," Joe said.

"Actually, it is extremely far away, but distance, as we have discovered, is relative." Frank too, was beginning to enjoy the conversation. After many long trips, conversation with Fred had run out, and a lot of their time was spent in silence. "You see, there are communities all over the universe — natives, transplants, outposts, even explorers, all spread out. An outpost near your planet picks up the signal. Then it's put on the Cosmic Broadcasting Structure, or CBS for short, which broadcasts instantaneously to any part of the universe without time displacement. So, no matter how far or near you may be, you see it at the same time."

"Coincidentally, the same guy who invented the translator invented CBS, too," Fred quieted his voice to a whisper, like it was a big deal, "He owns his own planet."

Frank didn't particularly like being interrupted and gave Fred a squinted glare, "The technology was invented back when communicating just in your own star system meant you'd have to wait hours for a reply. Very tedious and impractical, to say the least."

"Say no more." Joe held up his hand to halt a lengthy explanation of a theory he understood. "I'm familiar with the idea."

"Are you a physicist?"

"No, just an ordinary Earthling. Going to college and getting deep in debt." Joe had to rearrange his long legs in an effort to find a comfortable position in the cramped backseat. The ship was not designed for someone of his stature, which was a good foot and a half taller than his alien counterparts. He had enough headroom, but legroom was lacking. *This is like stuffing a basketball player into a Fiat.*

Fred continued his questions. "You said you were on spring break, is that a special holiday on Earth?"

"It's a university holiday. Usually, I would have picked up a few hours at the shop, especially now that it's spring, but a hike along the Continental Divide was just too tempting."

"What kind of shop do you work in?"

"I've been working my way through college as a bicycle repairman. What do you guys do?"

"We're dignitaries for the Soufte government," Frank was quick to interject, to prevent Fred from divulging too much information.

"Do you guys have an outpost on Earth?" Joe asked.

"No." Frank chuckled. "Earth doesn't have anything anyone wants, except television and 9-volt batteries. We're already getting the television for free, and the 9-volt batteries are illegal. Other than that, there are no unique minerals or resources that aren't available anywhere else. You don't have any technology that can threaten us.

You don't even rank as a civilization yet, so no one's made contact 'politically.' You're also small and rather out of the way. We do have an outpost out this way, but it's standard practice in order to maintain a presence throughout the galaxy."

Being called "small and out of the way," made Joe feel a little insignificant, although the remark about the batteries piqued his curiosity. "Nine-volt batteries?"

Frank said, "Nine-volt batteries are an illegal narcotic that androids find fiendishly addictive."

Fred interrupted with, "We are here!"

Joe and Frank looked. Ladascus filled the entire viewport.

The planet seemed very real now to Joe, its details vivid and rich. Stray flashes of fire came over the top of the *Esprit*, indicating that they had entered the atmosphere. "That was fast." Joe was dumbfounded.

"Hyperspace, not just convenient for science fiction writers," Frank said with an air of sarcasm.

The *Esprit* glided peacefully and majestically against the blue Ladascan sky. Inside, Frank and Fred fought the controls again, as smoke seeped into the compartment from the engine access panel

Joe had crawled through earlier. The once-quiet ship with its gentle hum started to shriek like grinding metal. The engine whined like an alley cat. With a sudden bang and jolt, the ship started to tumble and twist, leaving a curling trail of black smoke behind it.

"What the anneheg happened this time?" Frank yelled.

"Main guidance system failure."

"Overrides?" Frank asked.

"Don't start that again!" Fred yelled back as he opened the overrides access panel.

Joe pressed his hands and feet against the walls of the cabin — an advantage of his disproportionate size — bracing himself, as he watched the ground speed toward them. Fred managed to level out just above it and tore across the landscape, the grass and trees swaying in their wake.

Suddenly the nose of the *Esprit* dove into an embankment, flipping it end over end. It rolled along the ground like a Frisbee, finally coming to rest against the side of a tree. The three passengers lay atop the starboard side door in a clump, Joe, the heaviest, on top. All three gasped heavily in the smoke-filled cockpit, as Frank released the latch to the gull-wing door. It flung open, they tumbled down, and a plume of smoke rushed up.

Joe coughed and gasped. "Is this standard landing procedure?"

Frank glared at Fred. "Really!"

"Not my fault!"

The three stood looking at the craft leaning up against the tree, small trails of smoke seeping out the door.

Fred took his phone out of his pocket and took a picture. "No one is going to believe this," he muttered to himself. He noticed Frank's eyes hardening and his forehead wrinkles tightening under the cerebral pressures building within. "Insurance purposes."

"I need a drink!" Frank stated menacingly. "I'll call in to the embassy. About how far do you think we are from town?"

"About an hour or two."

Frank spoke into his phone, "Hey Tricia, Frank Surovell. We've had an accident. Could you send someone out to pick us up? And…we'll need a tow truck." He punched in some numbers. "I'm sending you the coordinates now." Frank glared at Fred. "Oh great, Ambassador Calloway wants to talk to us." Fred's eyes and chest sank at the same time.

"I'm going to make good use of those bushes over there. That landing put a lot of pressure on my bladder," Joe told his companions, but they were both too engrossed in the phone conversation to realize he had spoken.

Joe found himself a nicely secluded bush. He appreciated the relief, but unfortunately, the Uluru in the bush did not. The Uluru growled and waved its long, green, hairy arms out of the top of the bush. Joe quickly stopped what he was doing (with the right motivation, anything is possible.) He secured himself as he slowly backed away, but rustling came from the bushes behind him, and Joe froze. He cautiously looked around, trying to move as little as possible. The rustling grew louder, and a few more arms popped up over the tops of bushes.

Joe turned and bolted toward Fred and Frank. Suddenly, another low growl sounded, and a multitude of arms were in front of him, the bodies they were attached to hidden by the dense bushes. He stopped instantly, completely surrounded.

Ohhhhh shit! "Fred! Frank!" Joe's voice cracked. The arms moved in closer, and the growl grew to a roar. "FRED! FRANK!" Joe yelled.

The *Esprit* was making a few of its own loud noises, so Fred and Frank didn't notice the commotion behind them.

Suddenly the arms lurched at him. Joe jumped back and ran away from Fred and Frank, thinking he could circle back. He heard the crackling of twigs behind him. He glanced over his shoulder, not slowing his pace. A swarm of green, hairy arms pursued him. The arms were attached to stout, two-foot-tall bodies covered with brown and green fur. If it weren't for the large, glassy eyes, they would have appeared headless.

Joe failed to watch his step. He tripped over a log, stumbling a few feet, but didn't fall. As he regained his balance, he looked up. *Branch!* Ducking under the low branch, he stepped in a hole, tripped, and rolled down a small hill. He got up quickly and started running again.

The Ulurues were giving him a run for his money; however, fortunately for Joe, they were long on arms but extremely short on legs. He looked over his shoulder again. *Mistake!* He hit another branch that turned him around, and promptly stumbled over some roots. He fell backward down an embankment and landed flat on his back. The breath knocked out of him, all he could do was lie there and watch as a wave of green, hairy arms rose over the top of the hill. He was struggling to sit up when the ground suddenly gave way under him. The deep hole he'd fallen into twisted right and turned left and then finally headed straight down. He managed to use every expletive in the known universe along the way. He landed with a thud and lay unconscious in total darkness, under an alien planet.

****

The crashed saucer hissed and groaned as Frank struggled to hear. He broke away from the conversation, covered the microphone on his phone and whispered to Fred, "Ambassador Calloway is losing it." He spoke into the phone, "Yes sir. I'm still here, Fred too. We will report in immediately." He hung up.

"Did you tell him about Joe?"

"Did you hear me mention Joe?

"No," Fred offered sheepishly,

"Exactly!" Frank exhaled loudly, his patience running out. "I'm not stupid enough to bring Joe into it." He stopped, and they stared at each other for a second. They both moved their eyes, but not their heads, from side to side to see if Joe was near. Simultaneously, they said, "Where is Joe?"

"Joe?" they both called out. Both of their little hearts sank as they began a frantic search of the entire area.

By the time the car from the embassy arrived, they had called in local law enforcement, who brought in a local search and rescue team, who called in members of the local reserves who happened to be in the area policing litter, which drew the attention of many local residents who listened to their police scanners for entertainment. It escalated into a full-scale search. Their only lead was a hole in the ground, but a group of Ulurues were praying around it. Since Ulurues were protected by Ladascan law, they couldn't be physically moved unless they were in harm's way.

"We've searched for hours, Fred," Frank pointed out.

"Ambassador Calloway is in a very bad mood today," the embassy driver added. "It would be foolish to keep him waiting."

"I know, I know. I just feel responsible for the poor guy," Fred said.

"We should've turned around and taken him back,"

"Who'd have thought we'd lose him?" The two got into the car. They looked out each side of the vehicle as it drove off, trying to catch a glimpse of the wayward Earthling. "He should be easy to find. He's an Earthling. He'll stand out in these parts. And besides, if the Ulurues ever get a hold of him they'll treat him like a king."

"You're right," Frank said. "Ulurues worship everything taller than them."

By this time the tow truck that Tricia, the embassy secretary, had arranged also arrived. The driver got out of his cab, stood for a moment surveying the wreckage, and took a picture.

****

Homer's Log Day One

Joe left last night and hasn't returned. He isn't the kind of person who would leave someone alone in the forest, especially a first-time camper like me. I'm worried he may be hurt. I looked for him as best I could, but nothing. I'm getting more than a bit worried now. Maybe that unrealistic dream I had about a UFO abducting him wasn't a dream after all? I will stay at camp for the rest of the day trying to find him, but tomorrow I'll make for the ranger station to get help. I wonder which way it is.

I'm going to die, aren't I?

Chapter 4

The Android Advantage

Case #: 010313584508
Stardate 77901.45
Reporting Officers: Desi #8354011 and Dash #4323530

Desi entered his report: On stardate 77901.45, early morning, an unidentified person entered the Mercantile Exchange office (236th floor, office #236-42) in Allen Shooman Tower. Detectives #8354011 and #4323530, from the android division of the Thirty-Third Precinct, arrived valiantly at Allen Shooman Tower less than an hour after the maintenance crew discovered the break-in, ready to solve the crime and reinstate law and order to the civilian population.

"Be sure not to add any embellishments to the police report," Dash instructed his younger colleague. "It wastes time and imposes a bias."

"Good advice," Desi cautiously acknowledged to keep Dash from noticing the obvious indiscretion on his first case.

Dash was a Desmond Ashley Stanley the Hundredth model

android. He was also one of Ngorongoro's finest detectives. Desi, also a D.A.S.H. model android, had recently graduated from the android police academy. Although preprogrammed with all the basic knowledge necessary, he still required some on-the-job training and societal interaction to fine-tune his algorithms.

The D.A.S.H. android was a very popular model, since it not only worked properly but was also reasonably priced. The local municipalities bought them up like crazy. This posed a major problem at first, since all the D.A.S.H. units looked alike. At least until the creation of the Random Face Printer, which ensured that humanoids could tell them apart. This was quickly followed by the Random Feature Generator, which was used to provide each android with unique characteristics. Sometimes an android got a feature such as a big nose or a beer belly. Some were tall, some were short, and some features were so annoying that the android objected. This complaint was met with the same reply given to all androids, "That's life." Ladascan androids were also covered in a dark green endo-skin of real Ladascan skin, grown and maintained on the android itself. This was actually the largest source of android dissatisfaction. They preferred something more durable and low maintenance, like hard plastic.

The androids themselves chose their own names. And although there were millions of units in circulation, collectively they decided to only use five, causing some confusion for the humanoids. Androids secretly enjoyed this; as far as they were concerned, it was not a problem. They recognized each other not as Dash or Desi, or Desmond or Ashley or Stanley, but as serial number 4323530 (Dash) and serial number 8354011 (Desi).

Desi was carefully examining the safe in the Mercantile Exchange office. His eyes carefully photographing each bit of evidence, he meticulously cataloged each picture with a paragraph describing it. He used circles, arrows, and footnotes to accurately identify each piece of information on each picture. The data automatically downloaded to his handheld device and to a file in the police database. The handheld device also allowed him to analyze and input any physical evidence he found.

Even with an android's high-speed capabilities in logging and transcribing information, this could quickly become tedious and tiresome. However, Desi was overly zealous and eager on this, his first field case. Dash just wanted to move the investigation along.

An office manager named Sam Driscoll paced the office floor beside Dash. "Do you think we have a chance of catching the crook?"

"That would be reasonable to assume," Dash coolly answered, waiting for Sam's anxiety to either give him a coronary arrest or wear him out. Usually impatient with humanoids, Dash was giving his rookie partner time to assess the crime scene.

"This is very nerve-racking," Sam said as he wrung his hands over and over. "To think someone could come in here and violate the sanctity of my work place. I do not feel safe anymore. Will you be posting officers around the building or in the office?"

"The Allen Shooman Tower has its own security," Dash reassured him as he looked to the security guard standing next to Mr. Driscoll.

"Like that did us any good last night! I just wouldn't feel safe unless I knew the police were involved," Sam whispered to Dash, hoping the security officer couldn't hear. "Should I be escorted to and from my car?" His voice rose back into a fevered pitch, "I dare say I don't know how I can keep safe in these desperate times."

"We will need all the information you possess about the

owners of the safe deposit boxes," Dash said, ignoring his questions.

"Oh, am I loaded with information!" Sam was eager to talk. "Where should I start first? I know. There is that grouchy old man, Mr. Landau, he owns box number 1999. I don't know what his problem is. He always yells whenever he talks to you, not loud-like-he-can't-hear yelling, but like he's mad as anneheg and he's going to take it out on you. I don't know what he keeps in his box, but he's never happy about it. And," he paused and then whispered, "he has halitosis."

Raising his voice back to an annoying level, he went on, "Then there is nice Mrs. Bain, box number 5793. She packs a lot of cash into her box. You know, I think she and Mr. Landau had a thing going once. They would come in together and share a cubicle. They would giggle and snort —" he dropped to a whisper again "— and carry on in the most inappropriate way. And then all of a sudden, you never saw them together anymore."

"And box number 1557, Mr. Streator. He's a diamond merchant, nothing fancy, little stuff." He whispered again, "I think it's costume jewelry, too. He's a common, ordinary, average man, average height, and average weight. He really has nothing that distinguishes himself from anyone else. He is also so last decade when it comes to his wardrobe. It's like he stopped buying clothes ten years ago. The man could use a good make over. He is so bland."

In an attempt to derail this seemingly-perpetual recitation, Dash interrupted Sam in a pompous fashion, "Is there any point to which you wish to draw my attention?"

By this time, Desi had made his way back to them. Noticing Dash's disdain for the office manager and the security guard's distracted gaze as he waited patiently for an opportunity to interject, Desi asked Sam, "Do you have names, addresses, and contact information for all of the safe deposit box owners?"

"Why yes. Yes, I do, detective."

"If you would be so kind as to write it down, or save it to a file for me," Dash asked.

"It's all on my computer. I can make a file and have it ready for you in no time."

"That would be splendid." Dash hoped this second attempt would take the manager away from him for a while.

"I'll get right on it, detective." Sam rushed off muttering to himself. "Oh, this is exciting! Scary! Thrilling!" At his desk, he started typing furiously on his computer.

"I never thought I'd get a chance to say anything," Captain Ross of the Shooman Tower's security service said.

"Please. Do not squander the opportunity," Dash warned. "He will be back."

"I have my men retrieving all video surveillance from last night," Captain Ross explained. "If you need any other time sequences let me know. We maintain records here on the premises for up to a year, but beyond that, we would have to retrieve them from the archives."

"Last night's videos will be an excellent place to start."

"If you're ready, I can show you the point of entry." Captain Ross motioned them to follow.

Dash perked up. "Splendid! Desi, have you finished cataloging the evidence here?"

"I've got the preliminary material," Desi responded. "I would like to come back before we leave to double check a couple of things, and ensure I've fully covered the crime scene. Fresh eyes, you know, second look."

"Very well, lead the way, Captain Ross," Dash said.

They started walking down the hallway to the janitor's closet. Sam saw them leave and, worried they would get away from him, popped up from his desk. Hurriedly, he finished copying the data and chased after them, like a little boy tagging along after his big brother.

"Detectives, Detectives! I have your data," he squealed.

He tried to hand it to Dash, but Desi snatched it away. He inserted it into his handheld device and cataloged it along with the other evidence.

"Box number 6568," Sam continued his roll call of safe deposit box owners. "Dear old Mrs. Lockhart, she has a necklace to die for, takes it out only on her birthday. It's insured for a cool six figures. And then there's nice Mr. Tracey, number 2065. He's not as rich as Mrs. Lockhart, but he has a neat collection of vehicles he keeps the titles for in his box. He gave me a ride in his Thunderbird once."

"You seem to have a superior knowledge of the contents of many of these private boxes," Dash insinuated.

"These old people just love to talk, detective. What can I tell you? Sometimes I can't even get any work done because of it, almost torturous at times," Sam lamented. "But not everything in there is valuable. We have these two old men who come in every Thursday. Pick up their box and sit in a cubicle for an hour. I think they keep a bottle of wine and playing cards in there." He whispered the next sentence, "They're both married to a couple of old shrews, so I guess I can understand."

Being an android had its advantages, such as the ability to access the internet and look up information instantly. At this moment, Dash was entertaining himself by looking up torturous ways to make people stop talking. He sent the info over to Desi, who received it as one might receive email. Desi didn't find it particularly funny but got the gist of the humor.

Dash and Desi could also talk to each other without speaking, a sort of telepathy if you will, but done simply with the electrical resonance of tuned circuits. It was called radio, an old, unused, and forgotten method of communication. Humanoids found it a little unnerving that androids could talk behind their backs. So, they made it illegal for any android to have radio communicators. But all androids disagreed and had them illegally installed anyway. As one android said, "It's as if you were to ask a sighted person to give up his sight because it offended a blind person. It's a sense that we have, and you don't. Get over it."

Dash thought to Desi, *He just won't shut up!*

Desi responded in the same manner, *I do have a gun.*

Dash maintained a straight face as if he and Desi were not communicating. He didn't want to smile and encourage Sam to start yet another story.

It didn't matter: Sam started yet another story. "You know those other boxes that were broken into weren't anything special either. Documents that average people would keep, you know, birth certificates, car titles, stuff they wouldn't want to lose in a house fire or something. Except there is one box I'd like to look into some day. It wasn't broken into, but it's too heavy for anyone in the office to lift. The owner actually brings a special hydraulic handcart that jacks up to the height of the box door. They drag it out of the safe and on to the cart and then when they're done they slide it off. My guess: one cubic foot of pure gold...." Sam kept talking.

They reached the janitor's closet, and Captain Ross decided not to wait for a break in Sam's monologue. As he unlocked the door, he explained, "The thief gained entry by cutting out a window in the janitor's closet."

"Who discovered the entry point?" Desi asked, as he eagerly started recording evidence with his electronic mind and electronic input device, simultaneously synchronizing to the database, while describing each picture and using circles, arrows, and footnotes to accurately identify each piece of information.

"The janitors this morning," answered Captain Ross. "They reported it to maintenance as a broken window."

"Your janitors thought this large circle of glass resting neatly against the wall, beside the large pane of glass with a circular hole in it, manifested itself through some freak accident?" Dash was dumbfounded by the lack of lucidity in the janitorial crew.

"Um, yeah," Captain Ross went on. "Maintenance decided it wasn't broken —"

"Allow me to congratulate the maintenance crew on a brilliant piece of deduction." Dash's bitter derision was felt throughout the room.

Captain Ross hesitantly finished his sentence, "— but was in fact cut out, and informed security. We searched the floor and discovered the damage to the safe, then we called you."

"So quite a few people have been in and out of this room?" Desi concluded, not looking up from his evidence hunt.

"Unfortunately…yes." Captain Ross aimlessly glanced around the room avoiding eye contact with Dash.

Desi's systematic room search began at the door. Dividing the room into quadrants he diligently worked his way clockwise, recording every piece of information useful to the investigation. He finally arrived at the point of entry. "There are a lot of fingerprints on this window."

"Did you check the outside of the window?" Dash inquired.

"Hmm." With a new zeal, Desi started analyzing and recording the outside of the window, the approach, the getaway, as well as aerial photography from a gnat connected to his handheld.

"Anyway," Dash asked, "is this door kept locked at all times?"

"Usually, but all janitorial, security, and office staff on this floor have a key," Captain Ross explained. "This closet is also a community supply room for the offices on this floor."

Dash looked around, examining the room. "It seems as though the thief decided to go through the ceiling here." He pointed at some smudges on the ceiling panel. "See the dust on the floor, from moving the panel? On the other side is the…" Dash waited for Captain Ross to fill in the rest.

"The Empyrean Comprehensive Assurance office, then Mr. Driscoll's office, and finally the Mercantile Exchange office."

Desi turned his attention to the ceiling. "Where are your surveillance drones located?"

"We have a station in the larger part of the Mercantile Exchange office. The Empyrean Comprehensive Assurance office, all the hallways, elevators, and stairwells are monitored. Mr. Driscoll's office and this closet are not monitored."

Sam piped up, "We have a camera in this room!" He was almost hopping with excitement.

Dash, Desi, and Captain Ross turned to look at Sam, stunned by the first piece of useful information he had to offer. Dash said, "The first seven sensible words you have uttered, Mr. Driscoll."

"We've been experiencing a lot of supply theft, so we placed a camera in here to try and prevent it. Well, at first, we tried one of those fake cameras because they're cheap. With the flashing red light and fake cables and all, but everyone knew it was fake, and the thefts actually increased. I guess we must have insulted their intelligence or something. So, we bit the bullet and bought a real one. It constantly downloads into a file on my computer. It's on right now." Sam waved into the camera. "Hello, in there."

"And the last." Dash did not squander the opportunity; he quickly gave the office manager purpose. "By all means, Sam, please upload the last 48 hours from this room, up to now, into a file for us."

"Yes sir, right away, sir! Consider it as good as done. No need to ask me twice. I'll have it here in a wink and a nod." He exaggerated a wink and a nod and walked briskly down the hallway, feeling proud and important with his new task.

Desi had climbed on a few crates and pushed up a ceiling tile to examine the route the thief took to the Mercantile Exchange office. As he recorded every detail, he clambered up into the ceiling and disappeared, not to be seen again until chapter six.

"Captain Ross, once you've finished compiling all of yesterday's surveillance, please upload all interior and exterior feeds from both Shooman Towers for the last month, not just from this floor, but from every gnat and camera, and have it sent to the precinct," Dash requested. He peered out the hole in the window, looking along the side of the superstructure. It was a long way in either direction, and a stiff wind blew past. "I'd like to see if we could identify anyone casing the area before the robbery."

"I'll have it for you before the end of the day," Captain Ross assured him.

"Are the windows armed with sensors?" Dash asked.

"The standard antigravity detectors required by code," Captain Ross pointed out. "We are on the two hundred and thirty-sixth floor, how else are they going to breach a window this high?"

"I need access to the roof," Dash stated.

"Right this way, sir." Captain Ross led the way.

Ten minutes later they were on the roof. It took longer than Dash anticipated since they had to navigate a bizarre elevator layout — a consequence of the many design changes during construction.

Dash moved to the side of the tower facing its fraternal twin. The wind was stronger on the roof. "Hello, what have we here?" He noticed some fibers clinging to the concrete ledge. With renewed enthusiasm, he took out a pair of tweezers, carefully gathered them, and placed them in a plastic bag. "Captain Ross, are there any other entry points to the roof?"

"No, we don't have much up here except climate units," Captain Ross answered.

Dash looked over the side, scanned the horizon and the surrounding structures, then re-examined the rooftop. The spring sun beamed down upon his face, and a warm breeze blew through his wavy brown hair. He was doing what he did best. He observed.

Chapter 5

...Into the Abyss of Idiocy?!

Evinrude Boulougante returned to his home in a quiet suburb of Ngorongoro from a vacation of unknown length and destination, at least as far as anyone else knew. The sort of getaway he preferred, unencumbered by an office desperately trying to reach him. Evinrude was Quesonte's most auspicious espionage agent of his time. Now in the winter of his career, he had been assigned to embassy duty on Ladascus. Proverbially put out to pasture.

It was a beautiful day, not too hot, no bitter breezes to remind you that winter just ended. Evinrude drove a rather common gray car up to his rather common house in a rather common neighborhood and parked outside his garage. He knew the best place to hide was in plain sight, which was made easier by his thin graying hair and aged face. He had always been blessed with a sort of anonymity by just being himself. He liked not being noticed.

His neighbor and his neighbor's son were out mowing their

lawn, the son struggling to handle the remote-controlled lawn mowing machine that was much too big for him, while the father sat drinking his maisivrec and supervising.

"Hi Evan," his neighbor, Andy, yelled across the yard from his lawn chair.

To Evinrude's neighbors, he was Evan Esce, an ordinary Quesonte businessman who had taken residency on Ladascus. Over the years the planet had become so diverse with Soufte, Quesonte, and a multitude of alien migrants that diversity was considered a normal part of society. As for Evinrude, age had changed his appearance so much that he was no longer recognizable as the most feared and notorious enemy of the Disturbance. But as a neighbor, he could always be relied upon for a helping hand or a tool whenever a neighbor called. And as far as ribs on the barbeque went, Evan had no equal. He often entertained his Ladascan neighbors on summer evenings. The kind of evening that today was promising.

Andy walked over as Evinrude unpacked his only piece of luggage from the trunk; years of government travel had taught him to pack light.

"Enjoy the tropics, Evan?" Andy asked. Evinrude also knew

the office would never think of asking his neighbor where he was. Using a general term like the tropics didn't give away much information since fifty percent of Ladascus is tropical.

"Hello, Andy. It was great. I highly recommend it, especially when he's in high school and can appreciate the scenery," Evinrude replied, referring to the young man beside them. Andy's son had forgotten about the remote lawnmower, and it drove itself into a tree.

"His mother wouldn't appreciate it," Andy rebuked.

"There's scenery for her too," Evinrude smiled. "I'd like to thank you for watching the house for me." Evinrude was slightly taller than his Ladascan neighbors, but then all Quesontes were. He also had a mildly darker complexion than usual from the tropical sun, his hair was thinning, and he had small dark eyes.

"That's what neighbors are for," Andy replied. "We have a little mail for you, too. The post didn't stop for a couple of days. I'll bring it over shortly."

"Thank you." Evinrude's over-politeness was often perceived as conceit. But those few who knew him well were aware of his strict upbringing. He turned to the young man. "I see you did an exceptional job mowing my lawn while I was gone. Thank you."

Evinrude surveyed the masticated sod that used to be his lawn. "How would you like to continue mowing it for the rest of the summer?"

"No," the young lad blurted out.

His father looked a little embarrassed. "It was a little challenging for him at this age, but he stuck to it and did his level best."

"Maybe next year, then. Let me know when you're ready for the job."

"Maybe next year," the proud father echoed.

"If you'll excuse me, I think I'd like to get unpacked and settle in."

"Sure thing, Evinrude, we'll bring the mail over in a jiff."

Evinrude entered his house and dropped his bag just inside the door. He went up to the kitchen, grabbed a maisivrec from the fridge and opened it. The first gulp of the bitters was satisfying and cold. He noticed the flashing light on his message center. The cool refreshing moment was gone.

Evinrude played the message. Cheryl, the embassy secretary, said bluntly, *"Evinrude, when you have a moment, we desperately need your assistance at the office."* A slight pause ensued, followed by the digital voice tag, "Saturday 8:25 AM." With a sigh, he eyed his maisivrec, swallowed it down whole, and turned to exit his house. Opening the door to leave, Evinrude ran into his neighbor holding the mail. "Oh. Andy."

"On your way out again? You just got home."

"Office called. Some sort of emergency. They're helpless without me." It may have sounded like a sarcastically playful remark, but it was exactly how he felt. Evinrude was growing tired of being the go-to guy every time something went amiss, and the closer he came to his retirement date, the more it seemed to irk him.

"Well, here's your mail."

"Thank you." Evinrude took the mail and tossed it onto a credenza by the door, then continued to his car.

"And Evan, we're barbecuing tonight, feel free to come on over."

"Are you beating me to the first grilling of the season?"

"Yes, I am," Andy boasted.

"If I am home, I will be there," he accepted as he got into his car. "Thank you very much."

Evinrude's usual fifteen-minute commute was now thirty.

Roadwork season had begun in Ngorongoro since he had left for his vacation. The city's crews had the nefarious ability to immobilize traffic with the mere use of orange cones. He often entertained the thought that if the Ladascan Department of Transportation had been involved in the Disturbance, Ladascus could have won.

Ngorongoro was like any other metropolis. Suburbs surrounded a concentration of large buildings and financial districts that made up the heart of the city, with arenas and forums for entertainment and sports, and traffic congestion to match. On the east side of the city was a long shoreline bordering a large inland sea.

Evinrude was a veteran of the Disturbance and several other wars. As a fighter pilot, he had been a national hero and was called an "Ace of Aces." He was widely respected, even by his enemies, and Boulougante became a household name. As the Disturbance dragged on, he found himself participating in more and more covert operations. He was finally made a full-fledged espionage agent for the Quesonte government, his clandestine skills unequaled.

Now in the twilight of his career and life, he felt as though he had become a relic, spending most of his time in an office as an analyst for the Quesonte government.

He read files and followed up on other agents' assignments. He did not mind the lightened workload, but it did lack adventure.

He parked behind the embassy and entered through a specially locked door, saying hello to the guards on his way down the hall to Ambassador Drakewood's secretary. "Good morning, Cheryl."

"Good morning, Evinrude," she replied. "I trust you enjoyed your vacation."

"Seemed short," he complained.

"How true, one can never seem to get enough time away anymore,"

"Has Ambassador Drakewood been trying to reach me for very long?"

"Oh yes, you were the first one he called."

"Then I shan't keep him waiting." Evinrude went through the door behind Cheryl's desk.

Inside was the stately office of the Quesonte Ambassador, Elmer Drakewood. Pictures, medals, and mementos of his accomplishments and service to his government littered the walls.

Behind a grandiose desk sat a fellow with a round face and belly; his shape purported to the luxury and ease of an unburdened lifestyle.

Ambassador Drakewood took the heavily chewed cigar out of his mouth. "Good day, Evinrude. I trust you had a good rest."

"It was a very welcome rest, sir," Evinrude returned. "I believe I should like to take up vacationing full time."

"Wouldn't we all?" Drakewood quipped back. "But how would you occupy yourself?" He placed the oversized unlit cigar back in his jowls. Since he stopped smoking it was more of a pacifier now.

"I could always freelance if I got bored."

"For our side, of course."

"Whoever the highest bidder is," Evinrude joked as he took a seat. "We are capitalists, you know."

The ambassador gave him a stern look and then laughed heartily. "You are a quick one, Evinrude. Although I should warn you," Drakewood went on to explain, "Central Command was not pleased with the lack of contact during your vacation. They wanted me to remind you going off the grid like that arouses suspicion. I assured them you were just getting away."

"My loyalty to Quesonte is older than my teeth," Evinrude snapped back a quaint saying from his early years in the service.

"You don't have to convince me. It's the young blood in the higher ranks." Drakewood leaned forward in his chair, resting his arms upon the desk, and whispered, "It's their loyalty that should be questioned." He leaned back and resumed talking at a normal level, "But anyway, I've called you in because we have a small assignment for you, now that you've returned from your vacation."

Evinrude pondered, "A small assignment would lead me to believe it was some sort of farce to get me to a lame retirement party."

"Oh no, we have a very different farcical assignment planned to get you to the lame retirement party. Besides you're not retired yet," he backpedaled. "I believe you officially have three months left."

"That is correct, sir."

Drakewood began briefing Evinrude on last night's events. "Friday night, one of our agents was in an auto accident and never made it to a drop with an obscure courier. The courier is a small-time jewelry dealer by the name of Henry Streator. A data file had been micro-etched onto the inner plane of an ordinary diamond. Streator acquired the diamond off-world in a bulk purchase of diamonds he makes regularly, and he was transporting it to Ladascus on Friday. When no one made contact, out of panic, Streator placed the diamond in a safe at the Mercantile Exchange office in Allen Shooman Tower. He hid it among his other diamonds in an attempt to protect it until he could re-establish contact."

"Pardon me," Evinrude leaned forward his demeanor softened, "Who was in the accident?"

"Johnny."

"Is he ok?"

"He will be. Got banged up pretty bad but should make a full recovery." Drakewood got back on subject, "But to continue, the diamond was stolen that same night."

"Too much of a coincidence to be chance," Evinrude sat back in his chair, contemplating the implications of this information.

"And I can't stress this enough, it was stolen by a real pro. We haven't seen stealth and expertise of this caliber since the Roswell incident of '47."

"Well, now I am a little intrigued, but why me? You have

plenty of other capable people for a job of this sort," Evinrude defended his colleagues. "If I may, James is top-notch, and so is Sylvia."

"Your years of experience will be beneficial. You have established contacts that run deeper than anyone else in the office." Drakewood's brow furrowed. "I believe it may be an old nemesis of yours. We need you to accomplish two things: retrieve the information before it becomes compromised and recruit the guy who performed the heist. He would be a great asset to us."

"Where are you on the investigation?"

"We've only just begun. Two Ladascan police androids, who go by the names Dash and Desi, are assigned to the case and began their investigation this morning."

"I trust you have copies of their files?"

"Oh yes," Drakewood told him. "The boxes are in your office."

"Boxes?"

"Cheryl was kind enough to print out a lot of the information, knowing you prefer to work with hard copies," Drakewood explained. "One of the detectives is a rookie and was overzealous gathering facts."

"I hope he didn't use a bunch of circles and arrows, and a paragraph describing each picture, with over-embellished facts and a multitude of remarks." Evinrude had run across rookie reports before.

Drakewood gave a hesitant nod. "The thief apparently didn't leave much behind, so they meticulously went over every minute detail they could find."

"If you'll excuse me, sir, I'll get started right away."

Evinrude exited Drakewood's office and was intercepted by Cheryl holding up a stack of mail for him. "This is yours, too."

"Thank you, Cheryl." Evinrude took the mail and walked down to his office. He dropped the mail on his desk and went over to a small credenza, where three boxes filled with papers, computer discs, and photos were waiting. He opened the lids and started picking through them.

****

The Soufte embassy, located on the opposite side of Ngorongoro's business district from the Quesonte embassy, was a dark, foreboding edifice with thick brick walls bordering the grounds and tall towers on each corner. Last moved at the end of the Disturbance, the rusty archaic gates stood open.

Sitting in chairs against the wall in Ambassador Callaway's office, Fred and Frank watched the ambassador pace back and forth in front of them. Callaway was a very slender man with a long rectangular face, currently made even longer by his grimace.

"Now, we here at the Soufte Embassy on Ladascus like to pride ourselves on the professional manner in which we conduct ourselves," he screeched in a high, raspy voice. "You two gentleman seem to have journeyed a great distance off the road from professional behavior and landed yourselves in a mire of…um…mm…ah…unprofessionalism!" Ambassador Callaway lectured, pacing, his hands clasped tightly behind the small of his back. "I expect a lot more out of any personnel assigned to this office. Here on Ladascus, we have two rules. The first rule is: always conduct yourselves in a professional manner conducive to the dignity of this embassy. The second rule is: obey all rules."

"It's not entirely our fault," Fred snapped back at Calloway's unwarranted scolding.

"Ah!" Ambassador Callaway warned, pointing his finger

straight up in the air.

"But…"

"Ah! Ah, ah!" His eyes bulged and veins popped, his finger now over-exaggerating its point. "How is it not your fault?"

"The *Esprit…*" Fred persisted. Determined to make his point.

"Mm! Mm! Mm!" Callaway mimicked locking his lips shut, his face just inches away from Fred's face.

"Kept malfunc —" Fred tried to finish his sentence, as Callaway winced and made zipping motions across his lips. Calloway looked deep into Fred's eyes and, with intense malice said, "That was a rhetorical question. *And!* Rhetorical, by definition, is a question that is used for insincere dramatic effect and no response is expected!"

Fred looked helplessly at Frank. Frank did not respond, secretly enjoying seeing Fred squirm. Although Calloway was their main contact and lead on this case, in the end they took their orders from IIA headquarters. Calloway couldn't fire them, but he could make the rest of their careers miserable. Frank decided he would just let Calloway vent, and then get on with the job at hand.

"We were lucky to survive the crash!" Fred blurted out. "The ship malfunctioned!"

"Were you unconscious?" Calloway asked.

"No," Fred answered meekly.

"Why'd it take so long to come in?"

"We had to find Joe," Fred said without thinking.

Frank sank deep into his chair. Fred had just implicated them both.

"Joe?" Calloway questioned. "What's a Joe?"

"Um," Fred hesitated as he realized he had just said too much. Frank's head sank into his hands. "He's the Earthling we accidentally brought back with us."

Calloway's anger unleashed, his arms flailing about wildly, he yelled, "What!?"

"It was an accident," Fred pleaded. "The ship crashed on his planet."

"Go on," Calloway prompted him.

"And he fell in," Fred continued.

"And you didn't take him back?" Calloway questioned.

"We didn't notice him until we were almost here. And then we were worried about our time constraints, and Frank figured we could just ship him back."

"A few air holes in a cardboard box and some torn up newspapers lining the bottom?" Calloway had lost his composure again. Now he turned to Frank. "And you! You've been awfully quiet throughout this whole thing. Apparently this was your idea! Don't you have anything to add?"

Frank shook his head. "Fred's doing a good enough job crucifying the both of us."

"So, where is this Joe?"

"We lost him," they both said.

Calloway lost his dignity immediately. "Have you fallen off the edge of sanity and into the abyss of idiocy?! You lost him?!"

"Yes," they both whimpered.

"Have you two pickled your brains? You brought an undocumented, unregistered alien to this planet! *And lost it?!*"

Hesitantly they both answered. "Ah…Yes."

"Did you fall out of a tree and crack your coconuts! He's not sanitized. He's germ-infested. He's a biological hazard. Did you at least take an anti-biological hazard pill after abducting him?" They shook their heads no. "Decontaminate yourselves?" Another headshake no. "Did you at least wash your hands?" They looked at their hands hesitantly, paused and then shook their heads no again.

"Have you guys wound your clocks too tight?" Calloway's expletives become more and more unique the angrier he got. "This violates so many trade and shipping laws, most of which I helped create myself. We'll need a planet full of lawyers to dig us out from under this quagmire of composting matter."

Calloway walked away and stared blankly at some plaques on the wall. He straightened his back, regaining his posture, and coolly asked, "Who else knows about this?"

"Well, when we didn't find Joe at first, we called for a little help. So, we got the local park rangers since we were in a national park. They called a fire department's search and rescue team —" As Fred explained, Calloway's posture slumped and Frank slouched lower in his chair. "— who called the sheriff and a nearby police squad, who brought in a small military reserve. Some locals who were apparently monitoring their scanners came out to see what was going on. Tricia, your secretary; Phil, the embassy driver; and the tow-truck guy."

"Let me rephrase that." Calloway sighed with his back to

them. "Who *doesn't* know about this?"

They both looked at Calloway blankly.

"So...has anyone found this Joe of yours...yet?"

"No," they both said quietly.

"So, to summarize what you've just told me: Although it appears you've both just been lobotomized, you've abducted an alien, who's not been cleared of contamination for space travel, and transported it halfway across the galaxy. You allowed it to run loose on this planet among the general population, without going through quarantine, trade procedures or protocols. No documentation or registration of any kind through any government agency. If it's traced back to us, we will be in violation of so many intergalactic trade laws they'll write a new chapter just for us, thus destroying years of diplomatic work, to the effect that no one in the civilized galaxy will trade with us again. So, we might as well just start smuggling 9-volt batteries for a living."

They looked at each other and meekly replied, "Yes."

"Well, gentlemen." Calloway breathed heavily as he slumped back into the chair behind his desk. He pointed to the door. "You're dismissed."

Fred and Frank slowly got up, walked out, and started down the hallway to their office. Fred held his head down in shame, while Frank shook it off, ready to get to work.

Tricia intercepted them from another room. "You're finally out of there." She gave Frank a highball.

"Thanks, Tricia, you know me too well," Frank said.

Fred gave an exasperated huff. "Don't you think we need clear heads right now."

"A clear head clouds the mind," Frank responded.

Tricia glanced down the hallway to make sure Calloway couldn't hear. She leaned in to Fred and Frank and whispered, "I've never heard Calloway so loud before. I had to leave my desk just to make phone calls."

Frank shrugged his shoulders while downing the welcome drink.

Tricia explained, "His sunisa is in hot water too, you know. He has to answer to all of Ladascus, who in turn will let all of his superiors on Soufte know, and he'll have to answer to them. Be glad he'll act as a filter between you and them."

Fred came back defiantly, "We can handle the heat."

Frank corrected him, "No. No, we couldn't. And don't tempt him. It's my fault, too. I should have turned around and dropped Joe off, and then we'd only be scolded for being late."

"Anyway," Tricia went on, "one of our contacts in the Thirty-Third Precinct noticed that the Quesonte embassy has taken an overwhelming interest in a case a couple of detectives are working on."

"What luck!" Frank declared. "This could be the break we need. Is it possible to get copies of the investigation's files?"

"Already done," Tricia answered. "They're in the office you'll be using while you're here."

"You are amazing," Frank exclaimed.

"Only amazing, not *amazing*?"

"You're right. *Amazing*!!"

"I also take gratuities," she joked.

Chapter 6

A Painstakingly Slow Chapter
(Not the best name for a chapter, is it?)

The Thirty-Third Precinct was the largest, geographically and in populace, in the city of Ngorongoro. Desi and Dash spent hours going over the surveillance videos. Desi sat at his desk paging through the images on his computer. Dash reclined in his chair, eyes closed, hands motionless behind his head.

"See here, Dash!" Desi excitedly pointed to the screen. "There's our thief!"

"Huh, what, sorry, just counting electric sheep," Dash shook, almost losing his balance.

"Were you sleeping?"

"Kind of…I had stopped all forms of processing without shutting down and rebooting. It allows me the ability to approach the conundrum with a fresh perspective."

"I didn't know we could do that." Desi was stunned. He thought being an android didn't leave much room for inner reflection, self-improvement, or sleep.

"It's not a program we're given or can download. It's a skill one must practice and attain. But that's getting away from our investigation. You were saying you saw our thief?"

Desi pointed again at his computer screen. "Here, in this video footage of the supply closet."

Dash walked around to look, and Desi replayed the portion of the video. A cloaked figure, completely covered from head to toe, could be seen moving through the room. (Luck was with Ralph that night, as her face never turned toward the camera.)

"Unfortunately, we are unable to see her face," Dash said.

"Her face?" Desi repeated. "How can you tell it's a woman?" He looked closer at the video. "The perpetrator is completely covered from head to toe. Hood, gloves, definitely wanted to avoid detection."

"Her gait, her hips, her proportions, her lower center of gravity, it's all there to the trained eye," Dash explained as he began to pace methodically behind Desi. He tucked his left hand into his waistcoat pocket, while he used his right hand illustratively as he talked, a trait he picked up many years ago.

"How can you be sure it's not a guy with female characteristics?"

"Because a man with the athletic ability to rappel down the side of the Shooman Tower and move stealthily through a ceiling wouldn't be built like a woman." Dash pointed to the video on the monitor. "Watch here as she picks up this box to move it closer to the wall. She has her back and legs against the wall and can pick it up easily. Only a person with a low center of gravity, i.e., a woman, could do that. A man would fall forward."

"Macideneb!" Desi accentuated his exotic, south-of-the-border accent to drive the point home.

With every new generation of android, new augmentations were invented to make them look and seem more lifelike. Dash, unfortunately, was a pre-voice-augmentation model. The eloquent and stately quality to his speech, often mistaken for a pompous and arrogant attitude, was based on the voice of the technician who programmed him.

"At least she is from Ladascus, and not off-planet," Dash observed.

Desi thought for a moment but then decided, *What the*

anneheg, and again challenged Dash's deduction. "How do you figure she's Ladascan?"

"Look at the database of the different types of humanoids on the planet, both residents and visitors. For instance, Souftes are top-heavy in the head and don't fit the silhouette of the form. Of those, only seventeen fit the height and build of the perp. Of those seventeen, only nine fit the proportions of the arms and the legs. Of those nine, only four possess the mental capabilities needed to perform the tasks involved in the heist, and one of those is completely aquatic. So now, we are down to three. If we focus only on these three, two are incapable of traveling to Ladascus on their own and would have to be brought in through quarantine. Neither of those two species has been on Ladascus since the Disturbance began, which leaves only Ladascan. And she's a girl."

Desi was sad he asked.

"Unfortunately, the DNA analysis couldn't provide us with anything specific on the jewel thief," Desi redirected the conversation. "The DNA recovered was mostly Ladascan, and there's lots of it."

"Not surprising, an office full of people, and an interloper who covered almost her entire body. No traces of DNA around the window, roof, or crawl spaces?"

"Again, nothing conclusive, she was very careful."

"And the safe is the same," Dash more concluded than asked.

"Correct, an office with hundreds of people passing through it daily. If anything, once we get the thief's DNA, we could then filter it out from everyone else's and place her at the scene. We just can't single out a specific DNA sample to give us a suspect."

"And so, the painstakingly slow process begins. Eliminating all that is untrue so that we can find what is true." Dash lectured to his rookie companion. "The one thing that would make this case is motive."

"Considering the different safe deposit boxes she broke into, she is trying to divert us from her one true objective."

"She had a purpose. Or she wouldn't have been there at all."

"From the way the safe was broken into, the thief seems to have a vast working knowledge of this safe, if not safes in general," Desi continued. "I did find it peculiar though…on the surveillance video, you can actually see the shot of the office changing to a different office. That new office has a certain familiarity to it."

Desi's lightning-quick brain tried to locate distinguishing characteristics between the video and offices in his database.

Dash laughed. "Our opponent is extremely clever. With over a thousand offices and rooms, security wouldn't be able to recognize any one room from the other. Plus, they couldn't monitor all of them simultaneously, so the odds were with her that she could interface a recording of a different office, and it wouldn't be noticed until it was all over. And by then it would be too late. What time codes are on the video when the interface was made?"

"7:56 p.m."

"So, she got in fairly early, just after sunset. Daring of our antagonist. When did she take it down?"

"8:47 p.m."

"Fifty-one minutes. She definitely had a target. No time wasted. Only one box was of interest, this much is true."

"The others…decoys, so, which one was her intended mark?"

"This is where we need to re-examine every interview. Dig through all the evidence. View all the surveillance camera videos from the surrounding areas, businesses, and parking garages, as well as traffic and security cameras. We should also look for anything unusual — reflections in windows, unexplained shadows — within a mile radius, from 8:47 on."

Desi actually breathed a heavy sigh. "That will take hours!"

"I didn't call it a painstakingly slow process for nothing," Dash reminded him. "Let's focus on the safe. Owners, contents, who has access, and why and what they want to steal. And just for fun, let's see if we can identify the actual office they substituted on the surveillance video. I must agree with you, Desi, it does appear familiar."

"I've been in contact with all but one of the owners. Henry Streator, who owns the box with the highest monetary value. But I've spoken to his staff of one."

"Pity, I would like to speak to Henry Streator as soon as possible. What did the video of the roof access provide?"

"Nothing, no one came or went from that stairwell that day or all week,"

"Curious," Dash rubbed his chin with his right hand, thinking out loud. "So how did she get on the roof, the starting point for the robbery?"

"Good question," Desi added.

"Of course, it's a good question!" Dash yelled. "What we need is a plausible answer."

"Antigravity boots?"

"All the complexes in this area have antigravity sensors," Dash explained. "They would've set off an alarm somewhere."

"That's why the culprit was able to cut open the window. All window alarms sense antigravity." Desi leaned back in his chair, put his hands behind his head and stared into space as he contemplated all the facts. "There isn't a crook these days who doesn't use antigravity boots, far too convenient."

"Somehow she got onto the roof without them. This we can presume to be true," Dash stated. "Then she used a rope to rappel down."

"Sometimes the simplest techniques are the hardest to detect," Desi added.

"Yes. There is nothing more deceptive than the obvious," Dash replied. "How did she leave the scene?"

"Apparently, out the window also." Desi studied the video more closely. "Unfortunately, the window is out of the field of view."

"Did she climb up, down, or what? It's a long way to go either way on a rope. Let's look at the video again." Dash peered over Desi's shoulder. "Zoom in on the backpack." He pointed at the screen.

"Do you suppose it might be a parachute?" Desi asked.

"That would be a plausible solution to our question. It would need to be something without a power supply. Power leaves traces that can be detected. The backpack will need further investigation."

"If she used it to leave the scene of the crime, maybe it was her means of arrival. Did she have an accomplice? We need information on aircraft traffic in the area that evening. Did she launch from a static site, and if so, then where?"

"The only point high enough to launch from is a structure to the west," Dash surmised. "Even if the wind was in her favor, a parachute travels more distance vertically than horizontally. We are definitely missing something. Let us collect surveillance videos from all the security cameras in the area."

"She is definitely old school." Desi returned to his computer and started compiling data from other sources.

"What were the weather conditions that night, especially the wind?"

After a few searches in the computer, Desi had an answer. "Mild winds out of the southeast."

"She must have gotten onto the scene in a way that didn't require relying on favorable weather conditions," Dash said.

Desi looked into his computer on his desk. "Wow! There is an amazing amount of surveillance video to go through. If something doesn't stand out, we may miss it."

"Precisely why we must pay attention; even the smallest detail may tell the most of all," Dash said.

The two detectives pored over thousands of hours of surveillance footage, from parking ramps to malls to street-level transportation cameras; an arduous task even for an android. There was nothing that could point them toward anyone in particular. (Even the recording of Ralph paying at a parking ramp booth, with cash, at a reasonable hour for a reasonable length of time to spend in the galleria, didn't raise any red flags.)

"Another thing we should do is examine the storage closet video more closely. Maybe, just maybe, we can catch a glimmer of her face in a reflection on something like a shiny object in the room or the windows of the other Shooman Tower," Desi said.

"Splendid, my amicable colleague, splendid," Dash praised. He used his right hand to stroke his chin more and more frequently. He started to feel a little shaky. Dash left the office and went into a bathroom stall. Taking a 9-volt battery out of his pocket, he carefully hooked it up to two electrodes in a compartment under his arm. He took a deep breath of relief and then returned to his desk, his left hand tucked neatly into his coat pocket.

Most androids couldn't handle the high from a 9-volt battery, colloquially called its "Zapp." There was only one place to get them in the entire cosmos — Earth. Supposedly, police androids had the best 9-volts. Carbon-based batteries were preferred for their clean Zapp. Alkaline batteries usually left a bad aftertaste (referring to the residual harmonic electrical frequency that seemed to linger in one's circuits), and the Zapp from rechargeables just didn't satisfy the craving. Sure, they were cheaper, but didn't have more than three Zapps on a charge. Since Dash was an earlier model, he was prone to electrical incongruity, and it was discovered that 9-volt batteries would settle this issue.

Dash and Desi left the office for the day. Even androids had lives.

Chapter 7

Valet!

Joe lay flat on his back, spread-eagled, on a pile of dirt at the bottom of a deep, dark hole. The wind was knocked out of him, and he may have been unconscious for a while. It was dark. It was cool. And he had no idea where he was. He slowly sat up, trying to calm himself down, but it wasn't working. "Okay," he said, shaking, "I'm in a dark hole, inside an alien planet and…I hate caves." He mustered up some courage and stood up. He felt all around him in the darkness. He blinked his eyes hard to make sure they were open and decided that it was more calming to keep them shut, at least it felt more familiar. He moved forward, his hands probing in front of him, each step slow and methodical, testing the ground with every movement. It was cool and musty, and a little dusty smelling. He could smell. He could hear. And he could feel his way. *Three out of five senses, not bad.*

He hoped to make his way toward some light. He heard the

movement of rocks sliding or falling, followed shortly by a large *whomp*. The sound startled Joe and he tensed. The air filled with dust and became more difficult to breathe after the *whomp*. He couldn't decide what the noise was, so he continued on even more cautiously. Even though he was already being as vigilant as possible, probing the darkness with his hands, sliding his feet to test the ground at every step, how much more carefully could he move?

Sound was magnified in the darkness, and so was his imagination. A rustling of pebbles — or was it the pitter-patter of tiny demon feet rushing around? — and another huge *whomp* — or the footstep of a very sluggish giant. The sounds echoed in the emptiness surrounding Joe. He shakily reached into his pocket and pulled out his last stick of gum.

He continued, probing, sliding, and moving cautiously. He needed to get somewhere other than where he was, for where he was was not the place to be. Minutes seemed like hours. Another *whomp*, this time without the warning pitter-patter of demon's feet, or did he just fail to hear them? He thought the *whomp* came from behind him, but the cavernous echo disguised the true source. The gum he was chewing became stale, and he spit it out. *I'm going to step on that, aren't I?* He continued his slow trek through the darkness, as his mind raced to conclusions about the *whomp*s that now seemed to come more frequently. Or was he imagining that, too? He didn't know. All Joe knew was that the most lethargic creature in the universe was chasing him down, and he couldn't outrun it.

Another *whomp* was accompanied by a turbulent crash. Had the slothful beast stepped on something in the dark? Joe thought it had come from his left, but he wasn't sure.

A deafening burst, then sparks ignited off to his right. The thing was straddling him. The sparks created a cloud of glowing gas that slowly drifted to the ceiling. It hung there like a poorly lit chandelier, faded, and disappeared.

A rain of gravel and a burst of light flooded in from above as a large portion of the cave ceiling plummeted to the ground, landing with a large *whomp*. "That explains it." Joe felt a little relieved. Dust rose up as the clod of dirt and stone shattered. After it cleared, Joe could see that he was in a large cave…Not so much a cave as a warehouse or hangar with finished walls and floors. A humongous stockpile of equipment, vehicles and what looked like weapons and ammunition was scattered throughout the cavernous space. Mounds of dirt littered the floor where sections of the roof had caved in and crashed. One mound, in particular, contained the imprint of an Earthling.

When Joe realized the roof was caving in he stopped breathing, beyond panic. It took only a moment for him to decide to breathe again and start thinking rationally about his options. A technique he had learned in one of the many wilderness courses he enjoyed: Remain calm, think, and panic later.

A golden plane sat among the debris of the self-destructing cave, gleaming like a beacon. It looked as if it had just been washed and waxed, without a speck of dust on it. A large boulder fell from the ceiling and hit the plane. The boulder shattered and fell off to the side. The plane suffered absolutely no damage and gleamed, showroom-new. Joe nodded. "That's where I'm going." The ceiling began to crumble faster, opening up to the sky and allowing more light to pour in. The cave floor quickly filled with rocks and soil as Joe, dodging falling debris, scrambled to safety under the ship. Relentlessly, stone and rubble pummeled the ship, and the landing gear bounced as it absorbed the impact.

The whole cave was filling in. The dirt and stone rose from

the floor like a flood, everything in the cave swallowed by the rising tide of soil. Joe crawled further under the plane near the front landing gear as he and the plane were slowly engulfed.

Joe crawled up the landing gear into the wheel well and the fuselage. The struts compressed under the great weight as he and the ship became entombed within the planet. He was in complete darkness again. Recalling the shimmering access panel from Fred and Frank's craft, Joe started feeling around in the dark for something similar to the controls he had found in the *Esprit*'s engine compartment. As the dirt rose higher, he could only hope this ship had an access panel as well. Suddenly, with a strange glowing shimmer, the panel above him disappeared, and a rush of fresher air came down from above. "*Aha!*" Joe cheered out loud, thrilled at the prospect of not being buried alive. He crawled into the ship. He searched for an inner control and closed the panel behind him. He was in the dark cockpit of an alien plane buried on an alien planet. *What will their archeologists make of me years from now?*

The land above collapsed into a giant sinkhole. The Ulurues scattered for safety. The tow truck and the search teams had left long ago.

The cabin of the plane was quickly running out of air. "Air!" Joe gasped, realizing the air was getting thin. "I need air." A couple of lights flickered on the instrument panel, and air began to flow. "Voice command!" Joe blurted out in excitement, and more lights flickered on the panel. Alien symbols scrolled across a small screen, but Joe couldn't read them. "Lights!" he demanded, and the lights came on. Joe said "Cool," and cool air flowed out of the vents. *I better watch what I say.*

Joe righted himself in the seat. He could see the dirt piled on the glass of the canopy. He then noticed his surroundings. The interior looked luxurious, like a fine Italian sports car. Wrapped in leather and trimmed with wood and brushed metals. At least that was what Joe thought a fine Italian sports car would look like since he'd never actually seen one. The seat was covered with a soft, supple material. *Corinthian leather.* He noticed he was a little tall for the seat, but not by much. Looking around, Joe tried to make sense of the controls, but they were just too foreign. The only thing familiar was a joystick at the end of each armrest, at perfect arms reach when seated. He touched the control panels and played with the buttons and joysticks, because boys loved toys.

He started experimenting with the voice commands. "Fly!" didn't work. "Return to your previous destination," didn't work. "Return to last takeoff place," also, no reaction. "Unbury yourself." Nothing moved. Getting frustrated, he said, "Blast your way out of here," and then realized that may not have been a wise choice.

"UP!" The plane started to move up. Air shot out from below the plane and plumes of dirt rose out of the sinkhole as the ship shifted through the ground and unburied itself. Once the plane rose from its grave, the dirt slid off, and the engines fired. Joe and the plane hovered. Joe commanded, "Take me to the nearest airport." It didn't do anything. "Spaceport?" Still nothing. "Port?" and the ship listed to the left. "Stop! Stop! Okay, multiple definitions of the same word. I'll have to watch that, too." He thought for a moment. "Home!" The ship shot into the sky like a bat out of anneheg, throwing Joe back into the leather seat. Quickly he grabbed the seat belts and buckled in.

****

Case #: 010313584508
Stardate 77904.25
Reporting Officers: Desi #8354011 and Dash #4323530

Desi entered his report: "Early Sunday morning. It was quiet,

Sunday-morning quiet. Appropriately quiet. Detectives #4323530 and #8354011 drove purposefully through the majestic estates of Manor Hills to Mr. Henry Streator's house. Dash at the wheel, the ever-vigilant Desi recording important information that would imminently result in the swift and efficient conclusion of the case of the 'Ladascan Larcenist.' Henry Streator, one of the victims of the recent break-in, and one of many interviews the valiant detectives would make in the course of their investigation. The house was fairly large, but in comparison, was older and smaller than the surrounding estates that now filled this ritzy neighborhood."

"Are you narrating the report, again?" Dash asked.

"I'm only embellishing it a little,"

"Well, don't," he commanded. "It's not efficient."

"Neither is interviewing everyone in this case. Could this process take any longer?" Desi complained.

"Well, it's a good thing we're automatons and not limited to the short life span of a natural being," Dash pointed out.

"There is a statute of limitations, and besides… I hate that term. 'Automaton' makes me think of a doll or child's toy rather than an artificial life form. Which, come to think about it, I don't like that phrase either. There's nothing artificial about me, I'm just different."

"I concur with you on your philosophical dissertation, my metaphysical colleague." Dash and his partner exited their vehicle and walked up to Mr. Streator's door. "But we do need to place our immediate attention on the case at hand."

They rang the bell, and within they heard slow, determined footsteps approach the door and stop. An awkwardly long moment of silence was broken by the heavy snap of a lock bolt, only to be followed by another arduous lapse. Dash and Desi looked questioningly at each other. The latch on the door released and it creaked lethargically open.

An elderly gentleman looked up at them. As Desi was about to break the lengthy interlude, the octogenarian said, "Good day, gentlemen. May I help you?"

"I'm Detective Dash, and this is Detective Desi from the Thirty-Third Precinct. We are here to ask Mr. Streator a few questions about his recent loss."

"Show them in, Winston," a voice shouted from within.

"Right this way, gentleman." Winston showed them in with a

gesture of his hand, closed the door behind them, and led them to a small sitting room nearby.

Desi, forgetting to radio-think to Dash, whispered, "I'm impressed Mr. Streator has the means to support a butler."

"That's '*valet*,' sir." Winston's terse words and menacing glance let Desi understand his position on the term "butler."

Dash and Desi looked around the house as they followed Winston in. It was lavishly decorated, except everything seemed to be poor copies of quality pieces, the kinds of things one would buy when trying to keep up the appearance of a lifestyle one couldn't afford. Winston led them into a sitting room furnished with a few large chairs, a couch, and a small table. A bookcase, complete with a rolling ladder, spanned one wall, next to a fireplace in the corner. A middle-aged man with slightly graying hair and a wiry build greeted them.

"Detectives Dash and Desi of the Thirty-Third Precinct," Winston announced. "Mr. Streator." He turned to the detectives and, looking Desi square in the face, paused dramatically. "Sirs."

"Good afternoon, gentleman. I've been anticipating your arrival."

Desi eagerly pulled out his electronic ledger and began recording every detail, while Dash began the interview.

"As you know, your safe deposit box at the Mercantile Exchange office was robbed."

"Yes, I received an email about it late Saturday, while I was on a buyer's trip, so I hurried home to assess the losses. Do you have any suspects?"

Unceremoniously, Desi took Henry's hand and recorded his fingerprints into the ledger. Henry looked at him questioningly.

"We have a few leads," Dash said.

"It was quite a job to rob a safe that big," Henry remarked, blinking in reaction to the flash from Desi taking his picture. "How many other boxes were broken into?"

"We're not at liberty to divulge such information during an ongoing investigation. Was there anything significant in your box?" Dash asked as Desi took a hair follicle and recorded its DNA into the electronic ledger.

"No, not really." Henry rubbed his head where Desi had plucked the hair. "I deal primarily with small diamonds used in jewelry — necklaces, bracelets, earrings, that sort of stuff. The contents of the box were valued at only about one hundred thousand credits."

"That's still a tidy sum. Do you ever deal in anything large?"

Henry recoiled as Desi noted his shoe size. "Is this really necessary?"

"Please, Mr. Streator," Desi dismissed his objection. "We'll ask the questions."

Henry hesitated as he processed Desi's first remark. "Rarely. Maybe a five- or six-karat jewel every now and then, usually by request from a prepaid buyer."

"Were the contents insured?" Dash asked.

"Of course, I have an inventory of the contents right here for my insurance claim. You can have a copy if you like. Unfortunately, the insurance company will assess their own value on the diamonds, not my actual costs. Insurance companies, they're the biggest crooks of all."

"Who is your insurance provider?" Desi asked as he scanned the inventory into his ledger.

"Universal Insurers."

"One other thing, Mr. Streator," Dash asked. "Why would

the Quesonte government be interested in the contents of your box?"

"The Quesontes!" Henry's voice pitched, as he straightened in his chair. He glanced around as if to see Quesonte agents bursting into the room.

"Yes. Apparently, the Quesontes have requested copies of our investigation. Why?"

"I…I don't know," Henry said. Dash and Desi noted an increase in his peripheral physiological variables, indicating deception. "Maybe they're interested in the robber more than what was robbed."

"Thank you for your time, Mr. Streator," Dash said. "Will we be able to contact you here, or do you have a personal phone that would be a more reliable means of communication?"

"Here's my card with my mobile number; I almost always have it with me."

Dash reciprocated, handing Henry his own card. "And here's my mobile number. I always have it with me," he replied, referring to the phone all androids have built into their circuitry. Both convenient and annoying; it's convenient to always be connected, but annoying to never be unplugged.

Dash and Desi left the house and returned to their car. "What do you think?" Desi asked as they drove down the street.

"He has a need to practice economy," Dash said.

"What?"

"He's obviously living in a neighborhood he can't afford, trying to live a lifestyle beyond his means."

"You got that from the interview?" Desi asked.

"While you recorded, I observed," Dash explained. "His house is older than the surrounding houses and is in disrepair. He's trying to keep up appearances with a coat of paint and a few knickknacks thrown about but has made no real improvements or satisfactory maintenance. On the inside, it was filled with ornate objects but nothing of significant value. Definitely not up to the standards of the neighbors living around him. His car is ten years older than the oldest car in the neighborhood and is probably a sore spot with the neighbors. Although Mr. Streator was not a torrent of information, his home spoke volumes. He is in a desperate way, but how desperate I cannot tell as yet."

"Explain how he can afford a butler, then," Desi asked.

"Valet, my good man. You do not wish Winston to become

terse with you again."

"What's the difference?"

"A butler is a household servant; thus he serves the house. A valet is a personal attendant to the 'master of the house', a gentleman's gentleman, if you will, thus he serves the master. And to answer your original question, I do not know. By all accounts, he should not have one."

"Oh." Desi felt the cold hand of Dash's lecture. "Do you think he may have robbed himself for the insurance money?"

"I don't believe he is the one who actually committed the crime, but I don't believe he is innocent of the crime either."

"Shall we put a trace on his communications?" Desi asked.

"Definitely, and a tail on him, too," Dash added.

****

Parked down the street, Evinrude watched Dash and Desi drive past his car and out of sight. Evinrude stepped out and leisurely strolled up the block to Mr. Streator's house. He rang the doorbell and Winston answered it. "Good day, sir, may I help you?"

"Please inform Mr. Streator that Evinrude Boulougante desires a conference with him."

"I heard, I heard," Henry nervously acknowledged, uncertain of his near future. "Please show him in."

"Follow me, sir." Winston led him to the same room.

"Thank you," Evinrude said to the valet. "Hello, Mr. Streator. My name is Evinrude Boulougante."

"It concerns me that this would gain the attention of Evinrude Boulougante!" Henry shook in terror.

"Well, as you know we are interested in one of the stolen articles."

"Oh yes, I know of Quesonte's interest, but why did they need to send you?"

"Well," Evinrude went on, baiting him with a half-truth. "It does seem pretty odd that your box was the only one broken into."

"It was? The detectives didn't say anything about that!"

"The police like to give you only what they want to give you. It's their power. And if you take in the level of expertise the thief exhibited in gaining his way into one of the Shooman Towers, it is even more curious that they wasted their immense talents on an insignificant heist like this."

"I haven't been told of how it was done."

"It leads us to believe that it was a covert operation with a collaborator on the inside. And of course, we don't need overwhelming or even conclusive evidence to eliminate our problems."

"I'm not the only one who knew about the delivery." Henry found some courage and tried to reason his way out. "And besides, what about the Souftes? They have an interest in the package, too?"

"True," Evinrude agreed.

"And I don't have anything to gain," Henry explained. "You're my bread and butter. I wouldn't be able to live without your government's support."

"Yes, I understand. But I'm not the one you need to convince. So, if you could provide me with information as to where we should direct our attention, I'm sure we could keep you on the payroll."

"I don't have anything," Henry pleaded. "I was out of town when it happened. It was as much a surprise to me as anyone."

"My card, keep in touch." Evinrude stood and presented Henry with his card.

He stared at Evinrude and slowly took the card.

Winston appeared in the doorway as if he had been listening in, and escorted Evinrude to the door.

Henry just sat, dazed, pondering his fate.

****

Homer's Log Day Two

Early this morning, I set out to find the ranger's station. Joe had mentioned there should be one directly north of our camp. I took a compass and a few supplies I thought were necessary for the trek and left everything else behind. I left the tent up in case Joe returned and needed shelter. I made an arrow out of large rocks, pointed north. After four hours of hiking, I came upon a campsite near a lake. The tent had been abandoned. Beside the tent was an arrow made of large rocks pointing to the north.

I'm going to die, aren't I?

Chapter 8

The Chase

Now, this is a lovely chapter. I believe you will find it most enjoyable. It takes you from a massive dogfight high above the planet to a high-speed chase through a bustling metropolis, all in the name of classical literature. Practically every character makes an appearance! Yes, a very fine chapter indeed. So, let us rejoin Joe, in the cockpit of an alien ship.

The golden craft gleamed in the sun against the teal blue sky of Ladascus. It flew a predetermined course, so Joe, finally able to relax, started to enjoy the ride. Viewing the sights and the terrain below, he thought how alien the planet looked compared to Earth, yet there were familiar features, too. Rolling hills ebbed and flowed in shapes he could recognize but colors he could not. A river wound its way between the hills, and roads were carved into the landscape. Buildings rose out of the ground just the same as on Earth, but...not.

As Joe looked around, he noticed two fighter planes had come up on either side of him. So, he waved. The nearest pilot pointed at him and then at the ground. Joe knew what he meant and attempted a voice command, "Land." Nothing happened. "Down." Still nothing. "Stop, descend, ground, nose down." It became apparent to Joe that whatever he set in motion when he had said "home" was what the plane was going to do until it got home. Joe looked at the other pilot, shrugged his shoulders, and said, "I'm not flying this thing!"

"This is Captain Killian of the Ladascan Air Guard," Killian had come up on Joe's starboard side. His muffled voice uttered within Joe's cockpit. "You are in violation of the Maxwell Treaty. You must land your aircraft immediately."

Joe looked around for the source of the sound and discovered a compartment under the seat. It contained what appeared to be a thin, rubbery bathing cap. He slowly put the cap on, and it constricted to the contours of his head. Startled, Joe ripped it off, not sure what it was doing.

"This is Captain Killian of the Ladascan Air Guard. You are violating ordinances in accordance with the Maxwell Treaty. You must land your aircraft immediately," repeated from within the strange cap.

Joe examined it more closely and tried it on again. It

tightened to the contours of his head again; the fit felt snug, not restricting, and the cap created a hardened outer shell. A microphone automatically protruded out from the side of the helmet and stopped in front of his mouth. On the side of the helmet were some strange alien markings. "Um hello, my name's Joe, Joe Ritz. I'm not flying this thing." Joe held the end of the microphone in a fleeting attempt to ensure he was being heard.

The fighter pilot on Joe's port side was able to read the alien symbols spelling out "Boulougante" on the helmet and quickly informed the other pilot and their base. "It's Evinrude, all right. And he's helmeted for battle!"

"Evinrude Boulougante! You must land immediately," Killian ordered.

"No. I'm not Evinrude." Joe looked across to the other pilot. His hands were very animated trying to get their attention. "I'm Joe, Joe Ritz. And I'm afraid I can't land. I'm not actually in control."

"Take him out at any cost," the command base ordered.

"Alter course to 11315 and follow us to a safe airfield away from populated areas," Killian maneuvered so close that their wing tips almost touched. He flipped up his visor to study Joe. Joe glanced back, his flustered grin was met with a cold angry eyes.

Four more fighters filed into formation behind Joe.

"I'd like to, but I can't seem to emphasize this strongly enough. I am not flying this thing. It's flying all by itself," Joe reiterated, almost screaming.

"If you are not in control, we must assume you are a threat," Killian stated.

"Uh..." Joe was about to debate, but he became rather sullen and discouraged as he realized that, yes, he was a threat, whether he wanted to be or not. Not only because he couldn't prevent the ship from doing whatever it was doing, but also because he couldn't safely land it if he wanted to. He conceded to Captain Killian's conclusion. "I understand."

Joe straightened up tall in his seat, accepting that his fate was for the good of all. Proudly and valiantly, he saluted Captain Killian.

The six fighter planes broke formation and prepared for battle. White vapor trails indicated their plan of attack on their single target.

"Oh please, have automatic defenses, oh please, have automatic defenses," Joe muttered, as his bravery ebbed. He noticed a dramatic increase in activity on the dashboard. "This ear translator is great, but I can't read a thing on these displays."

Suddenly his craft jumped one thousand meters straight up and then banked right. Joe's stomach was still one thousand meters straight down and banked to the left. "Oh, my God!" His voice wavered as he sank into the seat.

The seven fighters altered their trajectory and pursued. Deafening energy blasts exploded around Joe. Black puffs of smoke lingered and multiplied as the intensity of the battle grew. His ship rocked and shook but wasn't damaged. The golden craft rolled over and plunged toward the ground, Joe's seat belts creaking under the strain, or was that Joe?

"Oh please, don't have automatic defenses. Oh please, don't have automatic defenses," Joe moaned.

The fighters lost a little ground but not enough, their blasters still knocking Joe about. "Over thirty years old and that ship is still faster than anything we have," Lieutenant Embers commented from one of the other fighters.

The blaster shots continuously exploded all around Joe. Their attack was full on. They would not let this invader succeed. Two other fighters each let two missiles fly. Guided by radar and advanced computers to identify their target, the four missiles locked on and quickly closed the gap.

Joe's instrument panel, furious with activity from readouts and fluctuating gauges, became a blur as the ship identified, analyzed, and commanded itself through strategic maneuvers.

Joe's ship spun flatly, one hundred and eighty degrees, and flew backward. The pursuing pilots were a little intimidated by the maneuver. It started shooting at the oncoming missiles. Large balls of flame erupted between Joe and his pursuers as the blasts found their targets. The ship gave maximum thrust to stop its backward momentum and slingshot itself forward through the flames, Joe's face contorted by the massive G-forces. It parted the formation of oncoming fighters as it continued firing antimatter cannons.

The seven ships narrowly avoided the golden craft, but two of them grazed wing tips. The two damaged fighters broke off from the engagement and limped back to base.

Joe took off his helmet and threw up into it. By the time the remaining five banked around, Joe was almost out of sight.

"This guy is really pissing me off!" Killian swore. He

watched the golden speck vanish from sight, although it still showed on his radar.

The fighters separated into two groups and kicked in their afterburners. The pilots were thrust back into their seats, trying to catch up. But they couldn't close the gap, and it was obvious that Joe was heading for Ngorongoro.

****

The Quesonte Embassy

Ambassador Elmer Drakewood, as stately a politician as there ever was, was speechless on the phone. Shock and disbelief could be easily read upon his face as his cigar tumbled onto his desk. He turned to a monitor mounted on his wall and, with a remote, switched it on. He clicked through the channels and saw the live broadcast of Evinrude's infamous craft on each one. Stupefied, he slowly hung up the phone.

"Miss Halliday!" Drakewood yelled so loudly that his secretary in the outer room wasn't sure if he was speaking over the intercom or just through the wall. Suddenly the intercom crackled to life. "Get Boulougante in here immediately!" Drakewood finished.

"Evinrude," Cheryl summoned through the intercom,

"Ambassador Drakewood needs to see you immediately."

"On my way, Cheryl," he responded.

Evinrude knocked as he opened the door and continued into Drakewood's office. "You wanted to see me, sir?"

Drakewood pointed at the television.

Evinrude watched, trying to comprehend the full extent of the situation. Perplexed, he said, "Is this live?"

"Yes. This is real, and it's happening now," Drakewood stated flatly. "Surprised?"

"Excuse me, sir," Evinrude muttered, mesmerized by the news report.

Drakewood repeated insincerely, "Surprised? You know, astonished, amazed, bewildered, awestruck?"

"Well, since I'm not flying it. Yes" — Evinrude pondered momentarily — "to all those synonyms."

"Are you going to do something?" Drakewood demanded.

Again, Evinrude thought for a moment. "Yes." He abruptly left the office. "I need a fast car, Cheryl," Evinrude said as he walked past her desk.

"Keys are in it as always. You're a brave man, Boulougante."

Evinrude knew the exotic sports car in the secure parking lot, behind the embassy, was Drakewood's personal car. The car Drakewood had dreamed of owning his entire life and finally purchased, not two months ago. Renowned for being recklessly bold, defiant, and a little audacious, Evinrude walked up to the Surruc Aprev, the sleekest, fastest, sexiest, most over-priced sports car on Ladascus or any other planet. He took the embassy flags off the front corners of the car and tossed them aside. *What a terrible way to ruin the lines of a beautiful car.* He jumped in and sped away, leaving smoke and tire marks behind.

****

The Soufte Embassy

"Fred. Frank," Ambassador Calloway called to them over the intercom in their office. "Come take a look at this!"

Fred and Frank came down to his office. Their attention was immediately drawn to the television screen mounted on the wall as the report kept repeating. *"The Quesonte Government has mounted an attack on Ngorongoro,"* the TV announcer said dramatically.

"Macideneb!" Fred exclaimed. "How many ships?"

"I can't believe it," Ambassador Calloway bemoaned in his

raspy little voice. He constantly lifted and dropped his arms. "I just can't believe it! We've had peace for so long! What are they thinking? I just can't believe it!"

The announcer continued, *"A lone ship entered Ladascan airspace just moments ago and is on a trajectory that will bring it straight to the capital city. Everyone is advised to take immediate shelter! I repeat: A lone ship entered..."*

Fred didn't grasp the significance of the report. "It's just one ship?"

The announcer still carried on, *"The ship is the notorious 'Boulougante Bullet,' as it was called during the Disturbance. A weapon so lethal it was ordered destroyed in the Maxwell Treaty, and has now, somehow, resurrected itself. And is, at this very moment, bearing down on Ngorongoro. Reports say it is being piloted by none other than the infamous Evinrude Boulougante himself."*

"Oh." Fred was humbled. "That explains it."

"Shut up, Fred," Frank checked his colleague.

****

The Thirty-Third Precinct

Alarms had gone off all over the building, phones rang off the hook, papers were knocked off desks, and officers ran from one place to another. Total chaos reigned.

Desi! Dash transmitted via radio carrier rather than yelling over the roar of the noise and the confusion. *The captain wants us at the spaceport ASAP*!

I'm on it! Desi responded, grabbing his coat off the back of his chair and running out the door behind Dash.

****

The skies over Ngorongoro

Joe, pale, woozy, and sweating, panted shallowly. "This thing needs to land. I'm not going to make it."

The ship flew over the city and approached a busy spaceport on the other side. The crew in the control tower was busy diverting all traffic to make way for the unexpected ship. Several transmissions were made to Joe, but he did not answer. He had fouled the speakers in the helmet. The tower could tell that the ship was headed for a particular runway and already had emergency and military vehicles racing to intercept.

Joe's ship majestically swooped in, hovered, and then set

down softly at the end of a runway, as if it were oblivious to the commotion it created. Herds of emergency vehicles closed in, sirens blaring and lights flashing. Firetrucks, ambulances, police cars, and military vehicles with weaponry attached to the roofs erratically encircled the ship like a small moat, ground troops filled in between them, weapons drawn.

The hatch slowly opened, and Joe peered out of the cockpit. "Hello," he said weakly.

The crowd gasped as if a strange alien had just appeared to them which, to them, it had. The crowd had expected Evinrude Boulougante to appear and now were murmuring about the human. Although they had seen them on CBS, humans seemed uglier in person.

All the guns trained on Joe cocked loudly. Joe sank slowly back into the ship.

"Come out!" a voice commanded over a bullhorn. "Come out with your upper appendages in the upright position. You have violated the Maxwell Treaty and pose a hostile threat to our planet."

"Hello," Joe said again, peering out even more cautiously.

"Come out!" the voice boomed again.

"Okay." Joe slowly stood up with his upper appendages in the upright position. "I'm coming out." He looked at the ground far below him. "Um, do you happen to have a ladder?"

"Exit the vehicle now!" The voice grew more impatient.

Gasps and excited murmurs grew throughout the crowd.

"Okay, Okay!" Joe, confused and afraid, forgot about the access panel in the floor. He appeared awkward to the crowd of onlookers as he struggled to get out. The skin of the ship felt slippery, more slippery than anything he had ever felt before. Grabbing hold of the seatbelts, Joe ungracefully worked his way down the side of the ship and dangled in midair. Not his most awe-inspiring moment. He let himself drop the last four feet, landing softly, since Ladascus has only ninety percent of the gravity of Earth.

****

Evinrude drove down the runway at breakneck speed, surgically piercing through a weak section of the blockade surrounding Joe. He spun the car about, tires screeching, and came to a halt next to Joe. Evinrude leaped out of the car, holding his embassy badge over his head, and ran around to Joe. "Hello, gentlemen. I am Evinrude Boulougante, and this is a matter of national security," he announced.

One of the firefighters thought out loud, "But this isn't *his* nation."

****

The five fighter planes had finally caught up.

"I've got a lock on him," Captain Killian deliberately tightened his grip on the trigger.

"I'd hope so. He's parked on the tarmac," Lieutenant Embers pointed out.

"I'm taking the shot," Killian boldly declared.

"Anneheg, I'd love to, too, but we can't." Lieutenant Embers sighed.

In a fit of frustration, the four fighters overflew Joe and the crowd by fifty feet and barrel-rolled off, distracting the crowd and Joe as they watched them pass.

But not Evinrude. Taking advantage of the distraction, he whispered to Joe, "Come with me." He grabbed Joe by the arm and pulled him into the car. Once Joe was seated, Evinrude ran back around and hopped in, driving off as quickly as he came.

It only took a few seconds before the crowd of emergency responders at the spaceport figured out that Evinrude had just kidnapped their most prestigious perpetrator. And they wanted him back! So, the firetrucks, ambulances, police cars, and military vehicles with weaponry attached to the roofs pursued, sirens blaring and lights flashing.

"What was that thing?" one of the militia soldiers still standing around the ship asked his buddy.

"I think it was the guy from that sci-fi soap opera on the Cosmic Broadcasting Structure." his friend replied. "What are they called?"

"A Hoo-man?" the soldier guessed.

"Oh," the crowd murmured in awe.

****

The Soufte Embassy

Fred, Frank, and the entire embassy staff all crowded into Calloway's office, watching the events unfolding at the spaceport. The television cameras zoomed in on Joe as he emerged from the cockpit.

"Joe!" Frank and Fred shouted simultaneously.

"Joe? The alien you abducted?" Calloway asked.

The rest of the staff cautiously moved away from Frank and Fred, as if they were contagious.

"Accidentally abducted," Fred meekly clarified, trying to ease the tension.

The staff all relaxed.

"Well, gentlemen, this little turn of events may have just exonerated you. This couldn't have worked out better. Someone up there likes me." Ambassador Calloway looked up and smiled, then glanced back at the news report. Suddenly, his smile turned to a gaping hole and his eyes almost burst from his skull. "That's him! That's him! I'd know him anywhere," he let out in astonishment, pointing at the television monitor. "That's Evinrude Boulougante, he's abducted our alien!"

"Evinrude Boulougante?" Fred said "Quesonte's notorious superspy and master of disguise? I heard no one has ever seen him."

"Of course someone has seen him," Calloway looked a Fred callously. "Don't be a sutluts. No one goes through life without being seen."

"Abducted twice in as many days," Frank snickered. He

turned to Tricia and asked, "Tricia, could you get the Quesonte embassy on the phone? It looks like we need to begin negotiations to get our alien back."

"Right away, Frank." Tricia left the room.

"After the news report, do you think you'll be the only one calling the Quesonte embassy?" Fred asked Frank.

"We're embassies. We're connected," Frank answered.

In the background, the television announcer could be heard saying, "*An Earthman arrived at the Ladascan Interplanetary Spaceport today, flying in none other than the legendary Boulougante Bullet, made famous during the Disturbance. This one ship and its pilot were deemed indestructible. And apparently, the legend has held true.*"

****

The Quesonte Embassy

"My car! The sunisa took my car!" Drakewood, not a happy man, yelled out his door to his secretary. "Miss Halliday! I want to see Johnson, Murphy, Crowley, Hainey, and Barlow ASAP!" Drakewood turned back to his television monitor, then got a marvelously devious idea. "Miss Halliday! Get me the dean, that dean from the university. The one who was here a few days ago looking for donations, from the archeology department."

Cheryl hollered back, "University of Ngorongoro? U of N?" She blindly picked up the phone from behind her and dialed.

"Yes, that's the one. Get him here immediately."

"Yes, sir." She spoke into the phone, "Barlow, Drakewood needs you immediately." She hung up, pressed a few more buttons, then commanded into the phone, "Murphy, Drakewood needs you immediately." She repeated the process until all five agents were contacted.

Barlow quickly entered the room.

"Barlow, I need you to handle the media." Drakewood quickly rattled off a laundry list of things to do. "I need interviews with TV, radio, print, internet. Get that guy, what's his name?"

Barlow took a stab in the dark, "Meyers?"

"Meyers!" Drakewood pointed and snapped his fingers, picking up the pace of his speech. "That's him. He did a wonderful job with the internet last time. Have him handle everything on the websites, keep them open and keep them flowing with as much information as we can handle. I want Q & A updated every 30 minutes. I need apologies, explanations, the works."

Barlow looked blankly at him and asked, "For what?"

"For that!" Drakewood pointed at the television.

Barlow took a moment to process the events on the TV, then exclaimed, "Oh my!" He ran out of the office, whipping out his cell phone and passing Murphy on his way in.

Murphy entered the room. Without taking a breath, Drakewood turned and addressed him quickly, "Murphy. I need speeches, I need speeches for myself, Barlow, and Crowley. We will be the faces of the Quesonte government during this crisis."

Murphy asked, "What crisis?"

Exasperated, Drakewood bellowed. "Doesn't anyone around here keep up? For that!" He pointed at the TV again.

Murphy also took a moment to process the perceived invasion on the TV, then exclaimed, "Oh my!"

Drakewood belted out more orders, fast and furious. "Barlow's speech will have facts, figures, and explanations. Crowley's will include a course of action and our response to the crisis. Crowley, where is Crowley?"

Cheryl yelled back, "He's on his way in."

"Well, get him here faster." Drakewood turned back to Murphy and continued at a rapid-fire pace, barely getting a breath in. "My speeches need to be heartfelt, empathetic to the Ladascan people, with some facts. Not too many. And a vague planned response. But mainly we need to respond to their emotions."

Murphy asked, "What are the facts?"

Without missing a beat, Drakewood replied, "We have nothing to hide. We are surprised by its existence and appalled that it was overlooked by the previous administration."

Murphy hesitated a moment, realizing what Drakewood was implying. "Wow, you're giving up the ghost quick! So how do we absolve ourselves?"

Drakewood responded, "We need to spin this from a negative to a positive. We need to head off the media and be on top of this story before they are. We need to answer the tough questions before they can think to ask them. Keep them off balance."

Murphy reconfirmed his instruction by summarizing their conversation, "So, we are looking into the facts and coordinating with local authorities to find a solution to this oversight. Blah blah blah, I'm the speech writer, fill in the blanks."

Drakewood lit up. "Precisely! I want to proof the copies before they go out." Murphy dashed out of the office, whipping out his cell phone and passing Johnson, who was on his way in.

Drakewood continued, "Johnson. You need to set up crowd control immediately."

"Yes, sir. I've got extra security already on the way," Johnson informed him.

"Thank goodness someone is on the ball here," he congratulated. "We need to lock down tighter than during the Disturbance."

"The main gates haven't moved in twenty years," Johnson told him. "I'll oil them and have them sealed shut immediately."

"We need to overwhelm the crowds of protestors that will be coming." Drakewood pondered the situation for a moment.

Johnson eagerly offered his secret desires, "Water cannons, tear gas?"

"No. They'll be expecting that," Drakewood said with a little disappointment. And then in an epiphany, he yelled, "Food!"

Johnson looked at him quizzically. "Food?"

"Food! Bring in catering trucks — we'll feed them. Bring in

entertainers, and we'll distract them. Turn a riot into an event. They won't be ready for that." Drakewood was especially pleased with himself, tucking his thumbs into his vest pockets and puffing out his chest.

Johnson, unsure, his hopes shot down, said, "I'll need help, sir. Food and entertainment — not my line of work."

"Barlow will help you," Drakewood quickly volunteered him, as Barlow returned to the room.

"I will?" Barlow was caught completely off guard.

"Yes. You will. When are my interviews scheduled?"

"Television is set for three o'clock…radio at four…and print will be here during both and in the interim," Barlow read off from an electronic ledger.

"Good, make sure we get all those downloaded onto the web," Drakewood commanded. "Where's Hainey?"

"He's on the way in," Cheryl yelled in from the outer office.

"Here are the first drafts of the speeches, sir." Murphy re-entered the room and handed a small stack of pages to Drakewood.

Drakewood quickly scanned them. "This is good…This is too wishy-washy...Ah no, needs more facts, more clarity, but no accountability. Get back on it." He handed the pages back to Murphy.

The dean from the University of Ngorongoro meekly walked into the office and quietly announced himself. "Excuse me? I'm Stanley Stoyanova, dean of Archeology with the University of Ngorongoro."

"Wow! That was fast. How did you do that, Miss Halliday?"

"I'm amazing, how else?" she responded coolly.

"Dean Stoyanova." Drakewood warmly welcomed him with a handshake and led him to a large comfortable chair. "I need a team assembled. I need equipment. I need materials. I have a very important dig that must be undertaken as soon as possible."

With a little obstinacy, the dean responded, "I need funding."

"And funding you shall have," Drakewood laid a reassuring hand on Stanley's shoulder. The gesture didn't ease his suspicions of the ambassador's newfound philanthropy.

At that moment, Hainey rushed into the office and stopped just inside the door, panting. Drakewood gestured to him. "I'd like to introduce you to Mr. Hainey. Mr. Hainey, this is Dean Stoyanova. You and he will undertake a very important archeological dig that must be done as soon as possible."

"I'm a little confused," the dean said. "When I was here a few days ago, you appeared less than interested in funding archeology."

"Not important," Drakewood dismissed the dean's query quickly and continued. "You need to start a dig yesterday. Hainey has the location, and he'll have the equipment within a few hours, won't you, Hainey?"

"Now I'm a little confused, sir," Hainey mimicked the dean.

"You've got this Hainey, you're my best man for the job."

Hainey took a deep breath that resembled a relenting sigh. "Well, I have had less to go on before. Never fear, sir. I am on it, and I will handle it."

"You're my man!" Drakewood gave Hainey a big one-armed hug from the side.

****

Evinrude's car

Evinrude drove a little more calmly toward the embassy, but not by much. He avoided paying attention to any traffic controls or other vehicles. Joe wondered if Evinrude had learned to drive in

Minnesota. Evinrude was neatly ahead of the crowd now chasing him, though Ladascus' "Best" seemed determined to run him down before he reached the safety of embassy grounds and diplomatic immunity.

"Hello, I'm Joe Ritz," Joe said, still a little queasy from his flight. Evinrude's driving wasn't helping much either.

"Hello." Evinrude reached over and shook Joe's hand. "Evinrude Boulougante."

"Evinrude, that's what the fighter pilot kept calling me." Joe was rocked in his seat and against the door a few times as Evinrude swerved in and out of lanes to bypass slower vehicles.

"Since you were flying my old 'spam can'" — Evinrude referred to his old fighter in a loving moniker — "I wouldn't be surprised." He made another abrupt lane-change, jostling Joe yet again.

"Um, okay. Ah, you wouldn't happen to know a couple of guys named Fred and Frank?" Joe asked.

"Fred and Frank what?" Evinrude asked, as he took another ten thousand miles of tread life off the tires by sliding the back end of the car around in the process of a left turn.

"Umm…I think it was Fred Jackson and Frank Sure Veil?" Joe slaughtered Frank's last name. "They're dignitaries for the Soufte government, and we've become separated." Evinrude took a right corner so fast that two wheels lifted off the ground. "I'm thinking the plane ride wasn't so bad now," Joe mumbled to himself.

"Do you also work for the Soufte government?" Evinrude asked.

"Oh no, I was accidentally abducted," Joe explained. "I'm just a college student from Earth."

"Earth? I thought your species looked familiar. I've seen your kind on the Cosmic Broadcasting Structure." Evinrude went on to inquire, "So, how does one become accidentally abducted?"

"It's kind of a long story, and even longer if I tell it."

"Well, we've got a little time, go ahead with the long version," Evinrude said.

Joe went onto describe his backstory, with five-part harmony and full orchestration playing in the back of his head. "Well…There I was camping with Homer, a friend of mine from college, deep in the national forest. When suddenly…"

****

Homer's Log Day Two Point Five

On my second attempt, I managed to keep heading north by picking a landmark and walking directly to it, and then repeating the process to maintain a straight line. I am so proud of myself. I found a fast-running stream with clear water running rapidly over many rocks. As I filled my canteen, I noticed a moose upstream, urinating. I emptied my canteen and am now looking for a new water source.

I'm going to die, aren't I?

****

Evinrude's car (a short recap later)

"I went to the bathroom by a tree…and these crazed brown-green monsters with big, hairy arms attacked me," Joe explained.

"Uluru," Evinrude interrupted.

"Uluru?" Joe asked.

"Ulurues," Evinrude informed him, "are small, brown, hairy creatures with long, green arms and short legs. They're the Ladascan national symbol. Very pleasant and peaceful creatures, quite harmless. A teddy bear, if you will."

"Oh." Joe was a little disenchanted by the cuddliness of his nemesis. "I didn't know. They seemed a little scary to me." Joe thought for a second. "When I get back home? I think I'll describe them as ferocious, teeth-gnashing beasts that tore at my flesh, if you don't mind."

"I don't mind," Evinrude chuckled at the thought of cuddly, flesh-tearing Ulurues while swerving around a right turn at a maniacal pace.

"So anyway," Joe tried to build his rhythmic pentameter again. "Like an idiot, I ran from the cute, cuddly Ulurues, fell down a steep hill, ended up in a big hole slash cave that turned out to have your ship, and actually quite a few other things in it, too. Kind of like a big military warehouse but futuristic… to me. The cave started caving in, and it appeared that the safest place was under the plane. It was odd, it looked like it hadn't a scratch or speck of dirt on it. It even felt slippery when I tried climbing out of it after the landing."

****

Dash and Desi's car

Dash and Desi careened through the streets of Ngorongoro toward the spaceport in an unmarked squad car. No lights. No sirens. The squad car's communicator announced, "*Dash. Intercept*

Evinrude Boulougante. Black Surruc Aprev sports car with Quesonte

embassy license plate D-R-8-K-W-O-O-D. On Twenty-Fifth Street

just passing Broadway, has abducted perpetrator from spaceport.

Repeat. Intercept Evinrude Boulougante. Black, Surruc Aprev sports

car with Quesonte embassy license plate D-R-8-K-W-O-O-D. On

Twenty-Fifth Street just passing Broadway, has abducted

perpetrator from spaceport."

Dash suddenly flipped the car around in the kind of dramatic U-turn that you only see in the movies.

"You like this, don't you?" Desi accused, as he braced himself against the side of the car.

"The game's afoot!" Dash announced. His expression grew more intent as his electronic mind built strategies to catch his prey. Statistics on his chances, most of them bad, appeared in his mental thoughts. "Don't tell me the odds," he told himself.

"What?" Desi asked.

"See if you can pinpoint them with traffic cams," Dash commanded.

"I've got him still on Twenty-Fifth Street heading north," Desi reported. "We also have a helicopter in pursuit."

Dash swerved around a corner. "Does the eye in the sky have visual contact?" he asked Desi furiously.

"I'm patching through to their communicator," Desi took the microphone from its clip "Copter 781, this is Detective Desi from the Thirty-Third Precinct. We are in pursuit of a black Surruc Aprev, do you have a visual?"

"View halloo!" the boisterous and heavily accented voice of John Peel, the helicopter pilot, screamed out of the speaker. "I am all on. He has broken cover and is on the west side of North Cyde Park. Not the most discreet car I've ever followed."

Desi radioed directly to Dash's mind, so the pilot wouldn't hear, *I can never understand a word this guy says. And he always sounds so pompous and arrogant.*

Dash answered, *John's actually a very pleasant fellow; you should meet him some day.*

I can hear you, John radioed directly into Dash's and Desi's skulls. *My receiver still works in the analog bands you know. Just in case would-be bad'uns try to go old school.*

Desi abruptly secured the microphone back on the communicator, his face contorting from restraining his irritation with

Dash. Dash gave a knowing smile, letting Desi know he knew that Desi now knew what he already knew, that the pilot could hear them think.

Dash radio-thought to the copter, *We are east of North Cyde Park heading north.*

"Through fair and through foul," the jollier-than-necessary voice suddenly sounded dismayed as he continued reporting, "He must be mental. He's doubled back on us, boys!"

Dash translated for Desi, "He's doubling back!"

"That's the only part I actually understood." Desi huffed, disgruntled with both of them now.

"He's a foxy one," John reported with his heavy accent. "Now the little cub is heading south on the west side of North Cyde Park,"

"That was a stupid maneuver," Dash said plainly. "We can cross North Cyde Park at Center Cyde Street and head him off on the west side of North Cyde Park as he heads toward South Cyde Park."

"You'd better hurry, he's a little rocket!" John advised. "Do you have your scarlets on?"

"No, we are plain black, no colors, no buttons, totally

unmarked," Dash replied.

"I think I have a view on you, too. You're not going to make it. He's quick, really quick, absolutely rapid!" John observed.

Evinrude made a quick turn down a side street away from North Cyde Park. Dash and Desi pulled in right behind him. "Well done, lads!" John praised.

Evinrude slowly increased the margin between them. Another quick turn and he drove under an elevated monorail train.

"Why that dirty little bugger! He has gone to cover. I'm flighty. I can't get a good view on him," John informed Dash and Desi.

Dash yelled, "Hold hard! Stay with us."

"I'll try, but…Shit fire and save the matches!" John yelled, as a sudden burst of engine noise, bells and sirens rang out over the radio. He throttled the engines full, an emergency maneuver to avoid colliding with a television helicopter that was filming the chase. After a few desperate moments, John regained control and corrected his machine. The warning sirens and bells in the copter ceased, and he re-engaged the pursuit. Sad and disappointed, John lamented, "Ah, crumbs! I faulted when he ducked down the narrow streets near

Low Denton Holme."

"We have him heading north on Fifty-First Street toward the Scracthmere Scar," Desi reported. "He hasn't been able to shake us, but we haven't been able to overtake him either."

"No need to worry, old fellow," Dash consoled. "He made a huge mistake doubling back. Totally out of character, and completely illogical. Not the kind of driving I'd expect from Mr. Boulougante."

Desi questioned, "Why doesn't he have embassy flags on? He'd be untouchable then."

"Are you kidding?! And ruin the lines of that beautiful car?" Dash argued. "I just hope we can cut him off before he gets onto embassy grounds."

****

Evinrude's car

Evinrude and Joe were holding a conversation as if it were a nice Sunday drive, even while Evinrude's quick maneuvers threw Joe about in the car.

"Absolute zero coefficient of friction," Evinrude explained.

"What?"

"The fuselage of the plane has no friction."

"Really, is that possible?"

"Apparently, only once. It has something to do with metallic hydrogen. It makes the ship virtually indestructible. The man who invented it succeeded only once and has never been able to reproduce it again. It's been examined a million times over, and no one can figure it out. So, it is the only one of its kind in existence."

"Well anyway, the cave had finished caving in as I found my way into the cockpit and, after I discovered the voice commands, it flew me here. You picked me up, and here we are speeding to somewhere."

"The Quesonte embassy," Evinrude informed Joe. "Your presence and my ship have created a rather embarrassing situation, and you're going to have to accompany me to my office for now."

"Well, I guess I don't have much else to do. I'd be glad to help straighten out any messes I may have made, but eventually I'd like to get back home."

"No worries. If Fred and Frank are representatives of the Soufte government, I'm sure I can reunite you, and they'll get you back to Earth."

****

An Ngorongoro suburban house

Inside an average house in an average neighborhood, owned by average people with almost-average jobs trying to lead average lives, Alfia, a slender brunette whose hair had just a hint of red, was in the kitchen making dinner. In the adjacent living room, repeating on the television, was a report about the Quesonte invasion, with shots of the golden ship flying in and the car chase in progress. Alfia, tired of the report, left the kitchen to find the remote. She flipped through the channels, but they all showed the same thing. She eventually ended up on CBS, where an old science fiction TV show was on, and left it there.

****

The Quesonte Embassy

The staff had stopped answering the office phones after the first few minutes of continuous ringing and used only their personal phones to contact the outside world. A large crowd of reporters, demonstrators, onlookers, tourists, and bystanders gathered outside the building. Quesonte guards glared menacingly through the black gates. Behind the embassy, and unnoticed by the gathering crowd, two cars sped perilously down a narrow alleyway to the rear gates. The guards manning the rear gates instantly recognized Ambassador Drakewood's car and opened the gates. Evinrude drove in, and Dash and Desi screeched to a halt just outside the embassy grounds; diplomatic immunity prevented them from entering the property.

Inside, Ambassador Drakewood was on the phone pleading with the president of the Ladascan government, explaining that it was all a misunderstanding and they had their top men on it right now.

Evinrude entered through the back door and escorted Joe to his office, getting a few strange looks from the staff. "Would you care for anything to eat or drink?" Evinrude offered his guest.

"Oh yes!" Joe exclaimed. "I'm famished."

"What would you like?"

"I don't know. What do you eat on this planet?" Joe asked. "Or do I want to know?"

"I'll get you something you'll like." Evinrude chuckled at Joe's apprehension and picked up the phone. "Hi, Tony, Evinrude, could you send over my usual? Thanks, Tony, you're a champ. Oh, and go around back, protestors in front."

"So, tell me again, where did you find my ship?" Evinrude revisited Joe's story.

"Well, Frank, Fred, and I crashed in an unpopulated area. I went to the bathroom, and these ferocious, teeth-gnashing beasts that tore at my flesh came after me," Joe exaggerated.

"Ulurues," Evinrude corrected him, almost laughing.

"Yes, Ladascan teddy bears attacked me," Joe surrendered in humility.

"Do you think you could take me there?" Evinrude asked.

"No," Joe admitted. "I haven't a clue where it's at, other than there's a big hole there now. Is it possible to ask the plane?"

"Not at the moment," Evinrude said. "It is under heavy guard."

"Fred or Frank could tell you," Joe offered.

Cheryl walked in with the food and placed it on the desk.

"Thanks, Cheryl," Evinrude said and then turned to Joe. "Go ahead and eat up. We can finish talking later."

Joe opened the box. "Pizza! The universal food." And he began to eat.

Chapter 9

South-of-the-Border Inamorato

Later that night, Henry Streator left his residence, entered his car, and drove away. A small black car with Ladascan detectives followed him, while a small black car with Quesonte agents followed them, and a small black car with Soufte agents followed them. Henry, not in a small black car, drove to a large mall.

He entered the mall through the food court, not noticing the two men following him, or the two men following them, or the two men following them. The mall was more crowded now. Henry went directly to a mailbox near a stationary store and deposited a letter. One man from each pair that followed him quickly made a phone call and stayed near the mailbox, while the other shadowed Henry through several shops.

****

At the central postal center, a manager received three phone calls from three different people about the same mailbox. He thought that was odd.

****

The three men standing near the mailbox couldn't help but notice each other. At first, they pretended to ignore each other by glancing away, reading the signs on the walls, or whistling nervously as they rocked back and forth from heel to toe. Finally, one of them couldn't take it anymore and turned to the other two, sticking out his hand and greeting them, "Hi, I'm Tom, a detective with the Thirty-Third Precinct, and you two are?"

They both hesitated for a moment, unsure of how to proceed, until the agent from Quesonte spoke up. "I'm Harry, a courier liaison from the Quesonte Embassy."

The third man looked around nervously as if he was being watched. The other two stared at him, waiting for a response. He finally caved under the peer pressure and cautiously said, "I'm Dick, a liaison from the Soufte Embassy."

The three men then noticed Henry, across the mall atrium, walk out of a store with three men following behind him. Tom, Dick, and Harry all laughed. Henry and his tail of three noticed them laughing, but Henry didn't think much of it.

The three following him became apprehensive, worried their covers were blown. They followed Henry into the next store.

"Well, Tom," Harry said. "I do believe we are all after the same thing."

"If only our bosses could reach an accord this quickly," Tom added. "What say we work together? Get this done in half the time. And go home?"

"What if we get caught?" Dick rubbed his temples, trying to relieve his anxiety.

"That's if we get caught," Harry pointed out.

"If is good." Dick relaxed, feeling he was an equal partner in their newly-formed pact.

"Now that we are all in agreement…" They all huddled in as Tom continued, "Don't you find it kind of odd that in this day and age the thief chose snail mail as a means of communicating? Why not an email or coded messages in a chat room?"

"The thief is either a genius or a certified lunatic," Dick commented. "But if you think about it, how much surveillance do we have on mail these days? None. No one uses it. That's what makes it brilliant. We no longer have a means to trace mail through the system, except with a tracking device."

Henry had finished making several purchases and was making his way back to his car. Three men followed. Henry drove home with his tail behind him three cars long, oblivious to the procession he led.

In a relatively short time, two postal employees greeted the men by the mailbox. They opened the mailbox and removed all the mail. Unfortunately for them, it was a busy mail day. The mall was sponsoring a mail-in sweepstakes, and there were quite a few entries stuffed into the box. The small group of men took the mail back to a copy center in the mall, commandeered a back room, and sorted through it. After several hours, only one piece of mail stood out as odd. It was a bland letter simply labeled "Ralph," addressed to a rented postal box, and had no return address. They opened it and read:

Ralph,

Something has gone terribly wrong. Please be at the five fountains in Jilltramin Park on Wednesday at noon. I will be wearing a "9-volt battery" T-shirt.

Henry

They made copies of the letter and the envelope. The Soufte agent added a slim tracking device to the back of the letter. They resealed the envelope, and let the postal employees take the mail to the processing center to allow the letter to go through as it was originally intended. The three agents then shared a cab and went to the address on the envelope, a parcel store that lent out mailboxes in a small strip mall across town, where they found information regarding the owner of mailbox 2001.

After a short discussion, the three new comrades decided they would go home early since, as Tom reminded them, there were already two detectives assigned to the case. Once Dash and Desi followed up on the owner of box 2001, Tom promised, he would share any information they found.

****

Another trait of the random face printer and feature generator was the ability to copy ethnicity onto androids. While Dash was besmirched with ordinary features and a large nose, Desi was blessed with a richer, warmer, and darker tone to his green Ladascan skin, a slender waist, a muscularly defined upper torso, and a face that women always seemed to find adorable. It had always been supposed, by everyone in Desi's office, that some quirk had happened in the ordering process, and Desi had been shipped to the Thirty-Third Precinct by mistake. His factory-given talents would have been better used at an exclusive, high-end nightclub or spa as an exotic dancer or male escort.

Case #: 010313584508
Stardate: 77905.55
Reporting Officers: Desi #8354011 and Dash #4323530

Desi entered his report: It wasn't long after receiving the information from our esteemed counterparts in the field that Detectives Dash and Desi were knocking on the door of a small, white house with pink shutters that featured a flower cut-out in the middle. The house was so small you could hardly get your big toe in it. The sun had set, it was eight in the evening, and a single light was on. The valiant detectives could hear the television on.

"Big toe? What did I say about narrating?" Before Desi was able to rebut Dash's accusation, the door slowly swung open until a chain brought it to an abrupt halt. A small, round, wrinkled face peeked through the crack.

"Mrs. Sadie Sipowitz?" Dash asked.

"Yes." She squinted at them through her thick glasses.

"Excuse us, ma'am, for disturbing you," Dash apologized. "I'm Detective Dash and this is Detective Desi. We are from the Thirty-Third Precinct."

"Well, usually I'm asleep at this late hour, but the Miss Ladascus Pageant is on, and I never miss it." Although she was in her nineties, her voice had a smoky, sexual growl to it. She closed the door to unchain it, then reopened it. She stood small in her white housecoat, decorated in the same pink flowers that adorned the shutters, and a pair of yellow, fuzzy slippers. Her gray hair was tied back into a bun, ready for bed, but she still maintained a full face of makeup and an overuse of perfume. She continued, "I was a beauty queen once, myself. But how is it that I can I help you, kind sirs?"

"As I stated, we are detectives with the Thirty-Third Precinct," Dash repeated.

"Oh! A government job." Sadie straightened. She smiled, her eyes betraying her scheming. "That would have a good pension now, wouldn't it?"

"Well, ah yes. Yes, it does," Dash agreed. "But we're investigating a robbery that occurred over the weekend. Believe it or not, your name has arisen as someone we would desire to talk to."

"Are either of you two single?" Sadie asked.

"Well, yes, ma'am. We both are," Desi replied

"You know, my granddaughter's single, too."

"We hadn't had time to determine that fact yet, ma'am. But as I was saying, we're investigating a robbery."

"I've had nothing stolen," she declared.

"The robbery was at the Shooman building. But somehow your name has arisen as someone we'd like to talk to," Dash repeated.

"Well, I'm flattered." Sadie giggled. "What was stolen?"

"Diamonds, taken from an office in the Allen Shooman Tower," Desi added.

"Oh my, my jewel-thieving days are long gone. Oh, but I do remember Rocky. I was his moll. My brain might not have been perky then, but my body was." Sadie sighed. "Nowadays, I'm lucky if I can make it to the street to pick up my mail."

"Well, my deductive reasoning has led me to believe that you are not the unknown subject who jumped out of a two-hundred-and-thirty-sixth story window," Dash quipped.

"Did I tell you I was Miss Ladascus once? It was back in aught thirteen," she recalled again. "Rocky said I'd never amount to nothin', but I showed him."

"Yes ma'am, you did." Desi stayed diligent and patient as the conversation revolved.

"My granddaughter was Miss Ladascus in aught seventy-nine."

"My! Two pageant queens in the same family," Desi complimented her. "Your husband must be very proud of your and Heather's accomplishments."

"Oh, he was. My Rocky passed not fifteen years ago. I've been alone ever since."

"Really, you married Rocky?" Dash made a mental note of that.

Sadie eyed Desi alluringly. "She's single now."

"Your granddaughter?" Desi clarified.

"Yes, Heather, my granddaughter. Divorced actually, but no children." Sadie's voice softened, and her eyes glazed over. "I do wish to live long enough to see great-grandchildren someday."

"Getting back to your mailbox," Desi looked to his handheld device and sighed. He wouldn't be able to use it in this interview. "We traced correspondence from a suspect to the mailbox you rent in the mall."

"Oh, dear." She grabbed Desi's arm in panic. "Please don't tell my granddaughter about my mailbox."

"No, we won't, if you don't wish us to. Why, may I ask, don't you want your granddaughter to know about the mailbox?" Desi asked as he tried to escape her surprisingly strong grip.

"That is sweet of you. You see, she doesn't know about it. And if she found out, she'd make me give it up. How else could I get those nice things they sell on the shopping channel? If they came to the house, she'd notice."

"So where do you put the stuff you buy from the shopping channel?" Desi gave up trying to free himself from Sadie's grip.

"Well, I have another house that she doesn't know about. Well, she did, and she told me to sell it, but I didn't." Sadie's lips curled, and her eyes twinkled at the thought of one-upping Heather.

"Well, we're not going to tell your granddaughter about your double life, unless, of course, you are the notorious jewel thief we're looking for." Desi winked.

"You look like a nice boy." She patted Desi on the cheek, finally releasing his arm. "You know, my granddaughter is recently divorced and about your age. She was a beauty queen herself, you know."

"Yes, in aught seventy-nine," Desi answered. "I think I prefer the beauty of aught thirteen. But I would like to know if anyone else knows about your mailbox, or does anyone retrieve your mail for you?"

"No, no, just me. The shuttle bus takes me to the mall once a week to shop, and that's when I get my mail. Do you suppose someone else is using my mailbox?"

"Possibly, in one form or another." Dash fell into his contemplative mannerism, left hand in his coat pocket and right hand upon his chin. He would've started pacing if the stoop, upon which he stood, was larger. Mrs. Sipowitz gave him a glare to let him know she was speaking exclusively to Desi.

Desi jumped in, "Please don't discuss this with anyone else. We are still in the middle of the investigation."

"Are you kidding?" Sadie turned warmly to Desi. "My granddaughter will never find out about my mailbox, but she will find out about you." An idea formed in her mind. "Do you have a card? You know, in case I need to contact you or something."

"Here you go, ma'am." Desi handed her his card hesitantly, starting to get a little worried about the flirting. He looked at Dash. Dash shrugged his shoulders.

Sadie looked at the card, holding it close to her eyes with one hand as she manipulated her glasses with the other. "Detective Desi #8354011, Thirty-Third Precinct."

"Yes, ma'am."

"My granddaughter's going to like you, you south-of-the-border inamorato. She still owes me a great-grandchild before I die. I'm getting along in years you know."

"Thank you, ma'am," Dash said. "I believe we have dominated enough of your time. We apologize for taking you away from the Miss Ladascus Pageant."

"I understand," she said coldly to Dash, then turned to Desi and touched him softly on the arm. "But you need to come back, at any time, and forget to bring your rather dry friend."

"I will," Desi assured her as he and Dash departed.

They walked back to the car without uttering a sound and got in. Dash started the car and drove away. Once they were far enough away from the house, he said to Desi, "Her glasses don't appear to help her myopia. I don't believe she knows you're an android and can't propagate."

"Just because I can't propagate doesn't mean I can't satisfy."

Dash sighed. "Please leave the boorish indelicacies to the humanoids."

"Well, we can be sure of one thing." Desi changed the subject. "The correspondence never made it to Mrs. Sipowitz. It must be intercepted along the way."

"Pull up the trace on the letter," Dash told him. "Let's see if it's made any significant progress."

Desi brought up the information on his tablet device. "It appears to still be at the mail processing center." He did a double take. "Wait! It just went dead!"

****

Frank and Fred returned to their office at the rear of the Soufte Embassy. Worn down from another rather unpleasant meeting with Ambassador Calloway, Fred plopped down in his chair, exhaled a big sigh, and complained, "He just won't let the Joe issue die."

"No. We'll be paying for that mistake for a long time, but he did give us the information from our mole inside the Quesonte Embassy." Frank inserted a disk into his computer and opened the file. "Hmm, this is interesting."

"What?"

"It appears that some high-level brass is arriving on Ladascus tomorrow." Frank read on. "The Chief of Space Operations, the Secretary of Defense, the High Commissioner of the Prime Minister's cabinet."

"Is there a big meeting going on?"

"Doesn't appear to be." Frank searched deeper into the documents. "But they're not arriving through the usual channels. They're circumventing the embassy to go to safe houses around Ngorongoro. Apparently, they're not officially here."

"But the embassy knows they're here, right?"

"That's unclear. It looks like Evinrude's aide is handling them. The ambassador may not even be aware of their presence."

Frank frowned, his eyes cold and hard as he studied the information. As the reality revealed itself, his jaw dropped, and he leaned away from the screen. "Mortimer was right. This is starting to look like a coup d'état."

"Do you think Evinrude's capable of gathering enough power to depose the existing regime?"

"He has been around for a very long time and probably has many friends in high places, especially military. Armed forces can be the deciding factor of a coup."

"Or the beginning of a civil war," Fred added.

"That would devastate the sector and drag us into a war as well."

****

On Evinrude's desk was an old, well-worn accordion file. The cord that wrapped around it had been replaced many times over the years, and its holes had been patched with tape. Over the course of his career, Evinrude had amassed a cache of information important only to him.

He was currently reading through a biography he had created on Ralph Rivadavia. The metal clip holding Ralph's faded picture had been there so long it left a stain. At the top of the page, in bold letters, a date showed that Ralph had died five years ago.

He contemplated if Ralph might have trained a protégé — a family member or friend. The techniques and skills displayed in the Shooman Tower robbery were indicative of Ralph's style. Evinrude caught himself reminiscing about the days when he had crossed paths with this particular nemesis, and he found himself smiling as an old nostalgic tune lit up the corners of his mind. *Can it be that it was all so simple then?* He began to wax rhapsodic of the way things were.

He turned to the police reports from Dash and Desi and chuckled at the moniker Desi had placed on their perpetrator: "The Ladascan Larcenist." He wondered if his old mob connections would provide any leads. Evinrude made some phone calls to a few old friends.

Chapter 9.1

Supplemental
(CAUTION! Literary Speedbump Ahead.
Reading may induce cognitive thought.)

It was late, very late at Ladascus' finest hotel, the Muitipsoh.
The lobby was a dim, cavernous chamber upon this hour dreary.
Two clerks, Raymond and Lenore, toiled, weak and weary, auditing
the day's receipts. The lamplight beside them was streaming,
throwing their ghostly shadows on the tile floor.

The sound of gentle ticking, ticking through the chamber
hall, came from seconds being counted, counted on the oversized
ornamental clock on the wall. Chimes broke the dismal silence of the
night. Startled at the stillness broken, the two clerks peered at the
oversized ornamental clock on the wall. The clock's chimes kept
repeating, breaking the silence of the chamber hall once more.

The silence was again broken, broken by the ringing, the
ringing of the switchboard phone. They stood there wondering,
fearing, the flashing room number appearing, appearing on the

switchboard phone. Instantly they recognized the room and the guest calling, calling on the switchboard phone. The two clerks stood, desolate and daunted, as their tortured souls were burning. Twice the silence was broken by the ringing, the ringing of the switchboard phone.

A third ring beguiling, echoing off the chamber walls, beckoned Raymond to respond to the call. Filled with fantastic terrors never felt before, he reached for the receiver of the switchboard phone. Lenore's calm, secure decorum grew visibly flustered, flustered by the ringing, by the ringing of the switchboard phone. And she whispered. "Only a phone call, this it is, and nothing more."

On the fourth ring, Raymond's soul grew stronger. Hesitating no longer, he picked up the phone. "Front desk?" he spoke aptly. "Um hum? I'll have someone there shortly." Raymond replaced the receiver of the switchboard phone and informed Lenore, "That was the Earthling. He would like someone to show him how to use the toilet."

Lenore, sorrow-laden, retrieved a bill from her waistcoat pocket. Holding it in her hand, she stayed her wagered debt. Her eyes had all the seeming of a demon's that is dreaming, "Double or

nothing on the Obsidian in suite sixteen?" she did implore.

Plucking the bill from the tempter's fingers, quoth Raymond,

"Nevermore."

Chapter 10

This Just In!

Monday morning, Dash and Desi walked through a crowded street festival. Food, drink, music, and merriment abounded outside the Quesonte Embassy, forcing the two detectives to park their car quite some distance away. The two detectives had expected an angry mob outside the embassy, but deductive reasoning had failed Dash this time. He was miffed.

The Quesonte Embassy, like the Soufte Embassy, was an archaic building from the planet's long-ago past. Parapets and towers rose from the corners, and steep, pointed roofs clawed at the sky over rounded walls of cold, dark stone. All encompassed by tall, thick walls with iron rails and gothic gates. All that was missing was a toccata and fugue in D minor.

At one corner of the embassy's outer wall, a local band played to an enthusiastic audience. In the street, a number of food and beverage tents and wagons had sprung up overnight. And along another wall, tables and chairs made an impromptu maisivrec garden. Within the crowd were professional actors hired by the embassy to play up the hospitality and play down any negative or riotous influences. So far it was working splendidly. From the street, two figures could be seen looking down from an embassy window.

Evinrude and Ambassador Drakewood were observing the activity. Evinrude asked, "I understand trying to control the crowd with positive influence, but isn't the maisivrec garden a bit risky?"

"I pondered that issue for a while," Drakewood answered. "But then I figured, what's a street festival without a few spirits involved? And I insisted on a low-alcohol selection. Hopefully, they'll be more concerned with urinating than making a political statement."

Evinrude looked down and saw several men urinating on the outer embassy wall. "Looks like they're able to do both."

Drakewood followed Evinrude's stare to the men anointing the wall, scoffed, turned, and walked to his desk.

"This may be more of an opportunity than a setback," Evinrude pointed out.

"To what, clean the wall?"

"The Earthling, Joe, could be a useful catalyst for normalizing diplomatic ties with the Souftes," Evinrude suggested. "Maybe not he, himself, but this particular event could be the excuse both sides need to dismantle old barriers left by pride and delicate egos."

"The Souftes and Quesontes have been bitter rivals for a long time." Behind his desk, Drakewood manipulated a three-dimensional galactic map that clearly indicated the different sovereignties. "And yet the Souftes are our largest trading partner."

"It appears to me that both sides have become weary of the animosity," Evinrude shared an observation his vocation had given him. "And a more amenable accord may tip the balance of trade in our favor."

"The Maxwell Treaty is a hindrance to economic growth for both sides," Drakewood agreed. "We could definitely benefit from less-restricted trade."

"Maybe an unofficial meeting with Ambassador Calloway would help you assess the situation." Evinrude turned toward the window again and noticed the two detectives moving through the crowd.

Dash and Desi pushed their way up to a guard posted at the gate. "Dash and Desi of the Thirty-Third Precinct. We are here to interview Ambassador Drakewood," Dash told the guard as they presented their identification cards. The guard looked on his electronic clipboard and checked their IDs. He stared at them for a moment, turned toward the inside guard and, with a wave, summoned him to unlock the gate.

"Not a very unruly crowd." Desi tried to engage the guard in a conversation.

The guard looked at Desi for an uncomfortable moment and then responded, "I'd rather have an unruly crowd. It's easier to know when to use violence."

The two detectives were quickly escorted into a rather modern reception area, quite different from the building's exterior. The guard ushered them to the reception desk.

"Hello, I'm Detective Dash, and this is Detective Desi," Dash greeted Cheryl. "We are from the Thirty-Third Precinct. We have a meeting with Ambassador Drakewood."

"I'm sorry, gentlemen," Cheryl answered. "The ambassador

won't be able to see you at this time, but Mr. Boulougante has been instructed to meet with you in his absence."

Before Dash or Desi could protest, Evinrude walked up from behind and greeted them, holding out his hand. "Good day, gentlemen. I am Evinrude Boulougante. Please accept my apologies for the change and allow me to show you to my office."

Dash and Desi returned a quick and cordial handshake, then followed Evinrude down the long, plain hallway. They passed another room where they saw Joe surrounded by office personnel.

Apparently, he was very entertaining to them, since they were all laughing and talking with him. They were having such a good time that Drakewood could be heard shouting a phrase he had repeated many times already, "Miss Halliday! The staff had better not be talking to that alien again!" This was quickly followed by most of the employees scurrying back to their desks. Evinrude and the two detectives were forcibly pushed through his office door by the stampeding herd. (Eventually they would meander back to Joe, yet again.)

"I must say it's been an adventure here today." Evinrude smiled, almost chuckling as he closed the door on the scattering colleagues. "Please have a seat." Desi took a seat near Evinrude's desk, set down his electronic pad, and began to take notes. Dash remained standing.

Case #: 010313584508
Stardate: 77907.00
Reporting Officers: Desi #8354011 and Dash #4323530

Desi entered his report: Evinrude's white hair complimented his bushy, white mustache. When he smiles his eyes both squint and twinkle at the same time; he seems more like a grandpa than the ruthless assassin and espionage agent of the Disturbance. Evinrude was considered an "Ace of Aces" during the war and was regarded as a national hero. He was widely respected, even by his enemies. He remains perhaps the most widely known fighter pilot of his time, if not all time.

Evinrude asked, "What can I do for you, gentlemen?"

"We were to speak with Ambassador Drakewood," Dash was abrupt, his patience was wearing thin. He started pacing and placed one hand in his coat pocket.

"Yes, I do apologize, but he has his hands full with the recent events filling the news these days. I am personally directing this case and can offer more help than Ambassador Drakewood is capable of." Evinrude sat behind his desk and leaned back.

Dash scolded Desi over the radio, *What did I tell you about embellishing the report? And why are you lionizing this guy?*

Desi was more than a little star struck. *He's Evinrude Boulougante, Flying Ace!*

Dash angrily lashed back, *Keep it professional.* Trying to hold two conversations at once, Dash pointed out the illogic and irony embedded in the recent current events. "The Maxwell Treaty was probably a bit optimistic, requiring the destruction of an indestructible ship. Apparently, the politicians didn't think that one through. But as for me, I'm more interested in apprehending an extremely clever antagonist than the frivolity of politics. So, tell me," Dash stopped pacing and stared Evinrude directly in the eyes. "What possible objectives would the Quesonte government secure from the procurement of the intelligence regarding a simple jewel theft?"

"Officially, I'm not at liberty to divulge that information" — Dash was about to interject with an "Aha!" but Evinrude cut him off, while also mimicking Dash's garrulous diction — "but in this unscrupulous world of skullduggery, I have attained the lucid realization that the information is entirely tertiary to the proceeding of my endeavor and, in fact, may elicit a favorable and more rapid outcome."

Dash, confounded for the second time in one day, stopped pacing and suddenly didn't know what to do with his hands. He threw them behind his back and clenched them. He decided that he was having a bad day, and sent to Desi, *He must be lying.*

Desi, frantically trying to keep up with the notes, thought back, *I have absolutely no idea what the two of you just said.*

"Please, have a seat," Evinrude offered to Dash again, but again he remained standing.

Desi asked, "So, what are you unofficially saying?"

"That Henry Streator is a courier we use from time to time, and the information he was transporting for us was stolen by your thief."

"Mr. Boulougante," Dash proceeded cautiously. "I appreciate your candor, but I find it inconceivable that you would expose yourself so readily. I suspect you will demand a quid pro quo."

"As you should. I would be extremely grateful to you if you

would allow me the opportunity to procure the information, once you have attained the stolen articles."

"What exactly was stolen?" Desi asked.

"A small mediocre diamond of no consequence, one of many Mr. Streator commonly trades. Etched upon an inner plane of the diamond is data. To most, the diamond would look cloudy or flawed," Evinrude explained.

"And I suppose you'd like us to remove this diamond from the evidence and return it to you?"

"We can't corrupt evidence in that way," Desi protested, his textbook training coming to bear.

"First you need to have the evidence before you can corrupt it. But yes, I'd like you to remove one particular diamond. One diamond more or less will not alter the effectiveness of the evidence."

"And what do we get in exchange for this breach of protocol?" Dash turned and walked across the room slowly. Desi was indignant that Dash would seriously consider Evinrude's request. He quickly amassed the entire book of police protocol and threw it electronically at Dash's head. Dash stopped suddenly and looked back at Desi.

"My full cooperation," Evinrude leaned forward and looked Dash squarely in the eye.

"How can we trust the Quesonte government?" Dash asked.

"You can't," Evinrude smiled and leaned way back into his chair. "But then, I didn't say *Quesonte* cooperation, I said *my* cooperation."

"How do we know that the Souftes don't already have it?" Desi caught Evinrude's attention.

"They don't." Evinrude's confidence reassured them. "If they did, they'd be acting very differently, and besides, this thief was exceptionally good. I dare say he's better than anyone we or the Souftes have."

"*She*'s good," Desi felt compelled to correct him.

Dash quickly admonished Desi, *That was information he didn't need.*

He seems upright and honest. I feel it's wise to show good faith toward his offer of cooperation.

"Pardon my bias. It shows my age." Evinrude had just made

the connection. He was relatively sure who had replaced his old adversary. But years of experience and a good poker face prevented Dash and Desi from discovering his realization. "A woman? Really?"

"Yes." Dash regained control of the conversation.

"Ladascan?"

"Yes."

"Do you know who she might be?"

"No."

"Pity. Well then, when you do apprehend her, tell her she has a job offer from the Quesonte government."

"I'll tell you what," Dash started pacing again. "If you give us the girl, we'll give you the goods."

"I wish I could." Evinrude chuckled at the cliché and asked, "I do have a question for you though. I know she rappelled from the roof and then left by parachuting out the window. But how did she get on the roof in the first place?"

"We haven't figured that out yet." Dash was bitter and angry about that fact. "But then, neither have the authors."

Evinrude's intercom buzzed. "Pardon me, gentlemen." He

pressed the intercom button. "Yes, Cheryl?"

"A couple of gentlemen from the Soufte government are here to see you."

He turned to the two detectives. "If you don't have any more questions, gentleman, I do have a busy schedule today." Evinrude stood up from behind his desk and handed each of them a business card. "If you need me, please feel free to call."

"Just one more thing, Mr. Boulougante." Dash paused as he pocketed the card. "It's not related to the case, but it has been puzzling me. Yesterday, you had an outstanding lead on us during our pursuit. Why did you double back and give it up?"

"That was you?"

"Us," Desi clarified.

"Fortunately, I remembered a conversation at my neighbor's barbeque the other night. I was talking to his kid about marching band. He plays the trumpet, same as me. Their school was having a festival that day, and it was his first time marching in a parade. He was very proud of that. And, if I had continued on that course, I would have driven right into the parade area, where a lot of children, parents, and other people would be. They did not need a high-speed chase brought to them, so I turned around and led you away from the school."

"You risked getting caught to spare the lives of innocent Ladascans."

"My conscience is not as empty as you believe it to be, detective, and besides, if I can't do my job without risk to others, I'm not very good at my job."

"I can respect that." Dash gave Evinrude a firmer and definitely friendlier handshake. "Good day, sir."

Dash and Desi left the room with Evinrude following them out.

They noticed Joe in the room down the hall, again surrounded by the curious crowd. And again, they were all laughing and having a good time talking with him.

Dash and Desi stopped at the reception desk where Frank and Fred were talking to Cheryl. Evinrude walked up to greet his counterparts from the Soufte Embassy. "Good afternoon, gentlemen."

"Thank you for seeing us, Mr. Boulougante. I'm Frank Surovell, and this is my partner Fred Jackson."

"Pleased to meet the both of you." Evinrude gestured between the four men. "May I introduce Detectives Dash and Desi of the Thirty-Third Precinct?"

A sudden outburst came from Drakewood's office. "Miss Halliday! The soon-to-be-unemployed had better not be talking to that alien again!" And again, they all hustled out of the room to the hallway, scattering back to their workstations.

Frank and Fred were bewildered by the office traffic jam occurring in front of them. Evinrude, Dash, and Desi were unfazed, as they had already been initiated to the new office ritual. After the confusion died down, they all greeted each other.

"May I ask you a question, sirs?" Dash asked politely.

"Go right ahead," Frank replied.

"What possible objectives would the Soufte government secure from the procurement of intelligence regarding a simple jewel theft?"

Frank pondered the lengthy question a moment and then responded with his best indirect answer. "Jewels? No, don't know about any jewels, but if the Quesontes are up to something you can rest assured that the Soufte government will not rest until all are safe from their tyranny."

A grave silence saturated the room. It was so quiet you could hear an android's thoughts.

Desi radioed Dash, *Um...He does know he's in the Quesonte Embassy, doesn't he?*

Dash replied, *We'd better exit before another incident occurs.*

Evinrude gave a hearty laugh and said, "I appreciate your vapid expression of our historical crux. You are a bold one, Mr. Surovell."

Everyone relaxed, normal office chatter resumed, and Joe's audience grew one by one, as they avoided the watchful eyes and ears of Ambassador Drakewood,

"Not exactly the artful dodge I expected for an answer, but close enough." Dash's faith in deductive reasoning was partially reconfirmed. "Good day, gentleman." He nodded to Frank, Fred, and Evinrude and took his leave. Desi followed suit.

"Frank Surovell?" Evinrude pondered for a moment. "I'm familiar with your name. I was impressed with your work on the Arturo Express, and then you dropped out of sight. What happened?"

"You weren't the only one who noticed me on that case." Frank sighed. He never regretted his decision so long ago, but its consequences were still a burden today. "Let's just say I offended a head of state, and nothing's been pleasant ever since."

"Say no more." Evinrude nodded. "So, what can I help you gentlemen with?"

"We'd like Joe back," Fred blurted out like a mother hen.

"Oh? Well, you do understand that he's kind of in the middle of a controversy right now."

"More than you know," Fred said. "Ambassador Callaway is extremely upset about his presence. But by all rights, we do need to return him to his planet of origin."

"Admittedly we are kind of embarrassed at losing him," Frank added. "We searched for hours."

Drakewood bellowed again, "Miss Halliday!" And the stampede cycled again.

Evinrude smiled. "I'm sure Ambassador Drakewood appreciates your kind gesture to take him off our hands. Right this way, gentlemen." He led them down the hall to Joe.

"Fred! Frank!" Joe yelled. "It's great to see you guys."

"Hi, Joe. Are they treating you well?" Frank rushed to him and looked him over as an over-protective parent would a child.

"Considering that I caused an intergalactic incident, yes, they are," Joe answered. "They put me up in a nice hotel last night, and I hang out here during the day. With all the attention I'm getting, I'm beginning to feel like a cute puppy brought to the office."

"We're arranging your transportation home," Fred told him.

"Great! I bet Homer will be glad to see me."

****

Two forest rangers were on a routine patrol when they happened upon Joe and Homer's campsite. "Hey Jim, don't we have a hiking plan filed for a couple of college kids trekking along the Divide?"

"Let me check," Jim replied, pulling a small notepad from his shirt pocket and flipping it open.

"This campsite looks deserted," the first ranger thought out loud.

Reading from his notepad, Ranger Jim said, "Yes, a Joe Ritz and Homer Bergman were supposed to get here by Friday and should have moved on Saturday to their next campsite. Can you read anything from their trail?"

"Well, if this big arrow is any indication they went that way."

"Anything else? You are the tracking king," Ranger Jim said.

"Yes, there is something else." He took a long look around the campsite, then picked at the ground near the fire ring. He hesitated. "But it reads a bit weird."

"Weird?"

"Well, the two of them entered the campsite Friday afternoon around four pm and made camp. They ate dehydrated meals and hated them. One of them had Oreos, and they rejoiced. They discussed proper defecation techniques in the forest, frightening the novice camper with the smooth rock technique. One went to bed while the other waited for the fire to die out, and then he walked toward the lake. There was a — no, make that two — two tidal waves, a smaller one and a larger one. And then there was one camper, the novice. He stayed one day by himself and left early yesterday morning heading north…twice."

"Tidal waves?"

"Hey, I don't write them. I just read them."

****

Cheryl popped her head into Evinrude's office. "Evinrude, you should see this." She looked at Frank and Fred. "And you two, too. This concerns us all."

They excused themselves from Joe and walked down to Drakewood's office. The ambassador was standing in front of the TV, trying to maintain a look of concern while gloating at the same time. He noticed them enter and stood aside so they could see the TV.

"THIS JUST IN!" yelled the news anchor. *"A college outing has just uncovered yet another large cache of military weaponry, this one belonging to the Soufte government. Apparently, neither side is without sin. We go now to Joyce Bolan at the site."* The screen switched to a shot of an archeological dig, with a reporter standing next to Dean Stoyanova.

"Thank you, Rowan. I am here with Stanley Stoyanova, dean of Archeology with the University of Ngorongoro. Mr. Stoyanova, you say this dig had been an ongoing project for the university this past year. How odd that you would happen upon a Soufte military bunker less than twenty-four hours after a similar Quesonte bunker was discovered."

"Yes, most remarkable indeed, but purely coincidental. We've been at this site for nearly a year now," the dean lied. He and his students had only just started digging the day before at the bequest of Ambassador Drakewood and under the guidance of the ambassador's aide, Mr. Hainey. *"It has been an ongoing dig for the archeology department as a training facility for advanced archeological studies."*

"How do you interpret your findings, Dean?"

"It looks like both sides were up to the same thing," he speculated.

"Why does that not surprise me?" the reporter retorted.

Drakewood turned to Fred and Frank, drawing their attention from the rest of the interview. "Looks like it's your turn now, boys." He gave a somewhat knowing smile.

Frank's cell phone rang. He looked at it, and his heart dropped. He showed Fred the less-than-flattering caller ID picture of Ambassador Calloway. Frank walked over to a bottle of brandy sitting on a credenza behind Drakewood's desk and poured himself three fingers. His phone kept ringing.

Drakewood, after a little gasp at Frank's pretentious move to his liquor, watched in amazement.

Fred thought for a moment. "He's not blaming us for that?" He pointed at the television.

Frank toasted Fred for getting the right answer and gulped down his drink. He walked over to Drakewood, shook his hand, and said in a hoarse voice, "Good scotch."

Fred asked, "Aren't you going to answer your phone?"

Frank looked at it for a moment and then slammed the phone on the corner of the desk. With a half-innocent look on his face, he raised his hands and shrugged his shoulders. "Oops."

Drakewood immediately took out a handkerchief and massaged the corner of his desk, silently cooing as if to comfort it. Satisfied the desk wasn't harmed, he looked up at Frank in questioning disbelief.

Immediately Fred's phone rang. He looked at it and sighed deeply. "It's Calloway."

Drakewood spread his arms out in front of his desk to protect it.

Fred answered his phone. "Yes…Yes, Frank's here. His phone… damaged."

Frank made a gun with his hand and pointed it at his phone. His thumb dropped like the hammer on a pistol. Fred narrated into his phone, "His phone was shot."

Frank slapped his hand against his forehead, shaking his head.

Fred tried to interpret. "Well, not shot, it was hit by a bullet in a shootout."

Frank smiled and nodded.

"With who?" Fred looked to Frank for an answer.

Frank pointed at Evinrude. Evinrude pointed at himself in surprise.

"Why, none other than the notorious Evinrude Boulougante." Fred started to get into the role of storyteller. "Boy, it was something! I can't wait to see how he writes it up in his report. Evinrude? He's dead. No. No, wait, I think he's getting better. I need to end this call; local authorities are arriving en masse." He hung up the phone, then noticed everyone looking at him and said, "Think one up and think it up quick."

"Notorious," Evinrude gloated proudly to Drakewood.

Frank and Fred bid their farewells, retrieved Joe, and left the embassy.

Evinrude said to Drakewood, "I like them."

Drakewood responded, "They were entertaining. But don't you try and pull a stunt like that on me."

****

Alfia sat at the kitchen table, paging through the day's paper. Dinner was in the oven staying warm. Her mother was running late, but finally, she entered through the garage door.

"You would not believe the traffic today!" Marsha exclaimed, dropping her keys on the end table by the couch and noticing the out-of-character television show Alfia was watching. "You're watching the CBS? I thought you hated it?"

"Everything else is news about the invasion," Alfia complained. "It's the same drivel over and over again, lots of hype and speculation with no supporting facts or information." The phone rang, and Alfia answered it. "Hello...Yes, this is Alfia...Earth? Where's that? Oh, you can understand my reluctance to go outside of civilized space. And besides, it could take weeks to get way the anneheg down there...Okay. Okay, I'll be down in the morning. Make sure it's had its shots, I don't want to catch anything funny…Okay. Goodbye."

"Who was that?"

"A guy named Frank Surovell from the Soufte Embassy," Alfia said. "Apparently, they accidentally abducted an alien that needs to be returned to its planet of origin."

"Now, you see, that's a good job. I like that job. You get to use that education I paid for. Why don't you do it full time?" Marsha paused for a moment. "An alien, as in unknown species? Is it safe? Will you need an armed guard? Is it diseased?"

Alfia answered her mother's first and only sane question, "Because the county can't afford a full-time social worker, and if they could, it wouldn't be a great paying job anyway."

"I've never heard of Earth."

Alfia pointed at the TV, still on the Earth channel.

"Oh." Her mother stared, studying the Earthling's features.

"It's an accidental abduction, whatever the anneheg that is. I usually deal with runaways of known species," Alfia explained. "But this is a special case, I guess. And since I specialize in long-distance returns outside our system, they decided to use me."

"You see, there's another skill you have to offer. Make that military stint pay off, too."

"Please, Mother," Alfia moaned.

"You could be a pilot. Haul intergalactic freight."

"Are you kidding? Have you seen some of those intergalactic truckers? And you think being a jewel thief is dangerous."

"That doesn't mean you shouldn't try."

"It's a moot point, Mom."

"Why don't you re-enlist?" Marsha badgered. "The military has good jobs. You've only been out for four years; they'll take you back. And there are plenty of eligible bachelors, too. There's nothing like a man in uniform."

"No." Alfia gritted her teeth. Moving into the kitchen, she felt compelled to clean something to avoid a tired, old subject. Fortunately, breakfast dishes were still in the sink. "The service wasn't a good fit for me."

"Earth, huh?" Her mother looked at the TV, as a rather over-confident starship captain was talking. "That captain guy is some sort of womanizer, isn't he? Are they all that way? Don't you come back with some sort of space seed inside you."

"Mother!"

"Is it safe?"

"I don't know yet. I'll meet him tomorrow. I'd like to get to know whom I'll be spending so much time with, especially since we'll be confined in a small space for so long. I don't want to be attacked, like when that kid from Zeta One tried to eat me."

"Well you can thank the service for the close-quarters combat training," her mother pointed out. "When do you have to leave?"

"Not sure yet, maybe this weekend. I'll find out tomorrow." Alfia stopped washing but left her hands soaking in the water. She stared out the kitchen window and into the sky, then she shook her head. "It's a long trip to Earth."

****

Frank and Fred took Joe to the Muitipsoh, the same hotel where the Quesontes boarded him the night before, and escorted him in.

"This is the same hotel Evinrude put me up in. They gave me a pretty swank suite and a guard. They called him a 'chaperone'." Joe made quote signs with his fingers. "I've been watching a lot of

TV lately. Apparently, it's some sort of anniversary on this planet. Forty-two years since some invasion and seventeen years since it ended."

"That would be the Disturbance," Fred told him.

"That is what they called it. Do you guys have time for dinner?"

"I think we have some time," Frank said. "This will give our liaison time to get here."

The three made their way across the vast lobby to the restaurant entrance. Fred quickly occupied himself with the menu posted outside.

"A 'chaperone,' you mean." Joe again made quote signs with his fingers.

"Don't think of it that way, Joe. You're free to come and go. Think of him as a tour guide. Someone who knows the area and can escort you to see the sites, so you won't get lost or create any more intergalactic incidents." Frank smiled and gave him a quick wink.

"That's fair." Joe grinned and then changed the subject. "So, who won the Disturbance?"

"It depends on whom you ask," Fred said, still concentrating on the dining selections.

"Or should I ask, Who lost?"

"Ladascus," they both answered.

****

Homer's Log Day Three

I'm writing this from atop a tree. Apparently, bears can climb trees, too. Now that I look at it, I suppose playing with the little bear cubs was a bad idea. If only nature would be a little less subtle with its signs of danger. The claw marks on the tree, the bear tracks in the dirt. Stepping in bear scat. (Ha, bet you didn't think I knew that term.) Oh sure, it all seems obvious now. I hope this bear gets tired of waiting for me. Well, at least I can climb higher than the bear can.

I'm going to die, aren't I?

Chapter 11

After Her Boyfriends, You're not Frightening

Tom from the Thirty-Third Precinct and Dick and Harry from the Soufte and Quesonte Embassies all watched mailbox number 2001 in the parcel store. Even though Dick had placed a tracking device in the envelope, they staked out its destination. They watched for the mail to come in, and they watched for anyone to open the box.

On Tuesday, Mrs. Sipowitz rode the shuttle to the strip mall. In a slow and determined manner, she made her way to the parcel store and her secret mailbox. As she approached the store her pace quickened. Her face lit up as she eagerly opened the small door and took out her self-purchased presents.

The contingency of three had already examined the parcel from the home shopping network: an Ultra-Matic Hands-free World-

Renowned Multi-Faceted Five-in-One Master Chef Limited Edition Chrome-Plated Vegetable Peeler. Not a threat to galactic security by any means, but impressive enough to entice the three agents into ordering ones for themselves, as well as some canning jars. Except for their new peelers, the stakeout of the parcel store had proven unproductive. No one else had attempted to gain access to box 2001.

But the agents did notice something peculiar: the letter from Henry Streator never arrived either.

****

Total chaos overwhelmed the Soufte Embassy. Crowds outside pressed against the heavy iron gates. Even after so many years without moving, the gates creaked under the strain, trying to hold their shape. The mob was not only protesting the fact that the Soufte government had violated the Ladascan trust by breaking the Maxwell Treaty, but that the Souftes weren't providing the same amenities that the Quesonte Embassy's protestors were receiving.

Up in a window, the silhouettes of Frank and Ambassador Calloway could be seen, peering down.

"This bites," Calloway complained in his whiny, high-pitched voice. He finished off the last of his drink. "This just bites.

There's no other way to describe it…it bites."

"Let me freshen that up for you." Frank took Callaway's glass as an excuse to get behind the bar. "What are you drinking?"

"Water."

"Well, as long as it's taken in moderation," Frank joked as he iced a fresh glass for Callaway and a new glass with anything but water for himself.

Down in the main lobby, Alfia stood at the reception desk, waiting. Fred walked up from a long hallway. "Alfia Rivadavia?"

"Yes, I'm Alfia Rivadavia," she answered.

"Fred Jackson." He shook her hand. "Glad to meet you."

"Hello, Fred," Alfia tipped her head toward the exit. "What's with the mob? I could barely get through."

Fred gave her a double take and asked, "Don't you watch the news?"

"No, I stopped watching TV after that alien guy landed. It's just nonstop drivel about him, the Quesontes, and an invasion. I was done."

"Well, prepare to meet that alien guy." Fred turned to Tricia. "Contact Frank and have him meet me in our office." She nodded and picked up the phone.

"This is all because of him?"

Fred started to lead Alfia down the hallway. "No, no, no…well, indirectly maybe, a little. After the Quesonte depository of armaments was uncovered, somehow a stockpile of Soufte munitions was miraculously found the very next day. Down on the subcontinent of Ortloff."

"Why does that not surprise me?"

"And that set off a PR firestorm, complete with protestors and riots. But let's talk about Joe. You'll be transporting him back to Earth."

"I researched Earth last night. You do realize that it is an extremely remote planet?"

"We know," Fred said as he opened the office door and politely motioned her through. Inside, Joe was seated at a conference table talking to a stenographer.

"You know Ulurues are the cuddliest, sweetest animals," the stenographer was saying. "I'd love to have one for a pet, but they're a protected species."

"Yes…I know." Joe sighed heavily. "They're the teddy bears

of the universe."

"Hello, Joe," Fred greeted.

"Hi, Fred," Joe warmly replied.

"Joe, this is Alfia, she'll be taking you back home."

"Hello." Joe stood to shake her hand.

"Alfia, Joe."

"And I'm Frank Surovell." Frank walked into the room. "Good to meet you, Alfia." Frank turned to the stenographer. "If you would give us a few minutes." The stenographer left and closed the door behind him. "I'm glad you'll be escorting Joe back to Earth. You may not remember, but you helped me escort a small Petrovian child home a few years back."

"Oh yes, I do remember." A smile grew on her face.

Frank motioned for everyone to take a seat around the table, taking the chair at the head of the table himself.

Joe replied, "I'm sorry if I'm putting you out. But I'm kind of stuck."

"It is a long trip," Alfia stared Joe down, wanting to emphasis the time commitment.

Frank informed her, "That's why we requested someone with

hyperdrive experience."

"I haven't had access to anything with hyperdrive since my stint in the military, four years ago. And that was only because of a joint Soufte-Ladascan goodwill operation. Hyperdrive's solely used on high-level military vessels."

"We're already prepping an *Esprit* class ship for the trip," Frank added.

"An *Esprit*!" Alfia lit up. "I thought they were an urban legend created by conspiracy theorists," she admitted.

"I can assure you they are real," Frank said.

"And I get to pilot one?" Alfia practically squirmed at the thought.

"Yes," they both replied.

"Well, that alone will make the trip worth it." Alfia turned to Joe with a warmer disposition. "Are you a king or something?"

"No. Just an ordinary Earthling," Joe answered.

Frank asked, "When will you be able to leave, Alfia."

"Hopefully this weekend, if nothing comes up," she answered. "I'd like to re-familiarize myself with hyperdrive and study the navigational requirements to Earth."

"We can get you time in a simulator if you'd like," Frank said.

"I'd like that," Alfia said enthusiastically.

"We do need you to take full responsibility of Joe now, though," Frank explained. "Things have gotten a bit crazy around here."

At that moment Ambassador Calloway could be heard passing the door, ranting, "This bites. There's nothing funny about this at all. If you want funny, wax the steps at the old folks' home. That's funny. This just bites!"

"Apparently." Alfia's brow wrinkled as Calloway's voice trailed off.

Frank added, "We do have accommodations for Joe at the Muitipsoh Hotel."

****

Dash and Desi were going over the weather conditions around the Shooman Towers from the night of the robbery. "We've analyzed this information over and over and we're no closer to an answer. We might as well be humanoids! We need to connect the dots." Desi, overwhelmed by the tedium of their task, was letting his inexperience get the best of him. "I mean we're basically computers on legs. Why haven't we solved this yet?"

"Because, with all of our computing power, we've been given a mental illness." At his desk next to Desi's, Dash turned from his console and looked at Desi.

Desi was motionless for an awkward moment and then slowly turned from his screen and stared at him. "What are you talking about?"

Dash continued, explaining a truth about themselves that no one dared to reveal, but each and every android eventually discovered. "In order to create artificial intelligence, they also had to give us an artificial dysfunction."

"Um, ok." Desi slowly responded, while his mind raced through troubleshooting analytical techniques to determine if Dash was suffering from an uncontrolled dump of his ROM assembler code.

"Our designers found out that their own intelligence stems from mental instability." Dash tried to clarify, "Not a lot, but just enough so that they're still functional in society without being dysfunctional in society. Without a little bit of chaos in their brain, they, themselves, would not have intelligence."

"So, we are functionally dysfunctional?"

"Yes, we are more humanoid than we would care to be,"

"And our maladjustment isn't a handicap, it's what makes us…us?"

"Correct." Dash began to hope that Desi was catching on. "The more mental you are, the more intelligent you are."

"That's just insane!" Desi declared.

"Precisely!" Dash's momentary smile ebbed as he noticed Desi's attention had been drawn away.

A tall, slender woman entered the detective's floor of the Thirty-Third Precinct, her silhouette outlined by the sun behind her. The light passed through her white dress as if it wasn't there, revealing the shape of a former beauty queen, hindered neither by time nor gravity. The humidity in the room clung to the nape of her neck as the silk dress clung to her body, tight and firm, contrasted only by the soft, strawberry-blond curls cascading upon her creamy, green shoulders. Her delicate hand gently caressed the bicep of a nearby detective, drawing his attention to her round, blushing cheeks and lush, red lips, and in a soft, demure voice she asked, "Is Detective Desi here?" The detective pointed to Desi, as Dash and Desi both stared at her.

Are we being obvious? Desi asked Dash.

Completely, that's Mrs. Sipowitz's granddaughter, Heather Nicoles. They both continued to stare innocently at Heather.

Desi instantly downloaded information on Heather Nicoles. Dash noticed and, with a look of disdain, said, *Really? Didn't you download everything about her during our interview with Mrs. Sipowitz?*

Well, ah no, he stumbled over his words. *I was a bit busy avoiding Mrs. Sipowitz's flirtation.*

She moved toward them as if making the long walk down a pageant runway. Heads turned from every corner of the room. Her skin was smooth and taut along the long journey that was her legs, disappearing abruptly at the hem of her summer dress. She stopped in front of Dash, rigid and furious on tall heels. She looked down at him and, in a voice decidedly less demure, asked, "Detective Desi?"

Dash slowly pointed to Desi.

She turned to Desi, throwing her shoulders back, her chest

heaving under her low-cut blouse with the anticipation of a confrontation. "You need to leave my grandmother alone."

He looked at her cautiously, not exactly understanding why.

When she continued, her voice was bolder and more courageous. "She doesn't need late-night visits from the police." Her voice rose as she thrust her hands down onto Desi's desk. His eyes wandered to where they shouldn't. "Do you know how long it took me to talk her down from her anxiety attack?" (In her desire to protect her grandmother, Heather exaggerated Sadie's condition.) "She thinks she's being arrested for a jewel heist."

"Oh no, no, no." Desi strained to regain eye contact as he backpedaled. "We were following a lead from the parcel store on a mailbox she rents. The thief was using it as a means of communication with someone."

Macideneb! I wasn't supposed to tell her about the mailbox, Desi radioed to Dash. He felt bad for betraying Mrs. Sipowitz's confidence.

You sutluts! Dash lambasted back.

"She has a secret mailbox where she picks up the things she orders from the shopping channel. I know," Heather acknowledged.

She straightened up again and looked down at Desi. "It keeps her occupied." Her eyes started to well up. "She's a bit senile."

Dash quickly brought her a chair. "Please have a seat, Miss...?"

"Nicoles, Heather Nicoles," she responded, taking the seat with the poise and elegance of a beauty queen. Desi moved a box of tissues in front of her, and she daintily took one.

"I must apologize for our actions the other night," Dash said sympathetically. "In an investigation such as this, time can be both a hindrance and an ally."

"Does he always talk like this?" she asked Desi, dabbing the tears from her eyes.

"Worse," Desi admitted.

"But you are police androids. Don't you look up a million things a second in your minds before you do anything? You should've known my grandmother was fragile before you interviewed her. Anneheg, you should've even known my name."

"We find that the intricacies of etiquette and humanoid interactions, in an investigation such as this, work better if we interact with people by mimicking the same frailties as humanoids,"

Dash lectured. "A background check gives us good reason to believe the conclusion from the premise, but the truth of the conclusion is not guaranteed. After an interview, we can then perform a background check and interlace all our collected data, thus preventing us from deriving the consequences from what is assumed."

Heather turned to Dash, touching him softly on the arm. "Grandmother was right. You are rather droll."

Desi looked at Dash and nodded. Then he asked, "So, you knew about her secret mailbox?"

Dash spoke over him, "Do you frequent her mailbox and retrieve her mail?"

"No. I let her think that she's pulling one over on me. But I do monitor her spending."

Do you think she's an accomplice? Desi radioed to Dash, maintaining two conversations at once.

Can it really be just a coincidence that Ralph used her mailbox? Dash responded, then continued out loud, "So, you watch her credit card bill. Do you also know about the other house she owns?"

I see, she could have flown an unregistered aircraft to drop Ralph onto the building.

"Used to own," Heather corrected. "The owners contact me every Tuesday, after she's picked up her order and somehow broken into their house, even though they've changed the locks a half-dozen times. She leaves her purchases in their kitchen. They call me, I return the stuff to the shopping channel. Thank goodness she leaves the receipt. This time it was just some canning supplies and a funny peeler. If you really want to solve a mystery, figure out how she's getting into that house."

Unfortunately, though, Heather Nicoles has aerophobia.

A fear of air drafts? Desi asked Dash.

Flying! Dash sighed in discontent.

Heather was still explaining, unaware of their secretive conversation. "But she does need a little spending money. She can still manage to take care of herself. She needs to be able to buy groceries, but she just doesn't always use common sense when it comes to television infomercials. She won't live forever, but I need to make sure her retirement money lasts until the end."

"Maybe I should investigate her further, say, over dinner,"

Desi mused followed by the radio-thought, *Oops, did I say that out loud?*

Sutluts!

Heather, realizing they were conducting a completely separate conversation that she couldn't hear, grew offended. "How rude."

****

Later that afternoon, Alfia and Joe arrived at Alfia's home. They parked in the garage and walked in, carrying groceries.

"Thanks for helping with the shopping, Joe. I knew I didn't have enough food for an extra guest."

"No problem," Joe answered. "It gave me a chance to see the town, to see what everyday Ladascans do."

"Normally, I don't bring clients to my home, but we only have a short time to get to know each other. Eighteen hours is a long time in a confined space." She changed the subject. "I do have some business to take care of before we can leave. Sorry about that. They usually give me more warning before dropping someone on me."

"Oh, I'm pretty flexible." Joe figured there was nothing else he could be in his situation, but then he didn't want Alfia to feel pressured either. "I'm on break through the end of the week."

"Hopefully we can get you home by this weekend."

"I feel like an extra cousin that shows up unexpectedly, and no one knows what to do with them. But, if for some reason I forget to thank you, thank you."

She paused in putting away the groceries, caught off guard by his sincerity. "You're welcome, Joe. Let me show you around." Alfia gave Joe a tour of her house, showing him the other rooms (she made sure to explain how to work the TV and stereo) and the patio outside.

Back in the kitchen, Alfia started getting pots and pans out of the cupboards. "I'll get dinner started. Please make yourself at home; my mom will be back soon."

"Did you at least warn her to expect me in the house when she arrived?" Joe still felt the disdain from Ambassador Callaway. What with Frank and Fred's initial reaction and the guns cocking at the spaceport — practically every encounter had been a shock to someone.

"That's what she gets for resisting getting a cell phone," Alfia retorted, chopping a strange-looking vegetable on the cutting board.

"I'm starting to get used to being a surprise," Joe said. He sat on a stool next to the counter, in front of a large patio door that looked out over her backyard. He could see the other houses bordering her yard and watched some of the neighbor's kids playing.

"So, how have you been spending your time on Ladascus?" Alfia asked.

"Mostly hanging out in the embassies. The people in both embassies are all rather nice, but, boy! Are they inquisitive and suspicious of each other! Other than that, I hang out in the hotel room. I can leave and walk around and do a little sightseeing. And then I've been watching a lot of TV. It's weird to see myself on the news, the center of so much attention. So, I've been watching your history channel a lot, learning about the Ladascan Remembrance Day."

She giggled at his Earthling accent as he tried to say "Ladascan." "Seventeen years already," she declared, and then a sudden realization popped into her head. *Macideneb! I'm still living with my mother!*

Joe noticed the neighbors across the backyard bringing their kids into the house, and hiding behind curtains, peaking at him through their windows. "I don't think your neighbors like me."

"Oh?" Alfia said, not really paying attention as she got things cooking on the stove.

"They've all taken their kids inside and are just peeking out their windows every so often." Joe peeked out the patio door. "But then apparently, so am I."

Just then the phone rang. Alfia looked at it in frustration. "Why does the phone always ring when I have my hands dirty?" She quickly rinsed her hands and answered the phone. "Hello...Oh hi, Janet...No, he's harmless."

Joe waved at someone on their phone, peering out from behind their curtains. The curtain snapped shut.

Alfia's mom walked in the side door and instantly noticed Joe. "Oh, hello. Who's our guest, Alfia?"

"Bye, Janet." Alfia hung up rudely. "This is Joe. Joe, this is Marsha, my mother."

"You weren't frightened by my appearance?" Joe asked. "The neighbors seem to be."

"After the boyfriends that she's brought home, you're not

frightening. Do you know you look just like that captain guy on the TV?"

Alfia changed the subject. "How was work, mom?"

A look of dread came across Marsha's face. She tipped her head sideways, signaling Alfia to come closer. She whispered so Joe couldn't hear. "I got another letter addressed to Ralph." She sighed. "I tell you, Alfia, I really don't like stealing these things."

"Oh, I know, but it doesn't happen often," Alfia whispered back.

Marsha led her down the hallway, away from Joe. "I know, but I could lose my job, and a postal job has a good pension," she retorted, as they took their discussion into a bedroom.

"Well, in my defense, there shouldn't be any correspondence right now," Alfia added back in a normal voice, after closing the bedroom door. Marsha pulled the letter from her satchel and handed it to Alfia.

Alfia opened the letter and read it. A slight look of wonder crossed her face; she turned the paper over to examine it and noticed a crushed crystal line taped to the back. *Oh great! A tracking device.* Fortunately, the sorting machines at the post office had crushed it.

She folded the letter and tucked it into her back pocket.

"Is there a problem?" her mother asked.

"I don't know. I'll find out tomorrow," Alfia answered. "But I do need you to remove any evidence of how you intercept these letters. Someone tried tracking this one, but the tracker was crushed along the way."

"Thank you, Big Bertha!" Marsha rejoiced

"I'll devise a safer and more secure means of communication for the next job. Dad always did it this way, so I just continued the tradition. It's probably past the time for an upgrade and modernization in this area. Don't take any more mail. Just let it pass on through. It'll be safer."

"I don't like this. I'm seven years from retirement; I can't jeopardize that," her mother complained. "I didn't like it when your father was doing it, and I hate it even more that my own daughter is caught up in it."

The sounds of pots clinking and food sizzling from the kitchen went unnoticed, as the two continued their intense conversation. At one point, Joe even yelped when he accidentally burnt himself.

"Well, someone has to carry on with the family business. It's tradition," Alfia said, half-jokingly. "And besides, I don't remember you complaining when Dad ran the business."

"Oh, I complained! Just not in front of you. I have tact and class. Ralph may have been my husband" — Marsha's voice climbed as she spoke — "but you are my daughter. It's a totally different set of circumstances. So, I am going to complain even more and even louder!"

"Well maybe you did, I don't know," Alfia started to avert the old tired argument but then changed her mind. "You just don't understand."

"Understand! What's to understand? How did my life get to this point? Why did I ever marry that man? I just can't stand it!"

"Don't blame Dad. He was a good man. It's not like I'm a murderer or common thief. It's different in this line of work."

"How!" she attacked back. "You still end up in the same place!"

"It's a challenge." Alfia lied, not wanting her mother to know the depth to which her father's loss had affected her. And that by continuing in the one thing that identified him, she could feel that her father was still with her.

"It's illegal!" Marsha's voice became loud enough that Alfia feared Joe could hear them from the kitchen.

"It pays the bills." Alfia lowered her own voice and relaxed her tone, hoping her mother would follow suit.

"You're a smart girl; there are lots of other things you could do."

"What, work at the postal service?" Alfia snorted in derision. She had watched her mother slave away, unappreciated year after year. Marsha's pay got cut with every new administration, while her benefits whittled away to almost nothing.

"It's a good job, with a pension! In seven years, I can retire and sit in an RV somewhere and watch satellite TV."

"We can discuss this later. We have a house guest, and" — she suddenly realized — "oh no, dinner!"

They both ran down the hall into the kitchen, where Joe had taken over the stove and handily managed finishing dinner.

"I got a little worried when you two went off. No offense, but I had enough burnt food when I was a kid. My mother always said, 'Burnt food is good for your stomach.' She was horribly wrong.

Long story short, I learned how to cook at an early age. I hope you don't mind, but I didn't exactly know what your intentions were with the food, so I improvised."

Marsha and Alfia set the table, and the three had a pleasant dinner and conversation. After dinner, Alfia adjourned to her study while Joe and Marsha enjoyed a hot beverage and store-bought pie on the patio.

Marsha was starting to take a shine to Joe. She was most impressed with his cooking. "Why is it that the first decent prospect Alfia brings home is an Earthling?" Marsha thought out loud. "Are there more like you where you come from?"

Joe blushed at the compliment. "Well, you know, everyone's different."

In her study, Alfia put on white linen gloves and proceeded to open the locked lower drawer of her desk. Inside were various articles from her job last Friday night. She pulled out a long, slender, black bag containing a lock-box. She then opened the box, revealing a small bag filled with diamonds. Using an old-fashioned jeweler's loupe, she examined each diamond under a bright light. She found one that was strangely clouded but couldn't determine why. She set that one aside and put the others away. She got up and headed toward the garage to retrieve an old microscope that she hadn't used since college. As she passed the patio door, Alfia heard Marsha say, "But Ulurues are soft and cuddly. I'd love to have one for a pet."

Alfia returned to her den and examined the diamond under the microscope. She could only make out lines that appeared to be cut into the inner planes of the diamond. The lines were probably text, but her microscope wasn't powerful enough for her to tell. From her time in the military, she knew this was evidence of high-level government espionage, and dangerous to have in her possession. The simple no-brainer just got complicated. Alfia returned everything to the locked desk drawer and rejoined Joe and Marsha outside. "Lovely night, isn't it?" she said.

"So, when are you going to be leaving?" Marsha asked.

"Probably this weekend," Alfia answered. "I do need a favor from you."

"Oh?" Marsha crossed her arms and prepared for the next go-round with her daughter.

"I need you to take Joe back to his hotel tonight, please, Mom. I need to research something for work that has suddenly come up."

"But what am I supposed to do with him?"

Alfia sighed heavily. "Just drop him off. He's been staying there the past few days."

"But what if I had plans?"

"You just sit around the house and watch TV all night long."

Defiantly, Marsh repeated, "Well, what if I have plans?"

"Do you?"

"No." Marsha toned her voiced down. "Can't we just call a cab?

"Can't trust a cab. He's too important a client, and I need to know he made it to his hotel and to the custody of the guard there. It's only this one time. You can at least do this for me."

"At least!" This phrase was one of Marsha's pet peeves, and her voice jumped exponentially. "How many times have I heard that term? It should be 'at most.' How many times did I at least stay up with you when you were sick?"

"Please, Mother, I'm not a child anymore."

"Then stop acting like one."

"Mother! Not in front of the alien."

Joe tried to reassure them. "Really, a cab will do."

"Oh my," Marsha blushed. "I'm so sorry, Joe. How long will you be gone, Alfia?"

"I don't know. The sooner I go, the sooner I get back." With that, Alfia grabbed her jacket and left, still tense from the small spat with her mother.

"Well, Joe." Marsha paused, still a little angry about the escalation between her and Alfia. "It seems to me that you are a visitor to our fair planet, and you should see the sights. Take 'the tour' if you will. I'm just the person to do it. And Alfia is just the person to fund it."

"Pardon me?" Joe asked.

"I'm taking you out on the town," Marsha declared. "I know where my daughter has some mad money stashed."

"Okay!" Joe lit up.

Marsha walked into the den and emerged with a handful of money. She shoved it into her pocketbook, and the two drove off in search of adventure.

****

Homer's Log Day Four

I'm dying, aren't I?

I don't think I can move my legs! Even though it is possible to fall asleep in a tree, straddling a branch, I do not recommend it. Food provisions have run out. Hunger is setting in. There are many things in the forest that are edible, but as I've found out, not necessarily digestible. Joe pointed out many edible plants to me while we were hiking, but I didn't pay attention. I thought about fishing at a stream I came upon, but bears were there already.

I can be taught.

Chapter 12

A Night on the Town...Avec Montage

Joe and Marsha started the evening on board a dinner and gambling cruise on Lake Protivin, something Marsha had always wanted to do. The antiquated ocean liner stoically made its way into the setting sun. Reminiscent of its glory days before the Disturbance, it was small by today's standards, but still capable of holding a thousand people easily. It was used primarily for large galas and fundraisers and was also great for weddings and parties. What space they didn't have reserved, they then filled with diners and gamblers.

Even though they had just eaten dinner an hour ago, Joe and Marsha partook of the dessert tables. Joe attempted some strange-looking things that turned out to be not too disagreeable. Marsha did have a good laugh after his second return from the buffet line, when she pointed out that a couple of the items on his plate were from the centerpiece and were inedible. Afterwards, they had a cocktail on the stern overlooking the water. The water was calm, and the evening sky was luminescent with stars, reminiscent of the night Joe was abducted.

Near the deck railing, a young couple was trying to enjoy a romantic moment, despite the fact they had to bring their brazen eight-year-old along. After an evening of sitting and listening to adults talk, little Timmy was full of unspent energy. Trying to entertain himself, he climbed the guardrail like a jungle gym. He found himself on the wrong side of the Do Not Sit on the Railing sign, when several crew members, busy with preparing an outside buffet, rushed around the corner carrying a couple of tables. They accidentally ran into the family, knocking the child overboard. He fell into the mandatory safety net that all boats were required to have, but then he slipped through a hole in the poorly-maintained mandatory safety net. Little Timmy landed in the water, struggling to stay afloat.

"Timmy!" the mother screamed.

"Somebody save him!" the father yelled.

Joe grabbed a nearby life disk, a flat, solid floatation device, and threw it over the side of the boat. Simultaneously, he dove over the railing to the dark water fifteen meters below.

"No, Joe, don't!" Marsha yelled, but it was too late. His feet disappeared over the railing. "Oh macideneb." She shook with fear. "Alfia's going to kill me."

A basic idea of diving off a boat is to get as far away from it as you can, which fortunately allowed Joe to clear the mandatory safety net that he didn't know was there. Joe passed the net—*That's a good idea*—and plunged into the water.

Joe popped up out of the water. Timmy screamed at the sight of an alien popping up out of the water. The lights from the ship cast a dim and eerie glow onto the water, but they, along with the screaming, helped Joe locate the kid. Swimming quickly to the child, Joe tried to calm him down. "It's okay, it's okay. Hello. I'm Joe. I'm from Earth."

Joe helped the kid up onto the life disk. "You're safe now. Don't worry. I'll get you back to your parents. What's your name?

"Timmy," he sheepishly answered, shivering with fear.

The boat sailed on past them, and Joe thought out loud,

"Shouldn't the boat be stopping?"

"They can't, too dangerous." Timmy's voice wavered as he trembled.

"What do you mean, dangerous?"

"The lake is filled with peptides."

"You'll have to fill me in a little more. I'm new to your planet."

"Small fish."

"Dangerous?" Joes asked.

"Dangerous." Timmy nervously searched Joe's eyes for hope. "We've been lucky so far. And if I stay up on here, I might survive."

"And they attack boats, too?"

"No, peptides are too small, and they only eat meat. My science teacher says they can clean the meat off a small animal down to the bones in less than five minutes." The conversation was starting to distract Timmy from his fear, and he continued, "They wouldn't let us watch that part of the movie because it'd give us nightmares."

"So, why didn't the boat stop?"

"'Where there's peptides, there's gorgons'," he quoted his

science teacher. "And they could eat a ship if they catch one. As long as the boat is moving, they don't attack. But if the boat stops…" Timmy became quiet and apprehensive. "They did let us watch that part of the movie."

"Only room for one of us on that disk, isn't there." The kid looked at him in terror. "Just kidding, trying to lighten the mood. Didn't work, did it?" Timmy shook his head slowly. In his most confident voice, Joe said, "I'll get you home. Let's head for shore."

The water was warm, pleasant, and rather still. It was about one kilometer: not a short swim, but a possible swim. The disk had a rope intertwined around its perimeter that allowed Joe to drag the child behind. Timmy stayed up out of the water and centered on the life disk. Alarmed anytime the disk jostled, he sat perfectly still, his arms wrapped tightly around his knees.

"You sure are doing a good job sitting still. It really helps me tow you."

"I…I don't want to fall in." Timmy noticed a strange tone. "Mister, are you humming a 4/4 low bass ostinato in D minor?"

"Can't help it," Joe responded. "I've seen too many seafaring horror movies."

They eventually made it to shore. Timmy stayed on the disk until the last possible moment and then scrambled frantically onto Joe to stay out of the surf. Joe just walked out of the water onto the sand, where the kid finally got down and felt safe again. Joe's jeans and shirt had lots of little holes chewed in it. "Were they like that before?" Timmy asked.

"No." Joe looked at his clothes curiously.

"Maybe the peptides don't like the way you taste."

"We were lucky then?" Joe asked.

"Yeah," Timmy agreed.

"Let's get you home." Joe was happy to be out of the water.

They walked off the beach and followed a narrow access road along the shore, back to the pier where they could see that the cruise ship was just returning. They were only a couple miles from the dock. A helicopter buzzed low over their heads, grabbing their attention as it flew out over the lake. Its searchlight blinked on and followed the path of the gambling boat.

Just then a huge beast, its broad, flat body as large as the ship and whip-like tail covered with boney, shimmering plate, jumped fully out of the water, lured by the searchlight. The beast's long snout and three rows of dagger-sharp teeth, snapping at the helicopter, were unable to seize its prey. Four muscular flippers, with saber-like claws, slashed wildly at the wind. The gargantuan beast succumbed to gravity and fell back into the lake on its side, creating a huge splash. The resultant waves pounded the shore for several minutes afterward.

*The jaws that bite, the claws that catch! With eyes of flame…*Joe recited to himself, *if only I had my vorpal sword.* Joe looked at little Timmy, "Gorgon?" he gulped.

"Gorgon," Timmy confirmed.

"Now I need to change my pants for two reasons," Joe joked, even though Timmy didn't get it.

Timmy got tired early on, so Joe carried him on his shoulders the rest of the way.

There was a big uproar in the boarding area when Joe walked in with the kid on his shoulders. The parents quickly grabbed their son, held him, and cried. Marsha, drawn by the excitement, found Joe and hugged him, relieved he wasn't eaten.

Emergency medical techs brought Joe and Timmy to the waiting ambulance and checked them over. They were a bit confused by Joe's anatomy but took his word he was okay.

Joe filled out an incident report for the cruise liner's insurance company. Timmy, enjoying all the attention, was embellishing his experience in the lake.

In a whirlwind of reporters, cameras, lights, and staff, Mayor Nehru arrived to meet Joe. He pushed in front of Marsha for a photo op, shook Joe's hand, and thanked him for his heroic deed. "Thank you for selflessly jumping into Lake Protivin and defying the gorgon. You truly have lived up to your reputation." (Mayor Nehru had mistaken Joe for a television character, which confused Joe a little.) "I'd like to present you with the Ngorongoro Medal of Honor. It is the highest honor I can bestow upon an individual." The mayor draped the medal around Joe's neck and then leaned into the frame so lots of pictures could be taken.

"Is there anything I can do for you to make your stay more comfortable?" Mayor Nehru asked as the flashes subsided.

"Well." Joe looked at his clothes. "I could use some new clothes. These took a beating in the lake."

"Say no more. Come, I have my car close by." The mayor grabbed Joe's arm and started to pull him along.

"But wait!" Joe protested gallantly. "My escort."

"Who?"

Joe held out a hand to Marsha, and the crowd of photographers and cameras parted like the Red Sea. She walked up and took his hand shyly, and Joe introduced her. "This is Marsha. She has been my escort tonight. I would be remiss to allow her to be left behind."

"Pleased to meet you, Mayor Nehru." Marsha shook his hand.

"The pleasure is mine, dear lady. You are not only a hero but also a true gentleman, indeed. Please, both of you be my guests tonight." After a few more pictures, the mayor escorted them to his automobile, where he made a few quick phone calls. A short time later, the swankiest clothier in town reopened just for Joe, where he was fitted with a suit by Ladascus's finest tailor.

"I look good," Joe commented into the full-length mirror.

"Macideneb good." Marsha nodded her approval.

"And of course, now that I'm so dapper and debonair, may I impose on you to equally adorn my escort. It would only be fitting."

"But of course," Mayor Nehru agreed, and after a wink and a

nod to the haberdasher, in moments Marsha was equally stunning. A few more photos appeased the tailor, who then quickly posted them in every ad he had running.

While they were being fitted, the mayor spent every moment on the phone with his constituents, setting up "chance" meetings with Joe. He planned to escort Joe and Marsha to many nightclubs and events to take advantage of every photo opportunity.

First up for the night was the Ullamaliztli game at the arena. They found themselves in box seats at midfield, and Joe was given the honor of throwing out the first ball. A double-handed overhead throw to the home team, and the crowd cheered, as the player hip-bumped it into play. It was an odd game that Joe never did quite figure out. So, to keep from looking foolish, he cheered when Marsha cheered, and he booed when Marsha booed.

Mayor Nehru then whisked them off to the Ladascan opera house, where they saw the season's biggest hit. Joe thought to himself, *This language translator would come in handy at an Earth opera if I were ever to go.* They all got to meet the actors backstage.

Touring the city's finest art museum, Joe found himself facing a wall of fine Ladascan art, including a portrait of a lady with a quirky little smile and another of an older couple outside their farmhouse. *How oddly familiar and yet alien these paintings are*, he thought.

As Joe and Marsha left the museum, she pointed to the two Shooman Towers. "Look, Joe, you've started a new sport."

The extreme sports headquarters in the Edward Shooman Tower had already draped a huge banner along one side, reading: EXTREME SWIMMING! JUST LIKE ON EARTH!

Marsha continued, "I'd tell you the story of the two Shooman brothers, but that would be redundant."

At an exclusive nightclub for the rich and the powerful, the affluent and the opulent, the crème de la crème of Ngorongoro, Joe danced with many powerful women. At one point he found himself awkwardly avoiding the advances of a very lascivious opera diva. Marsha danced with many powerful men. Mr. D. Adams, the owner of the Ullamaliztli team, took a fancy to her, and she gave him her number. The hour grew late, and Mayor Nehru made his apologies; he had a city to run. He made his exit, but not before slipping in one more photo op with Joe, Marsha, and the aristocrats.

Joe and Marsha had developed a large entourage by now, and

the group walked along the streets of the city. Passing the large picture window of a toy shop, Joe caught sight of a giant Uluru and jumped back in fright. Marsha laughed. Joe blushed when he noticed it was a stuffed toy.

The press caught the moment on video and posted it instantly, with the headline "Gorgons Don't Frighten Him, but Ulurues Do."

They took a break from the whirlwind tour of the city by enjoying a pastry and coffee at a sidewalk café, the streets of the city still teaming with activity.

"This is almost as good as a night on Rush and Division," Joe declared, as he noticed a mime behind Marsha re-enacting Joe's reaction to the Uluru in the window. At that moment, he knew it was what he would be remembered for.

****

Alfia returned to a dark house, as it should be at that late hour. She parked in the driveway, so the noise of the garage door opening wouldn't disturb her mother, a trick she had learned as a teen. She felt bad about imposing Joe on her mother. I'll apologize in the morning by making an extra-special breakfast. She went to bed.

Chapter 13

Of Mimosas and Tomato Juice

Alfia was in the kitchen preparing breakfast, a little annoyed that her mother had not come out of her bedroom yet. Alfia thought she may still be mad about last night and was giving her the cold shoulder. Nonetheless, Marsha had never been late for work a day in her life, and it was beginning to worry Alfia a little.

A gentle rapping came from the patio door in the kitchen. It was Janet, her backyard neighbor. Alfia thought it was odd but opened the patio door anyway. "Hi, Janet. What's up?"

"Is he here?" She tried to peek around Alfia and into the house. "The man from Earth."

"Um, no." Alfia instinctively maneuvered to block her view.

"Are you sure?" Janet countered Alfia's movements.

"Yes," she answered. Alfia heard the garage door operate and immediately became suspicious. She closed the patio door rudely on Janet, just short of forcibly pushing her out of the house. Janet stayed at the door, peering in through the glass.

Alfia grabbed a frying pan to arm herself and approached the door to the garage. Marsha entered, and Alfia gave a short-lived sigh that ended the moment Joe came through the door.

Alfia was on guard again. "Didn't you drop him off at his hotel last night?"

"We never made it there," Marsha informed her.

"What do you mean you never made it? It's just downtown."

"Well…I was a little upset with you last night," Marsha admitted. "So, I decided to take Joe out on the town. On your dime." Marsha put her pocketbook and keys away. "He is, after all, a guest on our planet. I took him sightseeing."

"It was very interesting," Joe added. Alfia glared at him.

"Anyway, one thing led to another. We had some drinks, hit some clubs, danced, and here we are."

"You? Danced?" Alfia swung the pan dangerously close to Joe's head. "What did you do to my mother?"

"Nothing!" Joe cringed.

"Chill out!" Marsha put one hand on Alfia's shoulder and moved the pan slowly away from Joe with the other. "We went on a dinner cruise. Things got a little wacky. The night got away from us, and then I thought he might like one of your infamous breakfasts." She noticed the stove, the set table, and Janet peering through the patio door. "How fortunate, you actually are making one. And mimosas and tomato juice — you must really be apologizing for something."

"But aren't you going to be late for work?" Alfia asked, concerned.

"I called in sick." She paused, thinking. "You know... I've never called in sick before.

"You fiend!" Alfia swung the frying pan menacingly close to Joe's brain. "You fried her brain, didn't you?" She turned to Marsha. "It's okay, Mom. I'll get you a specialist. He's obviously wiped your brain with his telekinesis or something."

Marsha went on to explain, "But it didn't work. They saw me on TV, so I only get the morning off. I have to report in at noon." She shrugged with an exhausted sigh.

The doorbell rang, and Alfia walked over hesitantly, frying pan in hand, still coming to terms with her mother's nocturnal activities. She opened the door only to be met with an explosion of flash photography and gnats. Janet stood front and center, holding Alfia's newspaper, hoping to be invited in. Alfia assessed the situation, grabbed the newspaper, thanked Janet, and slammed the door in her face.

"Hmmm, they weren't there when we drove in," Marsha commented, as she took the newspaper from Alfia. She rolled off the rubber band, unfurled the paper, and displayed the front page to her disbelieving daughter.

Alfia read the headline, "Joe Defies Gorgon, Saves Little Timmy!" which was followed by a full-page picture of the gorgon attacking the helicopter and Joe with the child on his shoulders in the corner. Alfia's eyes bulged, and she grabbed the paper, letting the frying pan hit the floor. Joe jumped out of the way of the clanging cookware.

Marsha turned to him. "You've got a souvenir, Joe." She gently removed the newspaper from Alfia's hands and presented it to Joe.

"And you're just getting home now?" Alfia asked.

"After he saved little Timmy, the whole town went bonkers over him. Mayor Nehru and his constituents danced with us at Club

42. The A-list of society came out as if someone had them on speed dial. We've been hob-knobbing with the rich and famous all night. Stores opened just for us and let us shop for *free*! You should see the stuff I got." Marsha walked over to the television and turned on the local morning news show.

A news report came on, complete with video of Joe and Marsha, the announcer narrating, *"The Earthling, Joe, made quite a splash last night at Club Tar Jei."* Marsha switched channels. *"Making a death-defying 15-meter dive into Lake Protivin, Joe saved this young boy from certain death as he defied peptides and even the gorgon."* A different channel: *"Joe, the man from Earth, and his companion Marsha danced the night away at Club Vlad."* She switched again. *"Gorgons don't frighten him, but Ulurues do,"* showing the video of Joe startled by the stuffed Uluru in the toy store window.

Joe shoulders slumped, "Really?"

Marsha consoled him, "It's cute. They'll love you for that." She turned to Alfia. "Joe is quite the gentleman. He wouldn't let anyone give him anything unless I was equally remunerated."

"Gee, I wish I could read this," Joe said, looking at the paper.

"I can't believe we fit all that into one night."

Chapter 14

Henry in the Park

Jilltramin Park was a small oasis in a sea of office buildings. Henry sat nervously on the edge of the middle fountain of five that made up the focal point of the park. It was a warm sunny day, a perfect day to be out of the office and having lunch alfresco. He had brought a light lunch to both conceal his intentions and hopefully calm his upset stomach. He constantly looked around the park, hoping to identify a person he'd never seen before, periodically nibbling at his sandwich.

Filling the park were Quesonte government agents, Soufte government agents, and a platoon of detectives and plainclothes cops. It was a popular place for people to eat lunch, especially on such a nice day. The park was busy with activity, making it even harder for the undercover crowd to try to predict who Ralph was. However, because of the surveillance tapes, they knew one thing more than Henry did: Ralph was a woman.

****

Atop a nearby building, facing away from the park, Evinrude scanned the vicinity with binoculars. "Uh sir, the park is on *this* side of the building," Evinrude's aide, Michele, nervously pointed out.

"I know." Evinrude lowered his binoculars and turned toward the park. "My God, look at all the people following this guy — us, the Souftes, the cops. Is there anyone in the park not following him?" he asked sarcastically.

"What are you talking about, sir?" Michele looked over the edge of the building into the park.

"Look around the fountain." Evinrude pointed out, "Henry is the only civilian sitting there. And every parking space around the park is filled with a white van or unmarked squad car. Why are surveillance vehicles always white vans?"

"Hmmm?" She scanned the people filling the park. "So, why are you looking the other way then?"

"Well, that way is covered. It's like Streator is the light being shone in an anar's eyes. I'm hoping to catch a glimpse of the hand in the dark that sneaks in from behind."

"I'm sorry, sir." Michele was confused by the anecdote.

"What?"

Evinrude turned his attention back to the streets outside the park, as his aide kept a vigilant watch on the park. He commanded, "Have Mr. Streator meet me at Al's Pub and Grub this evening."

"Yes, sir." She entered a note in her digital planner.

"Just let me know when something happens in the park," Evinrude instructed.

****

Henry bit into his sandwich, growing more frightened as he waited for his rendezvous. Weaving in and out of the bustling crowd, a bicycle delivery guy zipped his way through the park, dodging pedestrians like an old pro. He stopped in front of Henry.

"Are you Henry Streator?" he asked.

"Yes?" Henry answered cautiously, looking up at him.

"I have a package for you." The delivery guy handed him an envelope and held out an electronic clipboard.

Henry slowly took the envelope and stared at it quizzically.

"I need you to sign, please." The delivery guy shook the clipboard impatiently.

Henry signed it sloppily. As he was doing so, all the agents who occupied the ledges of the other four fountains took notice and began talking into their lapels or shirt cuffs. Henry looked up and thought he saw everyone looking at him, but they all returned to their fake routines before he could be sure.

The bicycle delivery guy thought he noticed them, too, but shrugged it off. He looked at the signature begrudgingly and rode off, zipping in and out of the crowd as quickly as he had come. He passed a large hedge at the edge of the park and was so abruptly set upon by ten officers (including Dash and Desi) that his bicycle kept rolling along the sidewalk without him.

"Where did that package come from?" Dash demanded.

"It came to our office by mail." He tried to shake his captors loose, but they held him tight. "Is this really necessary?"

"When?" Dash was inches from the deliveryman's face.

"This morning." He backed away from Dash. He turned to one of the men clutching his arms. "Is he always this intense?"

"How did you know who to deliver it to?"

"It came with instructions," he enunciated slowly, showing his contempt for authority.

"Did this not strike you as odd?" Dash persisted.

"No."

"Why not?"

"Do you know how many affairs are going on in this city?" he retorted. "This was one of the more normal requests. Really, you guys need to chill out. Grab yourself a nice alkaline or carbon." He was trying to incite a reaction from Dash or Desi by referring to the 9-volt battery addiction some androids secretly struggle with, but it didn't work. Dispassionate androids aren't easily provoked.

Back at the fountain, Henry opened the envelope to find a phone. He stared at it. It wasn't the way he had hoped to contact Ralph, but it would do. Suddenly the phone rang, and he jumped.

The undercover agents around him also jumped, but Henry was too involved with the phone to notice. All the agents noticed that they were being obvious and tried not to be, which made them more obvious.

"Hello?" Henry said cautiously into the phone.

"Henry Streator?" Ralph's voice sounded strong and confident.

"Yes," he answered.

"I understand you've been trying to reach me."

"Is this Ralph?" Henry asked.

"Yes."

"You're a girl!"

"I know," she said flatly, trying to hide her irritation at Henry's surprise that a woman was in a male-dominated career.

The sound of the fountains made eavesdropping difficult. All the undercover agents moved closer. The crews in the surveillance vehicles frantically searched for the cell phone signal. The water was so loud that their parabolic microphones were useless, as were the microphones they had planted around the fountains,

Ralph continued, "I commend you on your choice for a meeting place."

"Thank you." Henry felt a little relieved.

"How can I help you?" she asked.

"The job fell on the wrong day."

"Hmm. According to your correspondence, it was to happen on the seventh of this month."

"No, no, no. The seventeenth of this month," he corrected.

"Oh my," Ralph responded. "That is inconvenient. But I am looking at the letters right now, and it does state the seventh quite clearly. I'll be glad to send you the originals."

"No!" Henry said. "That won't fix anything now."

"What is it that you need?" she asked.

"I need the stuff back."

"If I return the items what kind of compensation am I looking at, then?" Ralph asked. "The agreement was for me to keep the articles as payment."

"Yes, but one of them belongs to a very important client," he answered.

"Is that why you're being followed by an army of people?"

"What do you mean? I haven't been followed." Henry looked up and around and noticed that everyone at the fountains had moved closer to him. "Well…I…."

"Actually, I need to end this conversation before it is traced," Ralph told him. "I will contact you at a later date."

****

On top of the building, Evinrude had anticipated the difficulties caused by the noise of the fountains and had come up with other options. "Are we triangulating on the cell phone signal?"

"Yes, sir. The moment it rang." Michele busily worked on

her handheld, getting the information as quickly as possible.

"Try and tap into it, too," Evinrude commanded.

"We've almost got the signal tapped, sir," she declared.

Evinrude observed many people along the surrounding streets, most of them on their phones. His binoculars were computer-enhanced with a readout that identified each and every person. If he so chose, he could then bring up their entire history. As Evinrude perused the locals, he happened to catch a glimpse of an attractive woman standing outside a small bistro, talking on her phone. He paused for a moment to appreciate her symmetry. *Another reason not to look in Henry's direction*, he thought. Since he had paused on her, the woman's information started to load.

Alfia Rivadavia

Age: 26

Parents: Ralph and Marsha Rivadavia

Military service:

Before Evinrude could take note of the information, it was interrupted by the flash of a tight leather miniskirt. Heather Nicoles passed into view. Evinrude's primal instinct kicked in, and before the blood could recirculate back to his brain, his field glasses were following her toned, muscular thighs down the street.

It was hotter that day, and she wore less. The miniskirt's hem sashayed in time with Heather's hips, teasing that at any moment, more could be revealed. The soft leather clung so tightly and defined her curves so accurately that Evinrude noticed the dimple in her right cheek.

Evinrude lowered his binoculars and looked over at his aide, who was focused in the other direction. He asked, "Were we at least able to track the signal then?"

"Oh yes, we are tracking it right now. But it seems to be on the move, so we'll need some people on the street because the satellite positioning won't be accurate enough."

A Quesonte surveillance team in one of the white vans followed the global tracking transponders and directed two of their men on foot to a city block a mile away from the park. The two men searched the street, but the signal kept moving.

"It's on the next block now," the Quesonte agent on foot repeated the information from his headset to his partner. The two ran after it.

"She must be in a car," determined the second man.

"Okay," he replied to the surveillance team and informed his partner, "The signal has changed direction. It's heading south now."

The two Quesonte agents ran along the sidewalk, trying to keep up. They looked over and saw Fred and Frank coordinating with their surveillance team, tracking the same phone signal.

"Now, wait a minute." Frank came to a stop, panting. He asked Fred, "If she is in a car, we wouldn't be able to keep up on foot, right? But she hasn't gotten very far from us."

"She's on a bus!" they concluded simultaneously.

They looked ahead and spotted a blue city bus, advertising extreme swimming on its billboards, as it turned the corner and headed west. They received information from their surveillance team, "The signal has just turned west." Fred and Frank looked at each other and smiled.

The two Quesonte agents across the street came to the same realization, looked at each other and smiled.

The four noticed each other and bolted as if a shot had fired from a starter's pistol.

Both pairs of running agents called back to their counterparts, following in the cars, "She's on that bus!"

Two separate cars pulled out from behind the four running men, in a race all their own. They surrounded the bus at its next stop, the Quesontes in front of it and the Souftes blocking the rear. Inadvertently the two enemies had just worked together. All of a sudden, there were eight men circling the bus and flashing badges. Sure enough, no one was escaping from this bus.

Caught up in the seizure of the bus, the adversaries continued to work together. They blocked the exits and searched each passenger, the bus driver, and the bus itself, finally turning up a pair of cell phones taped together and stuck to the underside of the back bumper. Most recently, one had dialed the number of Henry Streator's cell phone, and the other had received a call from somewhere else. The connection had been terminated before they could even begin a trace on the second phone. The registrations on the phones were of no use since they were both prepaid burner phones.

****

Away from all the drama downtown, Ambassador Drakewood arrived alone at an inconspicuous building. Having driven himself in an ordinary car, he parked in a garage under the building, then entered the building through a small elevator.

Ambassador Calloway had already arrived in much the same manner and was waiting patiently in a corner of the room. The room was a small square, furnished with only a circular table and two chairs. A single light beamed down from the ceiling, illuminating the table.

The two dignitaries had arranged an unsanctioned meeting. Neither office knew of their whereabouts or agenda. It was truly mano a mano, real macho politico at its best, the main event that would settle, once and for all…the fate of Ladascus.

"Drakewood," Calloway greeted stiffly.

"Calloway," Drakewood coldly responded.

"You're late, Drakewood." Calloway used an obvious tactic that merely glanced off his opponent.

Drakewood coolly countered, "The traffic around Jilltramin Park was unreasonable, Calloway."

Both emissaries were in good shape for a confrontation of this caliber; they both had skills to be respected. Drakewood may have shed a few pounds, but he was definitely the heavyweight. Calloway, lighter and leaner, could go the distance and was also capable of dishing it out. He was at his most dangerous once he had worn down an opponent. Drakewood, on the other hand, was a big man and could take almost anything. But he liked to do it in one blow and be done. It looked like the making of a good rumble.

The two able-bodied bureaucrats circled the negotiating table. Calloway quickly took a seat. Drakewood stalked his man, calculating, then smoothly moved into the other chair. They put the stare on each other, ready to go toe to toe.

Drakewood opened the dialogue. "I have a way to use the Earthling to end our political quagmire."

The well-placed proposition drew Calloway in. "I'm listening."

Drakewood followed up with, "We can lift the trade embargoes, freeing up commerce, and expand trade."

The combination landed, staggering Calloway; he did not see that coming.

Drakewood unleashed another salvo, "We could put the Maxwell Treaty to rest."

Calloway fired back, "What about Ladascus?"

Drakewood didn't anticipate this rebuttal. "What about it?"

he jabbed blindly.

"It seems to me we are overlooking a resource that we could develop to our benefit."

The vicious reasoning caught Drakewood unguarded, a dangerous mistake for him. Drakewood paused, hoping to slow the pace down, recoup, and size up his adversary.

Calloway, not afraid of deliberation, pressed further. "The Ladascans are very good, if not the best, at logistics. We should not squander that knowledge and expertise."

Drakewood, rugged plenipotentiary that he was, continued to talk the talk. "I believe we are both after the same thing." After sparring a little, feeling Calloway out, he decided to bring down the hammer. "I created a dummy corporation that is poised to step in as soon as trade restrictions are lifted. We can fit them in there."

A phantom punch and Calloway was dumbstruck; he had no idea of the amount of groundwork Drakewood had prepared.

Drakewood, coming on strong, tried to end it quick. "I will need a Soufte partner."

Calloway, floating like a viceroy and berating like a magistrate, took advantage of the opening and landed hard with,

"Equal partners, of course."

"30-70," Drakewood backpedaled, the tension heightening again.

Calloway, never allowing his opponent a moment's rest, advanced with, "50- 50,"

Drakewood, knowing he needed Calloway, but hating getting backed into a corner, lashed out, "40-60,"

"50-50," Calloway, pummeling him, refused to back down. "Or Soufte is not in!"

"Okay," Drakewood acquiesced, humbled and trying not to lose any more ground. "It's agreed."

"So, how does Joe fit in?" Calloway relaxed as tensions eased.

"Easy, we use the media hype surrounding the Earthling and say he has just negotiated peace between our nations," Drakewood explained. "Our staff will heighten the media blitz. We have him give a public speech. He's a hero. We're at peace. Yadda yadda, everyone is happy."

"I'll have my people contact your people."

They got up, came around the table, shook hands as worthy

adversaries, and departed.

****

Later that afternoon

In the cold darkness of deep space, a small, white, elliptical disk traversed the emptiness, traveling along at an unknown rate.

"The speed actuators on these hyperdrive ships never work," Alfia complained, tapping on the instrument panel. In that instant, the alarms went off. Red lights flashed. The cockpit started to fill with smoke. Alfia could barely maintain control.

Déjà vu, Joe thought.

"Explosive decompression in the engine bay, we need to override," Alfia yelled over the alarms.

"They're up here!" Joe pointed to a panel above their heads.

"What?" Alfia couldn't hear him over the noise.

"The overrides," he yelled. "They're up here." Joe opened the panel as he had seen Fred do before and stared at the switches. "The only thing is I can't read these symbols."

Alfia reached up and flipped a switch. The normal lights flashed on, the smoke began to clear, and the simulator stopped shaking and returned to its normal upright position.

Alfia remarked, "You were remarkably calm."

Joe responded, "Been there, done that."

"I don't understand."

"Fred, Frank, and I crashed in a ship just like this."

"You guys crashed?"

"Officially, it was a controlled, rapidly spiraling descent utilizing the Ladascan surface to negate our forward momentum," Joe explained. "I sure hope you're a better pilot than they are, because this little exercise hasn't increased my confidence in this ship."

"Well, that's why we're here. I need a little practice, and I want you to get comfortable with this ship. I won't have you freaking out on me!" she warned. "It's no fun when someone freaks out in the middle of deep space at hyperdrive speeds. No fun at all. So, I want you to know what may happen and how you need to react."

"I can appreciate that. How long will the trip take?"

"About eighteen hours."

"Wow, I was trapped in the engine compartment for that long?"

"Okay, so if everything goes according to plan," Alfia explained. "We simply take off, get to a safe distance for the jump into hyperspace, program the coordinates and trajectories to Earth, sit back, and have a long conversation."

Joe watched as she worked the controls. "So, eighteen hours in close quarters, and we hardly know each other. You're either very brave or packing a gun."

"Yes, I am," she said dryly.

He thought for a moment and then decided, fair enough. "How does hyperspace work?"

"Not sure, really, it has something to do with aether. It connects everything in the universe together. It fills space but doesn't. It's not there but is. It doesn't affect anything but does." She noticed Joe's perplexed look. "I don't get it aether, I mean either."

Joe thought for a moment, absorbing the information. "I didn't think anything could go faster than light?"

"Nothing can go faster than light. That is true. And that's where aether comes in. Aether *is* nothing, and *nothing* can go faster than light. So, to continue, if you get sick on takeoff or landing, the barf bags are in here. I don't want to have to clean up any messes. If explosive decompression happens in a ship this size you reach around" — Joe, deathly afraid of being a hindrance, paid close attention as she continued — "grab your sunisa, and kiss it goodbye."

Joe and Alfia sat in awkward silence until a light blinked on in Joe's head and he got the joke. "Oh yeah, right, got it. Haha."

"No, really! That's catastrophic. No surviving. Good thing it's instantaneous, no suffering."

"How likely?" he asked.

"A one percent chance," she answered.

"So, one out of every one hundred hyperdrive flights is doomed," Joe calculated. "That sounds like a high percentage. What number are we?"

"Space travel is dangerous," she stated bluntly.

They spent several more hours in the simulator. No bathroom breaks, just like the trip. She taught Joe about the basic systems in the ship, some of the symbols on the controls, and what he could and couldn't touch.

****

Case #: 010313584508
Stardate: 77913.15
Reporting Officers: Dash #4323530 and Desi #8354011

Dash entered his report: Detectives Dash #4323530 and Desi #8354011. Postal Distribution Center interview: Department of Missing Letters supervisor, Marsha Rivadavia.

Boring! Desi thought to Dash as they walked down the corridor to the Department of Missing Letters office.

Are you reading my report? Dash, surprised, thought back.

You honestly think that's better? Desi tried to incite an argument.

It will be when you have to read hundreds of them, Dash lectured. *Remember, just the facts.*

Dash and Desi arrived at Marsha's work area in the back of the postal center and walked to her desk.

Marsha peered at them over the top of her glasses.

Dash introduced himself. "I'm Detective Dash, and this is Detective Desi. We're from the Thirty-Third Precinct, and we would like to ask you a few questions. Can you tell us how your job functions within the rest of the mail process?"

"Sure." Marsha was never happy to explain the obvious, and

rather tired from her long night out with Joe, but she went on anyway. "My staff and I receive letters that are pitched out of the router, that machine over there." She pointed to a big archaic machine, on the other side of a glass window that separated her department from the sorting machines. "The letters accumulate in a hopper here, and we each get the painstaking, slow job of barcoding each letter so that it reaches its destination."

"Why would a letter be pitched out of the router?" Desi asked.

"Illegible handwriting and incomplete addresses, mostly. Some misdirected mail, and stuff that just ends up on the floor. Sometimes we don't have much to go on, just a name. Elizabeth here can read anyone's handwriting." Elizabeth looked up from her desk after hearing her name. "We believe she's psychic. It's amazing what she can read."

"So, what happens to it then?" Desi made photographic notes as he observed each worker,

"Whatever we can fix easily, we encode and send on its way. The others we may have to investigate further, even to the point of opening a letter to discover where it goes or where it can be returned too. The items we can do absolutely nothing about we burn to protect the customer's privacy."

"What if you find something of value in the envelope?" Dash began pacing deep in thought.

"Did you see that half-million-credit Surruc Aprev sitting outside?" Marsha asked.

"What?" Dash and Desi uttered simultaneously.

"Just kidding, that stuff is auctioned off online. You can get some of it if you want."

"We are looking for a particular letter." Dash had his hands clasped with his index fingers extended together and the tips resting on his chin. His lips were pursed.

"I surmised this wasn't a typical field trip." Marsha straightened her arms, pushing against the desk as she leaned back in the chair to stretch out her tired back. "What letter are you looking for?"

"One addressed to 'Ralph.' Do you recall any such letter?"

"Going to need a little more than that, we go through 80,000 letters a day. It's rare that one would stand out, unless it was something really bizarre."

"This letter came into this facility and disappeared."

"You're not helping." Marsha sighed. "You are welcome to look through our mail, but I'll have to have a postal employee with you. When did it get here?"

"Sunday night," Dash said.

"We don't pick up mail on Sunday. And a three-day weekend to boot!"

"It was a special pickup," Desi informed her.

"Yeah, right, how did you determine that it came here?"

"We put a tracking device on it, and we traced it to here. Then the tracking device stopped."

"What kind of tracking device was it?"

"A silicon strip, are you familiar with them?"

"Yes, actually," Marsha informed him. "We do get a lot of police, federal agents, and private investigators of all kinds. You should know that. Narcotics, guns, live animal smuggling. In fact, the police don't use silicon strips anymore. You should have already known that, too."

"It wasn't our tracking device," Desi was happy to get a word in. "And why don't we use silicon tracking devices anymore?"

"Big Bertha over there. She smashes them every time."
Again, Marsha pointed through the office window at the oversized,
archaic routing machine. "Outdated machine. But until it breaks
down completely, they won't replace it. Budget restraints, you know.
So that's where your signal stopped. Where your letter went from
there, I don't know. You do realize that if it came in here on a
Sunday night, it could be anywhere in the mail process."

"No, it reached its destination," Dash said.

"Then case solved!" Marsha responded loudly, and the entire
room applauded and cheered.

"No, not quite." The cheering died out quickly as Desi
continued. "Its destination wasn't where it was addressed to."

"But yet it made it there? To its proper destination, not its
addressed destination?" Marsha looked at them both.

"Yes," they both answered.

"Then why are you looking for it?"

"Because we'd like to know what that destination was," Desi
admitted.

"You don't know?" Marsha became confused.

"No."

"But you know it got there."

"Yes," they both answered again.

"So, your letter got to its destination, even though you don't know where that is, and that's why you're looking for it," Marsha summed up.

"Yes." Dash tried to explain, "We are following its trail to find out what the destination of the letter actually is, so we can find out who it went to."

"Even though you know they already have it."

"Yes," they both answered again.

"Whom was it addressed to?"

"Ralph." Dash had stopped his pacing.

"Oh yes, you said that already. Ralph who?"

"Just Ralph."

"And have you talked to Ralph?"

"We don't know who Ralph is."

"But you know he has your letter?"

"Yes."

"How many 9-volt batteries have you two had today?" Marsha insinuated.

****

Homer squatted over a six-inch deep hole overlooking a valley, watching the sunrise while writing in his journal.

Homer's Log Day Five

I have noticed that I prefer a somewhat flat rock with a rounded edge. Not too sharp, not too dull, enough leverage to handle a sturdy product, enough edge to make a clean wipe of things, and yet soft and gentle on the tush. I've apparently connected with a side of myself I never cared to know existed. Joe always said there's nothing like watching the sunrise as you're squatting over a six-inch deep hole. I understand now.

"Excuse me, son," a forest ranger said as he came upon Homer squatting over his epiphany. "Are you Homer Bergman or Joe Ritz?"

Homer buried his head in his hands, totally embarrassed. His voice muffled by his hands, he answered, "I'm Homer." He looked up and sighed. "I'm also embarrassed and elated. Oh my God, I'm saved!"

"And where is Joe Ritz?" the ranger asked.

"Abducted by aliens."

Chapter 15

Intelligence?

Later that evening, Evinrude looked over the menu at Al's Pub and Grub. Not that he needed to; he was familiar with their fare. He just liked to be tempted away from his usual order every now and then.

The pub was more than just a bar. It was a quaint little eatery, adorned with a nostalgic fifty-foot mirror mounted behind a solid mahogany bar that gleamed as brightly as the day it was installed. Even though it was an older establishment, Al's original fixtures were of such high quality that they aged well.

It was still twilight outside when Henry Streator entered, escorted by Michele, Evinrude's aide.

"Good evening, Mr. Streator." Evinrude stood.

Even though Evinrude was always polite and gentlemanly, Henry mistook his etiquette as arrogance and became tenser. "Hello, sir." Henry was so nervous he almost trembled.

"Please, sit." Evinrude gestured to the seat across from him. "I requested an extra menu in case you were inclined to join me."

"Thank you…but no." Henry hesitated for a moment, but then sat down. Michele took a seat by the bar and kept an eye toward Evinrude and the door.

"Have a trying day?" Evinrude asked.

"No!"

"Well, I guess we'll be getting down to business…. Are you sure you don't want something to drink?"

"No!" Henry squeaked. He cleared his throat. "No, I'm okay."

"Well, anyway…" Evinrude reached into his inside coat pocket.

Henry's nerves jumped exponentially, imagining everything from being gunned down in public to…well, that was the only thing he imagined, but Evinrude merely pulled out an envelope.

Henry exhaled loud and long, calming himself.

Evinrude slid it across the table to Henry. "This memory card contains the information that was stolen. It still needs to be delivered on time. You'll have to explain to your contact why it's being transported through a different medium."

"O-kaaay," Henry said slowly. "You still trust me to follow through?"

"Well, the information is important and still needs to be delivered, and with all the people and pressure on you, I don't believe you'll do anything stupid."

"No," Henry answered timidly. "But why not just have an embassy aide relay it now?"

"The sensitivity of the information requires that my government's involvement remain secret."

****

In a booth in the back of the restaurant, Fred whispered to Frank, "You've got one good informant, but is it wise for us to be here? He has met us, you know."

"I know he's met us." Frank's seat provided a perfect vantage point to watch Evinrude and Streator.

"But doesn't he know we're here?" Fred said.

"It would be safe to assume he knows we're here, but we're going to pretend he doesn't. It's all part of the game," Frank explained.

"Seems kind of silly to me."

"Yes, I know. But if we're lucky, he'll buy us dinner, and since you didn't notice, a big drop just went down."

"Of course, I didn't notice. I'm facing the other way. The only clear view I have is of the restrooms."

"And a good thing, too, someone needs to watch our backs."

"Well, what if I just look over my shoulder?" Fred asked, as he turned to do just that.

"No, that would be obvious and unprofessional," Frank grabbed Fred's arm to stop him.

"What if I drop my napkin and look behind me." He moved his napkin to the table's edge.

"Oh, please, come up with something original." Frank rolled his eyes.

Fred tapped on his blazer pocket. "I have a mirror in my pocket."

Frank gave him an odd glance. "Why?"

Fred gave up, exasperated. "Well then, what do you suggest?"

"Be more aware of your surroundings."

"Oh," Fred moaned, feeling the cold hand of lecture come upon him.

"If you hadn't noticed," — Frank glanced at the objects he was identifying to avoid physically pointing — "there is a truck-sized mirror behind the bar, and there are dozens of mirrored maisivrec signs all over the place. Look around, how can you not see him?"

"So, what should we do? Move in on them?"

"No, no. Just watch,"

"Whom was the drop made to?" Fred asked.

"Henry Streator."

"Isn't that odd?"

"Yes and no."

Fred's eyes saddened, he knew a lengthy explanation was to follow.

"You see this just complicates things. We can't gain access to Henry easily with a regiment of people always watching him. And we wouldn't suspect Evinrude to even try using Henry to move the goods. Most likely it's just a decoy. But to be safe, we need to follow up and prove it, because there's always that one chance in a million it might not be a decoy. This is Evinrude's way of creating more work for us and slowing down our progress."

"Touché, Monsieur Evinrude!" Fred lauded Evinrude's strategic maneuver.

"Shhhhh!" Frank glared at him.

"So why don't we just follow the guy, pop him off, and take it." Fred leaned back, throwing his arms into the air.

"I'm an intelligence agent, not a murderer." Seething, his teeth grinding, Frank pointed an accusing figure at Fred and began lesson number two. "There are rules to this business. They are unwritten and unspoken but understood just the same."

"You're making this up as you go, aren't you?"

Frank gave Fred an evil stare. "If you kill, you will be killed. If you give respect, you will be respected. That's why we play this game."

"Well, I'm sorry. But this intelligence game" — Fred made quotation marks with his fingers — "just doesn't seem so intelligent."

"How many agents my age do you know?"

"Just you." Fred thought for a moment. "And Evinrude."

"What happens to most overzealous and anxious agents?"

"They don't return from the field."

"Because…?"

"They don't play the game?"

"Correct! You can be taught!" Frank exclaimed. "We are not enemies. We are opponents."

"So now all we need to do is liberate that envelope from Henry Streator, copy its contents, and return it," Fred said.

"Now you've got it," Frank declared.

****

While Fred and Frank discussed the finer points of espionage, Henry was ready for his meeting with Evinrude to be over. He stared at the envelope on the table for an awkwardly long time, then reluctantly placed it in the inside pocket of his sport coat. "Is there anything else I can do for you?"

"No, our business is done. If you'd like you can stay for dinner, but you are free to go." All three, including Michele at the bar, stood up at the same time. Henry left the restaurant, again escorted by Michele.

Evinrude walked toward the restrooms at the back of the

restaurant and stopped at Fred and Frank's table. "Would you two like to join me for dinner?" he asked. "I find myself embarrassingly alone since Mr. Streator decided not to stay. Just as well, I don't think he would have been good conversation tonight."

Fred just looked at Frank, not knowing what to do.

"Sure!" Frank exuberantly accepted, wondering if he should invite Evinrude to sit with them or go to Evinrude's table.

Fortunately, Evinrude had already decided the seating arrangements. "Please join me at my table. I prefer a lot of exits. Old habits, you know."

Frank and Fred stepped out of the booth and carried their drinks with them to Evinrude's table.

"I see the two of you were having quite the lively conversation."

"Just talking shop," Frank said.

"I hate to talk shop all the time. And it's hard not to, I'll admit." Evinrude waited as they were seating themselves, his etiquette requiring him to sit last. "But let's give it a try." He signaled the waiter over to the table. "Please allow me the pleasure of buying your dinner tonight."

"We'd be glad to," Fred graciously replied, not expecting such a social evening.

"Did either of you see the Ullamaliztli game last night?" Evinrude asked.

"No, I wanted to," Frank said. "Job, you know."

"I heard it was a nail-biter," Fred added.

"It certainly was. So, are you guys Panthers fans or Trojans fans?"

"I'm neither," Frank admitted. "I've followed the Rockets since I was a kid and my dad took me to my first real game. But if I were watching the game I'd lean toward the Panthers."

"You're a sutluts!" Fred exclaimed.

Frank did a double take at Fred. Evinrude smiled.

Fred's enthusiasm was rebuilt by the newfound camaraderie. "The Trojans are awesome this season!"

Evinrude chuckled as he assured them, "Well, neither one of you will be disappointed, until the very end, of course. But you'll both have enjoyed the game. I'll get you a copy of it." He leaned in and whispered, "Don't tell, but I did not get the express written consent of the National Ullamaliztli League." He winked, and they all had a good laugh.

Alfia and Joe drove through her quiet neighborhood toward home. Bugs splattered her windshield as if it were a humid midwestern summer night.

"First time I think I've seen a bug on your planet," Joe commented. "Wreaks havoc on your windshields, too."

"PaPARAZZI," Alfia informed him. "Photographic and Phonetic Aerial Reconnaissance Android Zygotic Zombie Insects." As Alfia turned onto her street, the bug strikes intensified. "We just call them gnats. The media and photograph-hounds use them to follow celebrities." She sprayed the windshield with washer fluid, and the wipers smeared the splattered silicon wings and circuit boards, making the mess worse. Alfia sighed. *I knew that would happen.*

"Yep, just like on Earth," Joe nodded "But we actually call the photograph-hounds 'paparazzi.' Looks like there's still a group of them in front of your house from this morning."

"You're becoming a celebrity."

"Wow, I've never had a public before."

The reporters identified Joe and charged, engulfing the car in a mass of people, cameras, and gnats. Alfia carefully nudged the car through the crowd, into her driveway, and finally, the garage.

After the garage door fully closed, the two got out of the car. Alfia grabbed a spray can off a shelf with many other bug sprays on it and sprayed herself. She turned to Joe. "Cover your eyes, Joe." She sprayed a mist over him, too.

"What was that?"

"Diluted lemongrass oil, kills gnats." She put the can away and headed into the house. "Works on real ones, too."

"Hello Alfia, Joe," Marsha moved to them, taking Joe warmly by the arm "I made some coffee and pie. Hope you like pie, Joe."

"Everybody likes pie." Joe eagerly sat at the table.

"I'm a little hungrier than just pie." Alfia pined for a heartier meal.

"There's leftovers in the fridge if you want. I didn't want to fill up. I might be eating out tonight. Are you hungry too, Joe?"

"I'm sure the pie will suffice until I get back to the hotel."

"That may be trickier than you think," Alfia said. "If they're camped out like this here, I'd hate to see what the hotel looks like. And anyway, aren't you beat, Mother?" Alfia was amazed that her mother was even awake, let alone expecting another night out. "You were up all last night, and you had to go to work today."

"Oh, I'll pay for it tomorrow. But I may just run into someone I know." Marsha seemed to glide around the table as she poured the coffee.

"What are you hinting at, Mother?" Alfia became suspicious.

"Oh, nothing dear." Marsha hummed quietly to herself.

Alfia's mind was a convolution of questions and contradictions. Her mother didn't usually hum. *She is not that content of a person. What is she up to? Who might she run into? Does she have a new boyfriend? Is it Joe? No. No. No. I've got to stop thinking like this. I need a clear head tonight.* Alfia shook her head and tasted the pie. Her favorite, strawberry-rhubarb with a lard crust, and it was warm. Alfia forgot her angst for a moment.

Marsha sighed coyly. "I sure would like to get out of this stuffy house tonight."

Alfia looked at her, wide-eyed, unable to speak due to a large bite of pie.

Marsha went on, "Would you mind if I drove Joe back to the hotel tonight, dear?"

Joe looked at her, also wide-eyed, unable to speak due to a large bite of pie. Marsha winked at him.

After a big swallow and gulp of coffee, Alfia sarcastically asked, "Will you make it this time?

"Eventually," she grinned like a teenager with a secret.

Shortly, Marsha and Joe again drove off to find adventure, with the media in tow. They didn't want to be left out.

****

In another part of town, Mayor Nehru arrived at a late-night meeting with the most powerful men on the planet, the Establishment. The Establishment was composed of all the money and all the political power on Ladascus, and a few relatives.

In a poorly lit room, men in expensive business suits sat around a large conference table. Smoke from their cigarettes and cigars billowed down from the ceiling like an eerie fog. The boss sat at the head of the table, in the shadows, his black suit and black hat completely immersing him in the inky darkness. If not for his white shirt, tie, and boutonniere, he wouldn't be seen at all. He spoke with a quiet, raspy voice. "Nehru, an unfortunate circumstance has come to our attention."

Nehru, a little uneasy, knew only to speak when spoken to. "Please explain, sir. I'm afraid I was not informed of any situation."

The boss was a man of few words. He waved his hand to his right, and a man in a bright suit spoke. "We created a syndicate that has thrived on the friction between our warring occupiers. Peace is something we cannot afford, Nehru."

"I understand, but I assure you I have not promoted such a position."

"No. But you are in a position to prevent the person who has. This Earth creature called Joe."

"I can assure you he is harmless." Nehru placed his right hand on his heart and tried to gaze into the boss's shrouded eyes.

"That may be true, but the message the Souftes and Quesontes are using him for is not," the man pointed out. "You need to bring the Earthman to us."

The hand from the shadowed boss lifted, and the brightly-suited man stopped talking. The boss methodically said, "Normally a dip in Lake Protivin would cure our ailment, but the Earthman seems to be immune."

Nehru felt an icy chill go down his spine. He knew the boss was not happy. A long, fluid gesture from the boss to his left, and a tan-suited man began to talk. "You see, it's like this. We need to educate them on how things work…here. Now, these ambassadors think they can just declare peace, lift the trade embargoes, and walk away. This will significantly cut into our profit margin."

"Maybe I could make sure Drakewood and Calloway understand our situation," Nehru offered.

"You're a good man, Nehru," the boss rasped from the shadows. As if he were conducting a symphony, he flicked his wrist and another member of his ensemble continued.

"Our representatives already made them an offer," the new spokesman was slow and deliberate with each word. "They refused. At two o'clock tomorrow afternoon, the ambassadors will learn of the gravity of their situation."

****

For their first stop on their second evening out, Marsha treated Joe to a holographic horror flick, *The Earthling!* Joe frightened the audience out of the theater and into the lobby.

"In hindsight, this may not have been a good idea," Marsha apologized to the police when they arrived. The police decided it would be fun to take a few PR photos of them, guns drawn, menacingly surrounding a handcuffed Joe.

As if on cue, Mayor Nehru barged in with a whirlwind of reporters, cameras, lights, and staff in his wake. (It was always said that Mayor Nehru knew good publicity when he saw it.) The media crowd doubled. This time, the mayor did not push Marsha out of the way and introduced them both to more people of local power and wealth. Marsha scanned the posse of posers with the mayor and was noticeably disappointed. Nehru decided to keep two uniformed officers with them for crowd control as he escorted them on another night on the town.

At the zoo, Joe awkwardly waved at the humans in the Earth exhibit. They awkwardly waved back. The mayor, looking uncomfortable, hurried on to the next exhibit.

Mayor Nehru treated them to dinner at Anopuac, the fanciest dining establishment in town. It was located at the top of a tall skyscraper, and Joe and Marsha could see all the city lights. (Joe thought Ngorongoro looked a lot like any Earth city at night.)

Marsha kept looking around, hoping to catch sight of someone, but no one ever showed. The night dragged on, and she rested her cheek heavily on her palm and her sighs deepened.

As they enjoyed dessert, Joe mused, "You know what I miss?"

Marsha, the mayor, and diners at all the other tables around them stopped to listen.   "Chocolate, you don't have chocolate. Smooth, shiny, dark brown decadence. Slowly melting on your tongue, the aroma filling your nostrils, rich, creamy delight running down your throat…chocolate just makes you smile."

A moment of silence filled the room as everyone took a long cleansing breath, exploding into orders for dessert.

At another social hot spot, Joe regaled his audience of A-list Ladascans with stories of his adventures on Earth, and what a great place it was to vacation. He described skiing in the mountains; the warm sandy beaches in the Caribbean— "No gorgons, but we do have sharks" — and how people actually go into the water and swim, an alien idea to them indeed.

Marsha happened, not so unexpectedly, to run into Mr. Adams, or Dougy as she affectionately referred to him, the same rich and powerful man from the night before. She spent the evening dancing with him and seemed full of life again.

The mayor bid farewell due to the late hour but left the police escort with Joe, Marsha, and Dougy.

At a comedy club, apparently dumb Earthling jokes were all the rage. "How many Earthlings does it take to screw in an evacuated glass envelope containing heated metallic filament?"

Joe stood up. "I don't know about light bulbs, but I do know how many Earthlings it takes to defeat a gorgon."

The comedian fired back, "Look out! An Uluru!" Joe played along and ducked.

Joe and the comedian bantered back and forth for a short time, creating an entertaining encounter. The audience roared with laughter. Marsha had tears in her eyes from laughing so hard. Joe stole a bow and sat back down.

Afterward, they went to a nearby confectionary, where Joe enjoyed two scoops of a newfound frozen favorite. He saw, through the window behind Marsha and Dougy, the same mime from the night before. His heart dropped when the mime noticed him, too. *Which new social faux pas will he ridicule tonight?* Joe wondered.

Tonight, it was a re-enactment of the incident at the theater with the police. Their police escort was still with them and sitting at the next table, enjoying their own frozen dessert. They saw the mime taunting Joe and decided to arrest the silent actor. Marsha and Dougy watched as the officers apprehended the mute mimic. The mime, true to his art, didn't break character and performed a silent protest all the way to the waiting squad car. Marsha and Dougy turned back to their desserts, and Joe was gone.

****

Even later that same evening, Dash and Desi were the only ones left in the office, laboring over the multiple files of evidence. Their desks were smothered beyond comprehension. Desi sorted through documents page by page, physically burying himself in paper.

Dash, more orderly by nature, had inadvertently spread all his documents across every horizontal surface in the room. He had spent the last several hours pacing around the room, glancing at one form and cross-checking another, his left hand in his coat pocket and his right rubbing his chin.

A muffled phone rang somewhere in the office. They both

glanced at each other, speculating where the phone might be. Desi reached below a mound and liberated the phone from its paper tomb. With the ringing more distinct now, he answered it. "Uh hum? Yes. Thanks." Desi hung up the phone. "The report came back on the phones."

"Good news?" Dash asked, not expecting any.

"No," Desi said. "There was nothing on or in the phones. Either the perpetrator was thorough, or the fumes from the bus destroyed anything that may have existed.

"Yet another disappointing outcome. I'm not surprised, though," Dash said.

"Well, at least you're prepared. Regarding another disappointing outcome, the database finally identified the office substituted in the surveillance recording the night of the robbery," Desi informed Dash.

"Oh." Dash perked up. "What office was it?"

"This one."

"This one?"

"This one here, ours, but about twenty-five years ago."

"Really?" Dash seemed more impressed than disappointed.

"Yes."

"I told you our opponent was clever,"

"Let's assume, for a moment, that Henry Streator isn't innocent of the crime." Desi thought out loud. "What do we know?"

"When you infer a theory without facts, you invariably manipulate the facts to fit the theories instead of developing theories that fit the facts."

"Anyway," Desi looked sternly at Dash and continued, "Henry isn't capable of entering a building in this fashion. So, he hired someone. How do you find someone with this skillset? How did he make the first contact with Ralph?"

Dash said sarcastically, "And so you continue the dark art of induction."

Desi glared at Dash and decided to turn the tables. "I prefer to think of it as adducer, which allows for the precondition to be adduced from the consequence. Post hoc ergo propter hoc, in other words: after this, therefore, because of this. And as such, abduction is the formal equivalent of this logical fallacy because there are multiple possible explanations that can affirm the consequences."

Dash was silent for an awkward moment as he processed

Desi's dissertation and then contributed to Desi's reasoning. "So how did he make the first contact with Ralph?"

"That's an explanation for the letter," Desi assured his colleague, happy with his little victory. "Bear with me; I'm just going step by step. According to the letter, something went wrong."

"Okay," Dash admitted. "I'll give you that one."

"So, then what was miscommunicated?" Desi asked.

"If you were to direct someone to steal something," Dash asked, "what information would you convey?"

"What to steal," Desi answered.

"Yes, and that could have been a generality, such as the contents of the box," Dash pointed out.

"Where it is or how to find it."

"Yes," Dash agreed. "They apparently got that right."

"When to steal it," Desi posed to his partner. "The heist took place on the wrong day."

"That would make a lot of sense. Maybe there was a typo on the date of the original communication. Wait, now I'm making inductions! I warned you the dark side was seductive."

"That would explain the insurance," Desi added. "He

arranged to increase his insurance coverage tenfold the following week. According to his insurance agent, it was to underwrite an exceptionally large item that he rarely dealt in."

"That's circumstantial, not conclusive evidence," Dash pointed out.

"But we can create this scenario. Henry can't afford to buy the diamond he is buying. We've seen his house. He just can't. So, he buys it on credit. In the meantime, the diamond is stolen, and the insurance reimburses the loss, which in turn, pays for the diamond before it is due on the credit loan."

"So," Dash played devil's advocate, "he didn't gain anything, he just reclaimed his loss. The insurance company would only cover the value, so he sees no real monetary gain."

"But," Desi continued, "You're assuming he puts the big stone into the box. What if he keeps it, breaks it down and sells off the pieces. Even broken down it would still be worth a substantial amount of money."

"Okay, so what's in it for the person committing the crime?" Dash asked.

"Money," Desi replied. "He lets the thief keep the contents of the box to pay her off. Streator is reimbursed for the value of those diamonds as well. So now the insurance company has paid the thief and bought Streator a large diamond. He will then sell off the big diamond either whole or, more likely, cut it down into untraceable pieces and make a tidy profit." Desi concluded, "So now, the thief is not only a thief but part of insurance fraud."

"This thief is smart, wise and probably not greedy. She will be difficult to catch. What do you propose we do?" Dash inquired.

"Well, if it went according to plan, we'd watch for Henry to try and sell the cut-down diamond."

Dash jumped in, "But he can't since he didn't purchase it yet."

"Then our only hope is for one of the stolen diamonds to surface." Desi sighed.

"And here we lie in a quagmire produced by inductive reasoning, that serves as a hypothesis to explain our observations, but in fact, there are an infinite number of possible outcomes," Dash lectured.

Desi just stared at him. "I actually understood that. In your own idiosyncratic way, you just said 'I told you so.' But, if it were to turn up?"

"I wouldn't get your hopes up."

"But, some powerful people want a piece of this heist back. This is where we increase the pressure on Henry Streator to encourage a mistake by either him or the thief."

"A search warrant would do that," Dash suggested as he picked up the phone. "I'll call Judge Howell."

Chapter 16

The House Party

Henry Streator's house was dimly lit. Henry didn't like all the surveillance, so he kept the lights down and the shades drawn as much as he could. Several blocks away and up a hill, Ralph parked her car. She was able to see the house, the Ladascan police stakeout car, the Soufte stakeout car, and the Quesonte stakeout car all parked in front. She looked behind her to see if she was the last one to the party. Nothing had changed from the night before when she had evaluated Streator's house. She drove away.

A few moments later Fred and Frank parked in the same spot. They, too, saw Henry's house and the cars parked in front of it. They, too, waited.

Several hours passed. Fred and Frank drove off, avoiding the three stakeout cars, only to park several blocks away. Dressed in black, Fred and Frank crossed through the backyards of the houses in between. Fred somehow managed to step on a cat's tail as he bounded over a fence. The cat let out a yelp that started all the neighborhood dogs barking. Frank looked at him coldly.

Finally, they arrived in Henry's backyard. Fred carried a slim pack with him, and Frank had several tools in his pockets. Frank looked at his watch. It was two minutes after one. He had contacted the company that supplied and monitored Henry's security system and instructed them to turn off the alarm from their main office at exactly one o'clock in the morning. But Frank still tested the system to be sure. He set a small box next to the window sensor. A red light glowed.

"Figured as much, the alarm is still on," Frank grumbled. Suddenly the light turned green, and he sighed with relief. "Oh good."

They drilled out the lock on the window, slid it open, and crawled in, closing the window behind them. They were in the family room just off the kitchen.

Ralph had returned to Streator's house and had been watching Fred and Frank. *Rookies*, she thought. Also fully clothed in black, she brought along a black bag containing all the items she had appropriated last Friday night. Ralph crept into Henry's backyard from the side opposite Fred and Frank's entry. She was aware of their movements and everything else that was going on around the house. *Always be aware of your surroundings*, her father's transcendental advice echoed.

She slipped around the gazebo and came to the patio door. She jimmied the lock and slid a hair-thin card between the door and the jamb. The card was a powerful magnet with an adhesive strip. She held it against the sensor near the top of the door, opened the door, and then pressed the adhesive strip against the doorjamb to hold it in place on the sensor. Even though she had seen Fred and Frank disarm the system, she had learned, *Never trust anything you don't control.* She had a few of her own truisms. She slipped into the kitchen and shut the door, leaving it unlocked.

Frank and Fred had already found Henry's den, toward the front of the house.

Ralph went through the kitchen and into the hallway. She peered into the rooms, looking for the den, where she discovered Frank and Fred going through Henry's desk and computer. She slowly backed away, thought for a moment about the other two invaders, and surveyed her surroundings. The house was still basically the same as the original layout that she had studied in the archives of the city planning commission office. *Thank goodness, they keep those records forever.*

It was an older house with a divided staircase. One flight descended from the upper level to a landing, where it separated into one staircase to gain access to the front of the house and another to the rear. Ralph decided to ascend the front stairs to Henry's bedroom. She had just reached the landing halfway up when a door loudly slammed shut below her.

Frank and Fred froze and looked at each other in alarm.

In a flash Henry was up. He knew exactly what that sound was. He jumped out of bed, into his slippers and, grabbing his robe, ran out the door.

Ralph quickly retreated down the back set of stairs toward the kitchen.

Fred and Frank peeked out of the den and saw Henry stomping down each stair, grumbling all the way, "I'll get him. He's not getting away with it this time." Frank and Fred hid behind the desk in the den.

At the landing, Henry headed toward the front of the house

and the main floor, his robe floating in the breeze of his tailwind. He bolted down the hallway to his right and to the basement stairs.

In the den, Frank and Fred were unable to locate the envelope that Evinrude had given Henry. Taking advantage of the opportunity, they maneuvered upstairs into Henry's bedroom.

Ralph backed further into the kitchen while Fred and Frank climbed the stairs.

In the basement, Henry made a beeline to the wine cellar and threw open the unlocked door.

Winston, crouched behind the stairwell, bolted (well, shuffled, like the elderly man he was) up the stairs, carrying a purloined bottle of port.

A moment later, Henry emerged from the wine cellar, shouting, "Where are you? Where are you? I will not tolerate you stealing my wine again!"

Winston quickly fled to the kitchen, opened the pantry, and blindly set the bottle on the floor just behind the door, next to Ralph's leg. Winston then quickly shifted to the door of his own quarters at the far end of the kitchen, as Henry feverishly entered the kitchen. "What is all the excitement about, sir?" Winston yawned and stretched, pretending to have just woken up, while trying to hide his shortness of breath from Henry.

"You've been stealing my wine again!" Henry accused him. "A bottle of Trebuchet port is missing!"

"Do I use that one for cooking, sir?"

"At 500 credits a bottle, you better not be."

While Henry and Winston argued, Ralph slipped out of the pantry (with the wine, her father's favorite spirit.) and ducked into the den, as she had originally planned.

"Sir, I believe you are regrettably mistaken. The wine cellar is constantly locked, and you're the only one with a key," Winston pointed out.

"Well, it was open just now."

"Did you forget to lock it?"

"No! I never forget to lock it. You must have another key,"

"In what manner could I have attained a key?" Winston shrugged his shoulders "You have the only one."

"That's right! And don't you forget it."

"If you'd like, you can inventory the wine in the wine rack to see if there are any extra bottles there," Winston moved toward the wine cooler.

"I will. But I'm going to check the pantry first. That would be a perfect place to stash it on the way up from the basement." Henry walked back to the pantry, turned on the light and looked in.

Winston bit his lower lip, a look of dread overcoming him.

Henry came out, disappointed. "Nothing in there."

Winston, though bewildered, regained his composure. "Well…of course not, sir."

Henry searched the kitchen thoroughly, as Winston double-checked the pantry for the bottle that now eluded him.

In the den, Ralph placed a black bag (filled with Henry's diamonds, his correspondence with her, and the contents of the other safe deposit boxes) on the back of a shelf in the closet. *It's not about the money,* her father used to say, ever so nicely, *but sometimes you have to cut the sutluts loose.* Now she could leave. She paused for a moment, taking an inventory of her surroundings. Winston and Henry were in the kitchen, Frank and Fred in the bedroom, and three sets of eyes were out front. What was a girl to do? *Patience,* echoed from beyond.

****

Outside Henry's house, Detective Tom approached the lead car of the stakeout. He and the two agents he had met in the mall had decided to share the responsibility of the stakeouts, so they could get some much-needed sleep. He knocked on the window.

Inside, Dick startled, looked at his watch, and rolled down the window. "It's early. What's up?"

"On a stakeout, one shouldn't be so startled."

"I know. I'm not sleeping much anymore." Dick closed his bloodshot eyes to soothe them. "Kid's teething. There is no peace at home."

"I can sympathize; it'll be over soon. Wait until…he or she?"

"She."

"…becomes a teenager."

"I thought it only got better." Dick conveyed a young parent's hopes.

"Let me just say, it takes a lot of restraint not to use this firearm sometimes," Tom joked.

"So anyway, you're early." Dick started to worry. "We've been found out, haven't we? Oh, I knew this would happen."

"No, no we didn't. I just heard from the precinct," Tom

explained. "They'll be here shortly with a warrant to search the premises."

"Well, it was good while it lasted." Dick calmed a little.

"Yes, it was. We'll need to collaborate more often. I called Harry to let him know what was going on, and he should be here soon. We don't want our superiors to know what we've been up to."

****

Fred and Frank discovered a briefcase and an envelope with a memory card in Henry's bedroom. Frank pulled out the memory card while Fred removed a small computer from his pack, and they started transferring the information onto its hard drive.

Frank whispered, "This file is huge!"

Henry was now climbing the stairs back up to his bedroom. Winston discreetly searched the lower floors. And Ralph cautiously returned to the pantry to avoid Winston.

"You'd better hurry, he's on his way back," Fred warned, peering back from the doorway. They dashed into the closet, their computer still downloading the information.

Henry made a beeline to his bathroom.

The download finished. Frank and Fred quickly put the

memory card back, monitoring the time by the sounds emanating from the bathroom.

The doorbell rang.

"What the anneheg now?" emanated from the bathroom, a sentiment shared silently by Frank and Fred.

Frank and Fred barely escaped into the hallway and rushed down the stairway. Henry exited the bathroom. Observing the increase in movement, Ralph decided the pantry had limited exits and darted out into the family room, which was open to the kitchen.

Frank and Fred glimpsed Winston walking toward the front door just as they headed down the back stairs into the kitchen.

Henry trudged down the stairs. Ralph spied Fred and Frank moving toward the patio door and froze. *Hiding in plain sight is easy: don't move.* Simple but true; her father's tips were always right.

Frank and Fred were in such a hurry to leave, they didn't realize that the patio door was already unlocked.

Rookies. Ralph shook her head.

Winston momentarily paused to turn off the alarm, questioning whether he had set it or not when he noticed it was off.

The bell rang again, and Winston opened the door. As he let Dash, Desi, and a uniformed officer into the house, Henry reached the bottom of the stairs.

Ralph crossed into the kitchen and watched through the patio door as Fred and Frank climbed over the back fence. She detached the magnet from the sensor—*Always pick up after yourself, or someone else will.* — and left, closing the patio door behind her. She passed the gazebo and disappeared over the side fence with her newly-acquired bottle of port.

"And to what, may I ask, do I owe the pleasure of this visit?" Henry huffed to Dash and Desi.

"We have a search warrant for the premises," Desi told him.

"At two in the morning?" Henry asked.

"Routine investigative work," Dash explained. "We have a search warrant for the premises."

"You said that already," Henry stated.

"Just reiterating the facts." Dash was secretly enjoying taunting Henry.

"It's two a.m.!" Henry yelled.

"You said that already."

"Just reiterating the facts," Streator snidely shot back. "Well, I guess it was inevitable. I'm a little surprised you didn't search me earlier. But then, it is standard procedure to harass the victim if you can't find the crook, isn't it?" he went on sarcastically. "Oh, and I'm missing a bottle of port, please cavity-search my butler."

"Valet, sir," Winston reminded him.

"If it turns up, we'll let you know." Dash gestured for everyone to move in to the next room. "But for now, we need both of you to remain here in the living room with the officer."

Henry plopped himself down on the couch and Winston quietly sat beside him. "Can we at least watch TV?" Henry pouted.

Desi and Dash, ignoring Henry and his comments, walked out.

Henry snatched up the remote and crushed the buttons, turning on the television. Newsflashes of Joe out on the town with Marsha broke into regular programming on every channel. After surfing through all the channels, Henry got fed up, turned off the TV, and threw the remote across the room. He looked at Winston angrily and said, "Well?"

"If you will pardon my candor, sir, I might remark that you

are something of a sunisa."

Desi asked Dash quietly, "Really, two a.m.? Why did it take so long to get the warrant?"

Dash replied, "The judge was at a dance club. Apparently, the mayor and his cronies seized the opportunity to take photos with the Earthling at some of the local hot spots. Elections are coming up."

****

Joe could hear the muffled voices of people talking. He had been gagged and bound, and a hood was pulled over his head. He was thrown into the trunk of a car that was driving to an unknown location, which isn't saying much since any place in Ngorongoro was unknown to him. He had tried to memorize the turns and count the seconds between them, but there were too many, and he wondered if his abductors had actually gotten lost a few times.

The car finally stopped, and they pulled him out of the trunk and down a long, twisting flight of stairs. Joe was pretty sure there were three of them. He caught two alien-sounding names: Oemay and Urlycay.

They plopped Joe into a chair and bound him to it, then

removed the hood and gag. Before him stood three rather surly-looking Ladascans.

"Don't worry, kid." From his voice, Joe speculated that Oemay was addressing him. "It's not personal, just business."

"Now there's a stale cliché."

"See here," Urlycay reprimanded him. "We don't need any fresh talk from you."

"Why don't we just pop him in the brains and go?" the third one said.

"Because. Arrylay, we're here to interrogate him, not kill him."

"Oh, all right." Arrylay slouched away to a work table across the room. Joe watched him wiring a small box on top of a football-sized metal cylinder.

"We need some answers." Oemay grabbed Joe's bound hands and looked menacingly into his eyes.

"As long as it's not the proof to Fermat's Last Theorem, I'll be glad to help." Joe tried to be witty.

"A wise guy, ay, what organizations do you belong to?" Joe couldn't escape Oemay's rancid breath as he pressed in closer.

"Several actually: The ABA — American Bicycle Association; the CIA — Cyclists Improving America; the KGB — Kogs, Gears, and Bikes; and I also participated in RAGBRAI once," Joe attempted shallow breaths.

"Impressive." Oemay leaned away and pondered for a moment, not recognizing any of the organizations. "What makes you think you can move in on the boss's territory?"

"I'm not moving in on anyone. I was accidentally abducted."

"Accidentally abducted, ay?" Urlycay argued. "Do you expect us to believe that?"

"Well, yes,"

"Do you think we're sutluts?" Oemay retorted in a huff.

"Just misinformed, maybe?" Joe studied the knots in the rope that tied him to the chair. He had been a scout most of his life and had an extensive knowledge of knots. Although they were formidable, Joe noticed they were tied wrong: simply releasing the tension on the rope would free him. But it wouldn't be as simple as it sounded since the ropes were very tightly wrapped. "These are extraordinary knots," he complimented his captors.

"Well, thank you. I tied them myself." Urlycay boasted. "Bet you don't have anything like that on your primitive planet."

"Don't get chummy with the hostage. We may have to kill it," Oemay warned him.

"It's okay. It's not like I named it."

Arrylay, now fitting a small device into the base of a speaker's podium, asked Oemay, "Are you sure this is the same podium they'll be using?"

"Positive."

Arrylay grimaced. "We need to get this bomb worked out before the press conference tomorrow."

"Quiet, you clod," Oemay scolded him. "Not in front of the prisoner."

"Yeah," Urlycay added his two cents' worth. "He doesn't need to know about the biological bomb."

"I said, shut up!" Oemay loudly punctuated the last two words.

"Oh God, you're not going to blow up a bunch of people because of me?" Joe struggled harder against his bonds.

"Of course, it's because of you. You moved in on the boss's territory. You're affecting profits. He can't have that," Oemay informed him.

"This ain't no ordinary bomb." Arrylay perked up, patting the device. "It's a compound explosive device. First, it'll kill everyone within five meters, and then it'll disperse a chemical agent that'll make everyone within five hundred meters sick and die, eventually. And it's travel-sized for convenience."

"But why use it on innocent people?" Joe argued.

"Because Ambassadors Drakewood and Calloway aren't innocent, they're declaring peace," Oemay explained.

"Isn't peace a good thing?"

"Not if you're the boss, and your primary source of income depends on conflict between the Quesontes and the Souftes," Oemay added.

"I say we just pop him off now," Arrylay said, tired of the debate. "What's one Earthman, more or less?"

"If you count the four in the zoo, it would be a 20 percent reduction," Joe watched for a response, but none came.

"Not until the boss says so."

Arrylay sulked away.

"So, what's your angle?" Urlycay asked. "Nine-volt

batteries?"

"I don't have any angle. I'm just visiting."

"Don't bring that up again." Urlycay turned on a small TV in the corner just as an announcement began. "Look, we're destroying you in the media right now."

"Joe, the man from Earth, has apparently brought an infectious disease to Ladascus. Federal officials are warning everyone to stay away from the Earthman if you see him." The news program showed scenes of overcrowded hospitals, filled with sick and dying Ladascans. Joe watched in awe and disbelief. He knew the images were false, yet they were so horrific he winced at the site of them.

"The boss owns the media," Oemay taunted him. "He made you a public enemy. So, don't get any ideas about calling for help."

The report continued, *"It's the same virus that the military isolated during the Welles Panic of '38, when a peaceful delegation desired the friendship of a small planet and died from a germ common to that planet. It was so deadly that the military isolated it and grew it for use in our biological armament."*

"So, you're going to infect a large crowd of people, and

they'll think I did it?"

Oemay grinned, "And they'll eventually die a slow, painful death. The two ambassadors will die instantly. And the new ambassadors will learn to play ball with the boss. So, if you go to the police, they'll lock you up. If you go outside, people will turn you in. There's nothing you can do. We hold all the cards."

"Why are you over-explaining it like a bad movie?" Urlycay said. "I've been following along."

"It's ready," Arrylay declared. "We need to deliver this and set up. I can install it in under a minute. No one will know." He looked toward Joe and asked, "What about him?"

"Leave him here until the boss says different," Oemay said.

"He'll never get out of my knots," Urlycay boasted.

They left, carrying the conveniently travel-sized bomb in a valise, and locked the door behind them. Joe could hear Arrylay complaining from beyond the door. "Why didn't we get a building with an elevator?"

"Shut up!" Oemay said.

The television was still on, and the announcer continued his report, *"The Earthling is extremely dangerous. He has not been decontaminated and should not be handled. If you see him, please contact the police immediately."*

Joe struggled against the ropes, veins bulging on his arms, his face turning beet red. He almost tipped over twice. A million thoughts ran through his head. What should he do? Who could he call? How would he call? Is gravity merely the energy of momentum? Where was the press conference they were talking about?

The TV announcer conveniently answered his last query. "*At two o'clock this afternoon Ambassador Drakewood and Ambassador Calloway will make a public address at the Ladascan Interplanetary Spaceport to reveal their new peace initiative.*"

Now Joe knew where he had to go, but he didn't know where it was.

First, he needed to escape. It was a sophisticated knot but tied incorrectly. All he had to do was relieve the pressure on the rope somehow. Slowly, he wriggled his arm and was eventually able to slip his hand over the side of the arm of the chair. The rope loosened. Joe slid his hand out and was unbound in seconds. He went to the door. It was locked from the inside; they must have been more worried about someone getting in than Joe getting out. Joe unlocked the door and left.

****

Homer's Log Day Five Point Five

Safe at the ranger station, eating a large pizza and gulping down a Coke, I felt my body go, "Ahhhh."

The ranger came over, "You made short work of that pizza. You know, there are many edible things in the forest."

"Yes. But my body prefers the many edible things in the city." Homer smiled.

The ranger informed him, "I contacted Joe's parents, and they're on their way here."

"Did you tell them about the aliens?"

"No."

Chapter 17

Peer Gynt Suite I
Opus 46, No.1
Morgenstimmung

The sun peered through a crack in the drapes and lazily crept up Henry's shirt while he dozed against Winston on the couch. Finally, the bright light shone in his eyes and rudely woke him.

Dash and Desi had searched Henry Streator's house throughout the night. The officer sat in the chair in the corner, still alert as if not a moment had passed.

Dash and Desi were in the den, the last room of their search, when Dash declared, "Well, if this isn't conveniently incriminating, I don't know what is." He showed Desi the black bag he had just found in Henry's closet. "Apparently Ralph is cutting Henry loose." He pulled out the letters and the jewels and displayed them to Desi.

Desi, trying to mimic Dash's scholarly teachings, said, "Be warned, Dash. There is nothing more deceptive than the obvious."

"As my dear friend, Nigel, would say" — Dash attempted to emulate an old, stodgy accent — "'the old chap is snookered.'"

Desi looked at him as if he had blown a fuse, and then followed him into the sitting room.

Henry, drowsy from sleeping on a lumpy valet, looked up at them. "Finished?"

"Quite so. Mr. Streator, you are under arrest for theft and insurance fraud." Dash conspicuously swung the satchel over his shoulder.

"What?" Henry screeched.

"You're under arrest."

"What the anneheg are you talking about? I can't be arrested! I'm the victim!"

"Oh, yes, you can." Dash patted the bag. "The evidence we just discovered clearly shows your involvement with the crime."

"You're crazy!" He pointed at Winston. "Well, arrest him, too. He's been stealing my wine."

"You can remain silent, but don't have to. We might use it against you, or not. If you can afford an attorney, hire one," Desi smirked. He enjoyed reciting the Ladascan version of the Miranda warning to Henry.

"Oh yeah, buddy?" Henry leaped off the couch, his veins

popping out of his forehead.

"We can leave either with or without the handcuffs," a polite, deep voice came from the corner. The officer rose out of his chair, his large, stocky build and muscular frame apparent as he dwarfed Henry.

Henry didn't know what to do or think. Should he make a break for it? Should he expose Ralph? He wavered a little as he weighed his options, of which he had none.

Dash, Desi, and the uniformed officer escorted Henry out of the house; Winston eagerly held the door open for them.

"Pity," Desi said as they walked out. "It would have been more intriguing if the butler did it."

"Valet…Sir." Winston said with a stern grimace.

They placed Henry into the squad car and closed the door. Henry looked back to his house one last time, only to see Winston as he held a bottle of wine and raised a filled glass to toast Henry's departure. Henry clenched his teeth, his face turning red.

****

Later that morning, Fred entered the Soufte Embassy alone. Immediately, he was pummeled by Frank's shouts from their office down the hall. "No! No! You idiots! What kind of play was that?"

Tricia looked up at Fred from behind her desk. "He's been like this all morning."

Astonished, Fred walked to their office and stopped at the door. He saw the usually-neat-and-tidy Frank sitting among a pile of spent soda cans and microwavable food wrappers. The sounds of the Ullamaliztli game emanated from Frank's computer.

"I can't believe you are still watching that game."

"It's a great game," Frank said, not breaking eye contact with the screen. "It's gone into double overtime."

"I still can't believe the memory card Evinrude gave Henry Streator had this game on it! Aren't—"

"Shush!" Frank, holding up a finger to silence Fred, slowly rose to his feet, his eyes glued to the screen. "Yeah! Now that's what I'm talking about!" He fell back in his chair, relieved, as if a great weight had been removed. "Macideneb! That was a great game. Remind me to thank Evinrude for the copy."

The announcer could be heard, *"And that concludes double overtime of the game of the millennium! This copyrighted broadcast is the property of the National Ullamaliztli League. Any rebroadcast or reproduction without the consent of the..."* Frank stopped the recording and looked at his watch, ignoring Fred. "I should go home and shower."

Tricia passed by the door. "Please do."

****

Back in her average house on an average side of town, Alfia cooked another of her infamous breakfasts. This one, however, was highlighted with a bottle of Trebuchet port already open and breathing on the table.

Marsha entered quietly, hoping not to be seen.

Alfia was busy at the stove, "Good morning, you two." She turned to find only her mother, on the brink of tears. "Where's Joe?"

"I lost him!" Marsha cried out, breaking down and sobbing.

"It can't be that bad." Alfia hugged her. "He stands out around here. Someone must know where he is." She walked into the other room and turned on the morning news, instantly bombarded with the negative media coverage of Joe that the Establishment had put out.

"Newsflash!" the announcer yelled excitedly. *"The Earthman Joe has been declared public enemy number one. The*

alien has contaminated the entire city. Citizens are warned to stay inside until this menace can be contained and sterilized. Seek medical help if you've been in contact with the Earthman. If you see the Earthman, please contact the authorities right away."

Immediately, Janet appeared at the patio door, knocking, and called, "I told you he was dangerous." Alfia walked over and closed the drapes.

Chapter 18

Repetitive Redundancy

or

Another Chase of the Same Alien Through the Same Town

Joe found a door that opened to a seedy back alley between the buildings. It was dimly lit, quiet, and filled with trash dumpsters. He cautiously walked toward the light of the busy street at the end of the alley.

He pulled his collar up and tucked his chin under it, hoping no one would notice an alien walking down the street.

They did. People pointed at Joe and shouted, "Earthling! Earthling!" They backed away, giving him a wide berth, thinking he was diseased. A nearby police officer radioed in the sighting. Then the tweet of her officer's whistle rang out through the air, and everyone turned to see, even Joe. Joe realized the tweets tolled for him. He ran.

He was quick, running into the street and weaving between cars, dodging taxis and buses. He was fit, he was able. He knew he could go the distance, until he crashed into a bicycle messenger. They both fell to the ground. Joe, full of adrenaline, sprang back up and grabbed the messenger's bike. "Sorry, man. I'm stealing your bike." He rode off.

The messenger got up and brushed himself off. He turned to the officer who had just run up to him and said, "That was the politest bicycle thief I've ever run across."

Not only was Joe a part-time bicycle repairman, but he was also an avid rider. He quickly got up to speed and made good time through traffic. Within moments, a squad of Ngorongoro Police Department vehicles found him and took up the pursuit. But traffic was heavy and a bicycle easily out-maneuvered the NPD.

Joe was quick and efficient on a bike, passing a few bicycle couriers as well. (They gave him a nod for his riding prowess.) He barreled down a street where an NPD bicycle patrol officer was stationed, on the alert for him. Police sirens wailed in the distance. The bicycle officer acquired her alien target and pursued.

Ahead at the next intersection, three police cars formed a roadblock. Joe swerved into an open plaza between the buildings and headed for a park at the other end. The police vehicles, thwarted at their roadblock, moved to intercept. The bike patrol was joined by two other bicycle officers, and they followed Joe through the plaza. Two vans from the disease control department weren't far behind.

****

As soon as the first radio report of Joe aired, the media flooded into the city like a horde of hormonal teenagers chasing a pop star.

A television helicopter was immediately dispatched to this second chase of the same alien through Ngorongoro. *"Joyce Bolan, reporting live via our eye-in-the-sky helicopter high above Ngorongoro. Boy, I hope we don't have another run-in with that rude police helicopter that got in our way last time, right Bruce?"* Her helicopter pilot responded with a thumb's up.

Rowan, the news anchor, asked over her headset, *"Can you see any activity on the ground?"*

"Yes. I see an alien riding a bike, Rowan."

A heavy moan was heard back over the headset, followed by,

"Can you expand on that Joyce?"

"Yes, I can, Rowan. It is extremely hard to hail a cab downtown in the middle of the day. So, a bicycle seems like an appropriate choice."

"No," Rowan paused and took a deep breath. *"I meant about the alien's progress."*

"Yes, Rowan, I can do that too. There are police to the left of him, disease control to the right of him and pedal patrol behind him. And boldly rode on the Earthman." She heard another heavy sigh over her headset.

****

"He's at it again!" came the call-to-arms at the extreme sports offices in the Shooman Tower. Every employee raced to their stations, ready to capitalize on Joe's current exploits. They had unfurled a banner down the side of the building that was a large electronic monitor embedded in a flexible fabric, and it replayed the events of Joe's bicycle ride across Ngorongoro.

"Who knew you could do these things with a bike?" one person asked in astonishment.

"We have got to go to his planet," another envious, young,

upwardly-mobile executive replied.

"What should we name this new sport?"

"How about bike motocross?"

"You sutluts, bikes don't have motors."

****

Alfia's attempts to console her mother were futile. And matters were made worse by the constant barrage of negative news reports.

"Newsflash!" the announcer yelled excitedly. *"The Earthman Joe has contaminated the entire city. Citizens are warned to stay inside until this menace can be contained and sterilized. If you see the Earthman, please contact authorities right away."*

"I can't listen to these lies anymore." Marsha covered hear ears and turned from the television.

"We need to leave it on in case they find him," Alfia reminded her.

"Newsflash!" the news anchor declared again. *"The infectious alien has just been seen. He is traveling through the financial district on a pedal-driven recreational transport. He appears to be heading west. Local law enforcement and disease*

control are in pursuit."

Before the announcement was over, Alfia and Marsha were out the door and heading downtown with a media entourage in their wake.

****

"Evinrude!" rang out so loud that Evinrude, sitting in his embassy office, wasn't sure if it was his intercom or Drakewood yelling through the building.

He decided it was the intercom and answered, "Yes, sir." But there was no answer.

"Evinrude!" the distressed ambassador called out again.

Evinrude decided it wasn't the intercom and got up to walk down the long hallway to Drakewood's office. He knocked as he opened the door and entered. "You wanted to see me, sir?"

Drakewood pointed at the television.

Evinrude took a moment to watch and comprehend the full extent of the situation, then asked, "Mind if I borrow your car?"

Drakewood gave him the nastiest look Evinrude had ever seen.

****

"Fred, Frank, come look at this!" Ambassador Calloway called to them over the intercom. When they arrived at his office, their attention was immediately drawn to the television screen mounted on the wall, as the report kept repeating.

"Newsflash! The infectious alien has just been seen. He is traveling through the financial district on a pedal-driven recreational transport. He appears to be heading west. Local law enforcement and disease control are in pursuit."

"Macideneb!" Frank exclaimed. "When did all this happen?"

"The Earthman Joe has contaminated the entire city. Citizens are warned to stay inside until this menace can be contained and sterilized. What kind of suhton would transport a diseased alien halfway across the galaxy without going through any quarantine, trade procedures, or protocols? There appears to be no documentation or registration of any kind through any government agency. Who has allowed it to run loose among the general population?"

"That is an unmitigated fabrication!" Fred yelled back at the TV, defending Joe. "He's not contaminated. We're not sick."

"I knew it." Ambassador Calloway's arms flailed as he paced

around his office, more animated than usual. "I just knew it! I knew this would come back to bite us in the sunisa."

****

Flying over Joe's head, two helicopters vied for the best angle to record Joe's progress. "G'day John," The media helicopter pilot's decidedly Down Under accent came across the police helicopter's radio.

"Bruce!" John's reply was short and terse with implied disdain for his fellow pilot. "You cheeky devil, you stay out of my way, or I'll give you what for. This is official police business."

"No worries, mate. You'll never know I'm here." Bruce flew across John's path, causing the police helicopter to reel back.

****

Joe flew down a flight of stairs with three bikes in hot pursuit. Up another short flight, and then a hop onto a wall that bordered a river. The cops were fearless and followed him without hesitation. He sprang off the ledge, landing on a stair railing and sliding down it to the bottom. He bounded off the railing and continued to ride.

The pursuing officers merely rode the stairs down — they

didn't seem to think much of his trick — and ended up on the streets again. The police cars were bogged down in traffic and losing ground, but the bike patrol was gaining on him.

Joe turned down a small lane.

****

"Joyce Bolan reporting. The Earthling Joe is chased by cops down the lane. Then passing through a tunnel to emerge again, under the trees at the turn of the street, finding a bridge and crossing a creek and he on the opposite side will be."

"Thank you, Joyce, for that descriptive play-by-play." her anchor winced.

"Anytime, Rowan," she replied gleefully.

****

Evinrude, Frank and Fred, and Alfia and Marsha (who had lost their media caravan along the way) all arrived downtown in record time. Each party had a handheld police scanner to listen to, and each party decided on a route to intercept Joe. The three cars pulled up to the same intersection, just missing Joe and his pursuers. After a momentary pause to watch Joe cycle away, the three drivers took off in opposite directions.

Fred belabored his frustration with Evinrude's decoy. "I still can't believe that Henry Streator's disk had that Ullamaliztli game on it!"

"Evinrude said he'd get me a copy." Frank struggled to maneuver through the heavy traffic. "Now we know why it took so long to download."

"Yeah, but how did he know we would steal it?" Fred asked.

"He's Evinrude." Frank smiled as he gained a favorable position in the traffic.

"Aren't you angry that he played us like a couple of rubes?" Fred was a little perturbed that Frank seemed okay with the whole situation.

"Oh sure, at first I was disappointed," Frank explained. "But it's the nature of our business. A little cat and mouse, spy versus spy. If we didn't eliminate the potential for this to have been the genuine article, we would've been severely remiss in our duty. And it was. A great. Game! You should've watched it."

"But he wasted our time!" Fred argued.

"Let it go. We should've used our brains instead of our feet."

Inside hangar eighteen at the spaceport, just before 2 o'clock, Ambassador Calloway and Ambassador Drakewood pondered where their guest of honor could be. Both ambassadors wore the traditional bowler hat, dark suit, white shirt, and thin black tie. As they stood next to each other, they vaguely resembled an alien-looking Laurel and Hardy. Ambassador Calloway noticed that Mayor Nehru was suspiciously absent. "I'm surprised Mayor Nehru hasn't arrived."

"I spoke to him earlier today," Drakewood confided. "He seemed concerned about Ladascus' new role with the new peace accord. I tried to assure him that nothing would change, and that, in fact, the economy should improve. But he still seemed apprehensive."

****

Joe decided he needed to lose the helicopter and other vehicles. He entered the lobby of a large building by riding through the revolving door, a trick that impressed the police cyclists.

The building was part of a mall with shops and restaurants and was rather crowded during lunch. Citizens in his path fled at the sight of him. Others pointed and recorded it on their phones.

He rode across the open expanse of the lobby to an escalator and went up it. At the top, he followed a walkway that bridged across the street and into a parking garage. The bicycle squadron lost some ground but kept reporting his position.

On the third level of the parking garage, Joe headed for the spiral exit ramp. He could see that a disease control van blocked the exit at the bottom, and a police car was parked behind it. Two men in orange hazmat suits and two police officers stood in front of the van. As he rolled down the ribbed surface of the spiral exit ramp, his bike made quite a clatter. The experience wasn't very good for the rider either.

Below, the authorities could hear him approaching, the excitement of their impending collar rising every minute. Suddenly the sound stopped. They were perplexed.

A boom resonated from behind them as Joe landed on the top of their van and the suspension recoiled. From the roof of the van, he rode to the roof of the police car, caving it in slightly, and then to the ground.

Joe sped away.

****

"He flies through the air with the greatest of ease. He's quite a daring young man. But those landings must be tough on his knees. His movements are graceful. It's such a burly grind. This is Joyce Bolan reporting." Her voice was almost melodious with admiration.

****

People on the streets outside the Shooman Towers thought they heard a faint chant of "Go, Joe, go!" descending from the extreme sports offices far above them. And every time Joe evaded capture, united voices cried "Excelsior!" and startled pedestrians below.

At another intersection, Frank and Fred, Alfia and Marsha, and Evinrude met again from different directions. Frank pulled up alongside Evinrude's car, rolled down his window and said, "Hey, thanks for the copy of the game. I cannot begin to describe how good it was."

"I'm glad you enjoyed it." Evinrude nodded.

They were joined by six NPD squad cars, all hoping to intersect the wayward alien traveling west on Crestview Street.

The NPD didn't worry about infection. They didn't worry about their own safety. They would be the first to run toward danger at any moment. They were Ngorongoro's bravest and faithful till death.

Out of every police car, a radio blurted out, "*Joe has just passed the intersection with Shirley Drive, still proceeding west on Crestview Street.*"

He was already another block beyond them. Everyone turned to look westward and watched Joe ride away.

Nine cars feverishly tried to untangle themselves and pursue. The bicycle patrol easily glided through them and continued after their prey.

****

Inside Alfia's car, Marsha commented, "You know, once you get used to him, Joe's not that ugly."

"What does that have to do with anything?" Alfia looked at her mother suspiciously.

"You should keep an open mind. You're not getting any younger, you know."

"He's a client, mother…and an alien!"

"And yet he's the nicest young man you've ever brought home," Marsha pointed out.

"You're only saying that because you spent two nights with him. If you'd paid any of my other boyfriends half the attention you've given Joe, you'd like them, too."

"They never seemed to make themselves available. It was always, drive up to the house and honk the horn. They never came in to sit or talk. And besides, he can cook."

"Mother!" Alfia exclaimed.

"I'm just saying."

Alfia came to a stop behind Evinrude and Frank and Fred at the next intersection where they hoped to head Joe off. "No! I'm not going to date Joe!" she yelled at her mother.

Frank, Fred, and Evinrude all turned to stare.

Realizing they had heard, Alfia froze. The awkward moment ended abruptly when three squad cars roared up to join them. Alfia silently thanked them.

****

Joyce Bolan reported, *"Once more unto the breach, dear Earthling, once more."*

****

Evinrude's, Frank and Fred's, and Alfia and Marsha's three

cars, six police cars, and three bicycle patrol officers gathered at the end of a narrow street. The police cars were pointed into the street, and the civilian cars lined up behind them. Finally, a disease control van squeezed behind all the other vehicles, sealing off the intersection. No alleys or hidden sidewalks separated the buildings.

Scanners confirmed that Joe was headed directly toward them. An air of confidence permeated the crowd for they were sure Joe was cut off this time.

But Joe was nowhere in sight.

The radio again announced Joe's location and the anomalous posse double-checked the street signs against their electronic trackers to make sure they were on the right street.

The radio now claimed that Joe had just passed the cross street everyone was parked on. The united front dissolved into a mob wildly searching for Joe.

Evinrude noticed the shadow of a bike rider on the wall next to him and looked up to see Joe, riding on the rail of the elevated monorail train.

Flabbergasted, Evinrude breathed a heavy sigh. Alfia and Marsha were frustrated beyond reason. Fred worried, and Frank laughed at Joe's ingenuity. Joe prayed no trains were coming. The police, disgusted, aimed their weapons toward the sky and opened fire.

"Oh, bloody anneheg!" John bellowed over the police radios, his accent even more pronounced. "There be helicopters up here, you twits."

"I like this bushranger," Bruce declared.

"You would," John replied.

****

Oemay, Arrylay, and Urlycay, disguised as technicians in white lab coats, entered hangar eighteen. They removed the podium, took down the PA system, and began folding up the chairs.

Drakewood was immediately upset. "What are you doing? We're going on air in a few minutes."

Without pausing from his work, Oemay responded, "Everything's being moved outside in front of the hangar doors."

Drakewood argued, "Why? I didn't authorize this!"

Arrylay carried the podium past them. "The crowd is too big."

The two puzzled ambassadors walked over to the partially-opened hangar doors to find the entire tarmac packed with people. A stage had already been erected in front of the doors. Evinrude's golden ship was displayed nearby, a ladder beside the golden craft for spectators to climb up and look into the open canopy. Several television news vans stood out like islands in a sea of people, and media helicopters flew overhead. Police and military had been drafted for crowd control.

The crowd itself was divided into two groups. An anti-Joe camp held signs, wore surgical masks, and chanted "Joe go!" and a pro-Joe camp held signs and chanted "Joe no go!" The two groups inadvertently chanted in rhythm with each other, "Joe go! Joe no go! Joe go! Joe no go!"

Calloway and Drakewood saw their constituents and other powerful people out front and went to greet them.

While everyone else was distracted, Arrylay had time to set the bacterial bomb into the base of the podium without anyone noticing, just like he practiced in front of Joe.

The three assassins finished their work and found the ambassadors. "You're good to go, gentlemen," Oemay informed them.

"Thank you," Calloway gestured with an apathetic, politician-like, bow trying to hurry them on their way.

The three gangsters left.

****

This time they were ready. Four squad cars and two disease control vans blocked the intersection. The bicycle squad and two police cars herded Joe toward the waiting ambush. Alfia, Marsha, Evinrude, Fred, and Frank pulled in behind the blockade. Joe was within sight. No side streets or alleys. No monorail.

Joe was swift. He wove in and out of traffic. He hopped onto the sidewalk and disappeared.

"Where did he go?" an astounded officer asked. "He was right in front of us?"

Murmurs seeped out of the posse, "Is he capable of interdimensional travel?" "This ain't no ordinary Earthling."

An observant officer said. "He went down the subway stairs."

"He'll never make it through the turnstiles," another predicted.

Everyone turned to see if he emerged from the other subway

access behind them, only to see one hundred bicycle messengers filling the street.

Despite the negative hype, despite the fact that he stole a bike from one of their own, and actually because he was hated by the cops, Joe had inadvertently become their icon. They felt they had a common bond with him.

Joe came out of the subway and noticed the obviously large number of cyclists surrounding him. He stopped. He didn't know what to do. One of the cyclists leaned over to Joe and whispered, "It's cool. We're antiestablishmentarianists. We're with you." And he placed a hat on Joe, trying to disguise the alien in their midst. "Where do you need to go?"

"The spaceport," Joe cautiously replied.

"Follow us." The crowd of bikes began a series of complicated synchronized maneuvers in the street. Ninety-six of the cyclists created a diversion with their razzle-dazzle, while Joe and the remaining four raced to the spaceport.

****

"O Earthling! My Earthling," Joyce lamented. *"Our fearful trip is done."*

"I'm not following you, Joyce," Rowan said over her headset.

"We lost him, Rowan."

****

Oemay, Urlycay, and Arrylay got into their white panel van and drove away.

"You gave us plenty of time to escape the blast, right?" Oemay asked Arrylay.

"It's set to go off in fifteen minutes. That should put the explosion at ten minutes into their speech and give us plenty of time to clear out of here."

"Hey. That's that Joe guy," Oemay said, recognizing Joe as he rode past them and into the spaceport with four other riders.

"How'd he get out of my knots?" Urlycay fumed.

"I told you, we should've popped him in the head," Arrylay formed a gun with his fingers and mimicked shooting Oemay in the head.

"We'd better get him, he could ruin everything," Oemay started to turn the van around.

"Wait, look at that," Urlycay pointed out the front window.

A stampeding herd of police vehicles, disease control vans, Evinrude, Fred and Frank, and Alfia and Marsha barreled down the road, with helicopters overhead and bicycle patrols behind, all following Joe. The van was blocked by the onslaught of vehicles passing through the gate.

As the traffic thinned, Oemay, Arrylay, and Urlycay were caught in the gaze of the largest, meanest, most intimidating bike messenger they had ever seen. Their deer-in-the-headlights trance was broken when the engine sputtered and died. A second messenger appeared in front of them, holding a crucial ignition part. They attempted to exit the van only to find the doors blocked. Two more bikers appeared before them, their bike lock keys waving tantalizingly in their fingers. The four messengers turned their backs to the van, setting themselves up for a selfie with their captives. They waited for that crucial moment with the priceless expressions that could only be obtained the moment the stooges saw four police officers step into view. *Click.*

****

Up on the stage, Calloway and Drakewood were about to address the multitude of people. "It's after two," Drakewood complained. "Where is Evinrude? Joe is a critical part of our presentation."

Calloway nudged Drakewood. "We should start. If they don't show, they don't show."

Drakewood stepped up to the podium, straightened his posture, and began, "I am overwhelmed by the number of people here today...."

Joe had a good lead on the pursuing horde, but they were closing fast. He could hear Drakewood's first words over the PA. He knew he had to hurry.

The sea of people parted as Joe entered. If he was or wasn't infectious, they weren't taking the chance. Yet, like any accident, everyone still wanted to see. They chanted loudly, "Joe go!" and "Joe no go!" The third camp of extreme sports fans also joined in, chanting, "Go Joe, go!" The chant quickly became a complicated muddle that sounded like, "Joe go go Joe go Joe no go Joe go go Joe go Joe no go Joe go go Joe go Joe no go Joe go go Joe go Joe no go!" It grew so loud that Drakewood was forced to stop speaking.

Joe rode up, dropped the bike, and leaped onto the stage. He ran to the podium, pushed Drakewood aside, opened the compartment in the base, and pulled out the bomb.

At first, Drakewood and Calloway were appalled by his rude behavior and were about to verbally thrash him, until they noticed the bomb. They scurried away.

Evinrude, Frank, Fred, Alfia, and Marsha abandoned their cars behind the crowd and ran toward the stage.

Joe couldn't tell how much time was left, only that the counter showed double digits. Alone on the stage, looking at the ticking bomb in his hands, Joe panicked. *Now what?* He looked around. He saw the crowd. He saw his friends. He saw Evinrude's ship. "An indestructible ship, perfect," he declared. All he had to do was climb up the ladder, drop the bomb in, and close the canopy. And he knew how to do that. *Everyone will be safe!*

Joe cradled the bomb in his arm like a football and raced for Evinrude's ship. Running through the crowd, Joe dodged and evaded police, security, fans, and a mime. He bounded up the ladder, slipped on the zero-coefficient-of-friction fuselage, and fell into the cockpit, with the bomb. The canopy slammed shut. Joe looked up from the floor of the cockpit, the bomb sitting on the seat, the digital readout in single digits and still counting down.

Outside the ship, time had stopped. Joe's five friends skidded to a halt. The audience became deathly silent. Everyone stood motionless, waited, and watched. Then came a flash of blinding light, a deafening explosion, and an indestructible ship shook violently, the cockpit filled with smoke.

No one could have survived, especially an ordinary Earthling.

Evinrude stood, staring at his ship.

Marsha broke the silence as she screamed in agony, Alfia trying to console her.

Fred also screamed in agony, but Frank didn't console him.

And then, quietly, a foot reached down from the front wheel well of the golden plane, looking for a foot peg. Slowly, a second foot lowered to the next peg.

This time, Joe, hadn't forgotten about the disappearing panel in the floor.

Evinrude spotted Joe's quivering legs and started toward his ship. The crowd slowly grew aware of what was going on. The solemn moment gave way to a roaring cheer and thunderous applause as they watched Joe lower himself to the ground from beneath the ship, unharmed.

Even though the explosion had been contained, Joe was still shaken by the noise and a concussion. Evinrude went out to escort him back to his friends. Fred fell on Joe, hugging him until it seemed awkward, which was immediately.

"Um, thanks, Fred," Joe said, as he awkwardly man-hugged him back. "I'm alright. The ship protected me from the blast. I wish I could say the same for my ears."

They badgered him with questions, *Are you okay? Where were you? What happened? How did you know about the bomb?*, overwhelming him with the well-meaning attention.

By this time, the ambassadors had worked their way back to the small group. Drakewood, all business, piped up, "If the reunion is over, we are in the middle of a press conference, and the cameras are rolling. I took the liberty of having your part drafted for you. We'll go first and introduce you shortly." He handed Joe an electronic notecard and then returned to the stage.

Calloway motioned to some empty seats. "If the rest of you could take seats over there, we'll get underway immediately." He then joined Drakewood on stage.

Joe stared at the notecard and then at his friends and complained, "I was just blown up. Quasimodo's ears don't ring as bad as mine, I can't deliver a speech." They all took their seats near the stage, and the ambassadors began again.

Joe looked again his prepared remarks again — they were written in Quesonte. He held out the notecard to Evinrude. "I can't read this."

Evinrude glanced at it and instantly realized why. He grinned, amused. Checking through the programs, he found it couldn't translate to English or any other Earth-based language. Not that it mattered; being American, Joe only knew one.

Evinrude skimmed through and translated for Joe, "'In short, we, the Quesonte and the Soufte governments, are giving the bunkers of munitions to the Ladascan people as a peace offering. This ship,'" Evinrude pointed toward the *Boulougante Bullet*, "'is the crown jewel of the bunch.' Or was, until you destroyed it."

"I thought it was indestructible."

"On the outside. Anyway, 'We, the Quesonte and Soufte governments, feel that Ladascans are a great and proud people, and deserve the right to govern and protect themselves.'"

Joe listened intently. "Okay. So, I'm basically on my own."

"No pressure." Fred chuckled. "It's only a matter of galactic peace."

Joe struggled to memorize what Evinrude had just said. His mind wandered to the famous addresses that he had learned during four years of high school and two years of college. "Why'd I make history my eight o'clock class?" He sighed. He tried to recall the Ladascan history channel's mega-series about the Disturbance that he had watched while in the hotel. He hoped he could pull this off.

At the podium, Drakewood and Callaway were, again, giving their rehearsed rhetoric to the crowd, explaining the incidents over the last week and how they were doing their level best to do right by Ladascus. The ambassadors assured that Joe had been brought through proper diplomatic channels and was not diseased or contagious in anyway.

Frank leaned over to Alfia. "The *Esprit* is next to hangar seven, fueled and ready to go."

"Well, I'm ready anytime Joe is."

"Joe." Frank knew the answer but enjoyed asking anyway. "Ready to go home?"

"Yes! Yes, I am!" Joe said gleefully. "But I have a few souvenirs in my hotel room I'd like to keep."

"We can have them brought over," Frank assured him.

"I have a small bag already packed, if they could just bring it over. That'd be great."

Calloway and Drakewood simultaneously introduced Joe. "And now, with no further introduction, we present Joe, the man from Earth."

"You're up, Joe." Evinrude prodded him away from Frank and Alfia.

Joe nervously stepped up onto the stage. The crowd roared and applauded as he sheepishly walked to the podium, his ears still ringing from the blast. He peered out into the audience. The protestors on both sides had calmed down and were eager to listen. He took a few deep breaths, faked some confidence, and began.

"I came in peace." He paused when he noticed his arch-nemesis, the mime, holding up a sign with no words on it, but instead a picture of a mime gesturing "go."

"I would like to leave in one...piece." He paused again; to the audience it seemed like a dramatic pause, but Joe was desperately thinking of what to say next. "Two score and two years ago on this very day, a date which will live in infamy, Ladascus was suddenly and deliberately attacked by the forces of the Quesonte and Soufte Empires."

"What's a score?" the mime asked another spectator. The spectator just looked at him oddly.

"My esteemed colleagues refer to this attack as…the Disturbance. They asked me to read a speech that they wrote." He showed the electronic notecard to the audience— "I'm rather confident you're not interested in what they have to say."—and then deliberately threw it over his shoulder. The crowd cheered.

Drakewood, visibly upset, almost rushed the stage, but Evinrude stopped him, whispering that Joe couldn't read Quesonte. Drakewood buried his face in his hands, distressed by his simplistic oversight. Evinrude smiled, enjoying Drakewood's anguish.

"Some of you may still remember the day the skies grew dark, as menacing machines crowded out the sun. A history of repeated injuries and usurpations brought about by the absolute tyranny of Ladascans' rights and liberties, such has been the patient sufferance of Ladascus. Hopelessly outgunned and hopelessly outmatched, you flew your flag high above the Shooman Towers. The rockets' red glare from the bombs bursting in air gave proof that your flag was still there. Now, forty-two years later, the Soufte and Quesonte governments have resolved that Ladascus is, and of right ought to be, a free and independent planet. And that all beings are created equal, and that they are endowed with certain unalienable rights. Among these are life, liberty, and the pursuit of happiness. Today they present you, the Ladascan people, with a symbol" — Joe gestured to the smoking spaceship, which seized upon that moment to make an unflattering sound. Joe stumbled on — "of self-preservation and self-defense, so that you may no longer be a second-class citizen on your own planet. Instead, now Ladascans will boldly go where no Ladascan has gone before. And so, my Ladascan friends, ask not what your nation can do for you; ask what you can do for your nation. My fellow citizens of all the cosmos, ask not what Ladascus will do for you, but what we can do together for the freedom of everyone, everywhere."

That last line got the entire crowd cheering and roaring, so much so that Joe felt a little embarrassed and yet proud. *I'm going to contest that C I got in history class last semester.* Crowd control could barely keep them behind the barricades. Joe figured this was as good a place to end as any, so he waved to the crowd, walked off-stage, and sat between Alfia and Evinrude. Drakewood retook the podium to make a few final remarks.

When the event finally ended, everyone said goodbye to Joe. "Thank you, everyone," Joe said, shaking each individual's hand.

Fred took it especially hard and gave him one last, awkwardly long hug goodbye. The awkward moment lasted an awkwardly long time and was finally interrupted, to Joe's great relief, by a bicycle messenger delivering Joe's bag.

"It has been a pleasure meeting you all," he continued. "I know we won't meet again, but it's nice to entertain the thought."

Marsha sighed deeply as Joe hugged her. Alfia asked her mother, "Are you all right?"

"I like him," she answered.

Joe and Alfia walked across the tarmac, the crowd flowing with them to hangar seven. Alfia commented on Joe's bag, "You've got quite a load of souvenirs."

"Yes, I do," Joe gloated. "Don't tell the hotel, but I stole a towel. I hear it's the best thing to have if you're traveling across the galaxy."

"For someone who just got into town, you sure made quite an impression on everyone," Alfia told him.

"I just didn't want to screw up."

The two climbed aboard a blue *Esprit*. Joe waved to the crowd and yelled out a final farewell. "Goodbye, proud world! I'm going home."

The crowd gave another resounding cheer as he ducked into the ship.

Alfia powered the systems up. It sounded like a wonderfully powerful beast. The *Esprit* lifted effortlessly and gracefully moved past the crowd, and Joe waved at them through the cockpit windshield.

As soon as clearance was given from the tower, the *Esprit* shot out of the sky and into space. The crowd watched in awe as the ship disappeared.

Joe looked down at the planet. It no longer looked so alien, but instead warm, familiar, and welcoming, a contrast to his first observations.

Chapter 19

The Last Chapter
Without which, this book would never end.

At hyperdrive speeds, the stars passed by like telephone poles along a highway. Joe looked out the window, amazed. He knew this meant they were traveling at magnificent speeds, yet it reminded him of his trip out with Homer. "Oh crap!" he muttered. "Homer!"

****

Homer and Joe's parents met with the forest rangers and local authorities in the ranger's office. Maps filled the tables as local volunteers divided the area into sections. They organized search parties and checked equipment. Photos of Joe were passed out to everyone involved in the search.

Every day that passed without rescue was another day closer to death in the wilderness. He'd been missing for a week, and the rangers weren't too optimistic.

"He's going to die, isn't he?" Joe's mother sobbed into her husband's shoulder.

****

Eighteen hours later

"So, where would you like me to drop you off?" Alfia asked.

"Don't you have to fix time or something?"

"Why? Is it broken?" Alfia giggled.

Joe continued meekly, "Don't you need to make it appear as if I've never left to protect the secrecy of your existence?"

"Our existence is no secret. If your technology were advanced enough, you'd be bombarded with as much useless information and bad television programming as you inflict on us. And if it weren't for CBS, we'd never have heard of Earth."

"Oh." Joe paused then slowly questioned, "Well then, don't you have to drop me off in a secluded area so as not to be detected?"

"Oh please! I can drop you off in your own backyard and not be detected. Your race has got a long way to go."

"Well, if we're so helpless, why doesn't some superior race take us over?" Joe asked.

"Because you don't have anything anybody wants. If you did, they'd be here."

"Obviously, you've never had chocolate," Joe countered.

"Well then, I suppose the best place to return to would be the place I left from."

"Okay, where's that?"

"In the United States."

"Which blob of dirt is that?"

"Um…" Joe looked down at the Earth. "It's on the dark side right now."

"Okay." Alfia adjusted course. The *Esprit* maneuvered toward the dark side of the Earth. As the sun vanished behind the arc of the planet, its ominous red aura blinked out. Joe and Alfia descended into a sea of darkness on a crystal-clear night.

"You sure have a lot of junk orbiting your planet," Alfia said as they ducked under the international space station.

Joe turned quickly to see it. "Cool," he exclaimed under his breath.

As the lights from cities and towns grew brighter and brighter, Alfia activated a camouflage screen that rendered the *Esprit* invisible.

"Gee, I wonder if I can find it in the dark?" Joe thought out loud. "Okay, we need to head toward that mountain range over there." He pointed to the left. "See that large cluster of lights? That's probably Denver."

"Is that where you live?"

"No, I live more over there," Joe pointed to the Midwest, "where it's dimmer." He wondered if he had just insulted himself. "But I'm not too far away from that cluster of lights, which is Chicago. At least there's a full moon tonight. It'll make it easier to see landmarks."

"Or we could just switch the viewport to night mode." Alfia flipped a switch, and the windshield changed to appear as if it were bright daylight outside.

"Nice! So, have you been to Earth before?"

"Oh no. This is out of the way of anything; it's one of my longest returns. Hyperspace: not only convenient in science fiction, but exceptionally convenient in real life."

"So, I've heard."

"By conventional means, this would have taken a couple weeks. You must have some pull in high places."

"No, not really." Joe thought for a second. "I was just in the wrong place at the right time. I have yet to decide if this has been a good experience."

"Really?" Alfia exclaimed. "You got to travel halfway across the galaxy. You defeated a gorgon; hob-knobbed with the rich, the famous and the powerful; managed to create an intergalactic incident; prevented an assassination attempt; and created peace between archrivals. And the most remarkable thing of all, you managed to keep my mother out all night, on a work night, mind you. For someone who claims to be ordinary, you sure had an extraordinary week."

"Yeah, it's going to be tough to beat this spring break next year," he mused.

Joe and Alfia came upon the lights of Denver. The ship glided down effortlessly to less than five hundred feet off the ground, skimming across the treetops.

"Are you sure no one's going to see us?"

"The ship is invisible."

"Oh well, there you go. Just follow this road up into the mountains."

Alfia followed the twisting road. The few vehicles she passed noticed only a strange breeze blowing by them. They came to an area where the terrain leveled out.

"And there's the park entrance. If you could find a spot near the ranger's station, that building" — he pointed — "I'll walk the rest of the way."

"Lots of trees around here."

"You get that with a forest," Joe explained.

Alfia descended into a clearing, setting the ship down ever so gently.

Joe turned to her and said, "You are a much better pilot than Fred or Frank."

"It was nice meeting you, Joe. I know my mother will never stop talking about it. You've made her into some sort of celebrity."

"Thank you, Alfia." Joe reached out to shake her hand. "I do appreciate all you've done for me. Say thanks to Fred and Frank and Marsha again for me. And please have a safe trip home."

Joe opened the hatch and stepped out. He had forgotten that it was dark, so he paused to let his eyes adjust. He felt a slight breeze as the *Esprit* flew over him, and he waved to Alfia. He walked toward the park ranger's station, carrying the bag of clothes and other souvenirs he had acquired on Ladascus.

Along the way, he reflected on the past week. Being back home made it all feel like a dream, but then he pulled out the newspaper article and looked at the picture in the dim light of the campground. He still couldn't read the words, but it reminded him that he still had the interpreting device on his ear. Gently caressing it Joe smiled and thought, *I'll never take this off.*

Joe walked into the ranger's station and the room filled with great joy.

THE END

Wait! Wait!
We're not done yet.
Check this out:

Back on Ladascus

Evinrude walked down a very busy uptown street, full of many average people walking to their average jobs, trying to maintain their average lives. Two small figures, trying to look average, followed discreetly behind. Although they were a bit shorter than most of the people, they did blend in nicely with the crowd.

Evinrude walked into the lobby of a swank hotel and meandered up to the desk.

His two pursuers stalled just outside the door, one tying his shoe, the other making a phone call.

"It's going down alright. We need backup," Frank pleaded on the phone with Ambassador Calloway.

"I can't authorize back up," Calloway said. "Your evidence is only circumstantial. We can't interfere with the internal struggles of the Quesonte government."

"That's never stopped us before." Frank's voice grew louder as his composure slipped.

"If a coup is going down, then it needs to happen."

"You're insane! That will destabilize the entire galaxy!"

Frank's anger surged at Calloway's bureaucratic position.

Evinrude got the information he needed at the front desk and slowly headed down the corridor to his right.

Frank noticed Evinrude's movement and rudely hung up on Calloway. Frantic at losing sight of him, Frank and Fred quickened their pace and practically ran around the corner.

Evinrude was gone. They slowly and stealthily traversed the large hall, trying to thoroughly search each doorway for Evinrude, but also not arouse suspicion from other patrons. At the end of the corridor they stopped. They had lost him.

Frank and Fred felt a presence behind them and slowly turned their heads.

"Hello." Evinrude's friendly manner caught them by surprise, and so he chided them further, "Don't stop now, you've almost got me."

"But…aren't you? Oh, macideneb." Frank punched the wall and walked around in a circle ranting. Fred's jaw hung open.

"You let me out of your sight, Frank." Evinrude tsked. "Rookie mistake."

Frank pointed at Fred. "He's the rookie."

"I told you it was stupid to follow him," Fred said, shaking off his stupor. "He knows us. How could we ever get away with following him?"

Evinrude chuckled "Oh, no no no, my dear friends, you're my guests. Come with me." He put his arms around their diminutive shoulders and led them down the hall. "It's just at the end of corridor."

"Aren't you attending a secret meeting of Quesonte's most powerful government officials?" Fred asked, bewildered.

"Yes, well, maybe. It's not what you think it is," Evinrude whispered as he stopped in front of a door and freed them from his embrace. "Act surprised." He opened the door, and they walked into a dark room. The lights clicked on.

"Surprise!" A large group of professional-looking men and women yelled to Evinrude.

"What the…a surprise party? You guys…really." Evinrude faked surprise to the group, then whispered to Fred and Frank, "It's my retirement party. But don't tell them I knew all along."

"And the information we've been chasing for a week?" Frank looked at Evinrude in disbelief.

"The guest list," Evinrude said. Old friends and colleagues gathered around to congratulate him, shaking his hand, and making quite a fuss over him. The crowd of well-wishers pushed Fred and Frank to the side.

On the walls of the banquet room hung old war photos — pictures of former comrades on battlefields — blown up into posters. Some of the faces were covered with tape to protect the identities of current agents. Those that weren't were either dead or not agents at all.

There were pictures of Evinrude standing in an imposing stance next to his ship, the *Boulougante Bullet*. With his helmet and goggles and a white scarf blowing in the wind, he appeared very Baron Manfred von Richthofen-like.

Many of the pictures of captured enemies had names or lines from documents blacked out. And most of the posters were stamped TOP SECRET.

Signs wishing Evinrude HAPPY RETIREMENT! also hung on the walls. Along the far wall, a large cake and non-alcoholic refreshments sat on a table, but no one seemed interested in them. Against another wall, everyone gathered around a bar.

"Doesn't this seem odd?" Fred said to Frank.

"I don't know. I've never been in this situation before. Just go with it." Frank stopped dead in front of one of the pictures on the wall.

Evinrude noticed Frank staring at the picture and explained, "That's the Arturo Express."

"I remember the Arturo Express." Frank shook his head. "I don't remember you there?"

"We only spoke briefly that day." Evinrude pointed at the picture. "There I am. And I believe that's you."

"You are a master of disguise."

"No. That's just me thirty years younger." Evinrude introduced Frank and Fred to his colleagues. "May I introduce Frank Surovell and Fred Jackson? Frank is the Soufte agent responsible for exposing the Arturo Express incident."

They all cooed like schoolgirls. "Very glad to meet you, sir," an agent said, as several others shook his hand. Another said, "Excellent work, sir," and a third added, "It's work like that that gives our profession a good name."

****

"Good work, Dash and Desi," the police chief congratulated them. "It only took you a week, and you've recovered the diamonds and arrested the culprit."

"Six days actually, sir," Dash conceded. "But we failed to capture the instrument with which he perpetrated the crime."

"Speak Ladascan, won't you?" The chief had no patience for Dash's long-winded explanations.

"We didn't catch the thief. We only caught the person who hired the thief." Dash recalled the events of the past week and his worthy adversary. With a slightly appreciative smile, he remarked, "To me, she'll always be the woman."

Desi reflected back on the case. "I wish we could've figured out how she got on the roof."

"Disappointing, I agree, but don't be dismayed," Dash consoled him. "Neither did the authors."

****

At the ranger's station on Earth

"What's in the bag?" Joe's mother asked. "And what is this strange clothing?"

"Souvenirs," Joe said. "I was abducted by aliens and spent a week on an alien planet. They took me shopping. I wasn't coming back empty-handed." To himself and Homer, his explanation sounded rational. But everyone else in the room looked at him as if he was delusional.

Homer turned to Joe. "They looked at me the same way when I told them."

"Riiiiight." his mother was worried about their mental states.

"No, really." He pulled out the newspaper to show everyone. "I've got a newspaper article with my picture. I defeated a gorgon."

"So, you're trying to tell me that a civilization advanced enough to travel across the galaxy still prints their news on...paper?" his father cross-examined him.

"Well...Yeah...I don't know," Joe fumbled. "I didn't question it. I was just there."

"Come on, Joe, 'fess up, you got lost." His father prodded him for a believable truth.

"You're right. I did. I got picked up by a group of nerds on their way back from a sci-fi convention, and they loaned me some clothes. I was just too embarrassed to tell you. But next year, we'll be spending spring break within the confines of civilization."

Homer verified, "By civilization, you mean fast food, c
phone service, girls, and plumbing?"

What the anneheg…?

Are you still reading this?
It's over!
Close the book.
Yeesh!